THE SWEET SPOT

A Tasty Temptations Novel

MONICA MYERS

To
Aunty Jac

Enjoy!

lots of love
from
Monica Myers
(Carmelle)

ROSEWOOD
BOOKS

Published by Rosewood Books

ISBN (eBook): 978-1-83756-033-2
ISBN (Paperback): 978-1-83756-034-9
ISBN (Hardback): 978-1-83756-035-6

Previously published as Sticky Treats by the author.

CHAPTER ONE

Erin

"Oh my gosh, that is the most exquisite pussy I've ever seen."

Several heads turned towards our table when they heard Madison's delighted squeal. Her half-eaten waffle sat forgotten on her plate as she admired the contents of the open cake box.

"Maddie," I gritted, feeling myself flush. "I appreciate the enthusiasm, but I think you might be scaring the other diners."

Madison snorted.

"Let 'em stare," she said defiantly. "My best friend is a genius, and I don't care who knows it."

She caught someone's eye over my shoulder and pointed at me like I was a prized exhibit.

"She's a genius!" she yelled. "I mean, seriously," she added, lowering her voice and turning back to me, "you made it WET!"

I didn't need to look over my shoulder to confirm that we were, once again, the center of attention. I could feel eyes on the back of my neck. After ten years of friendship, I had resigned myself to the fact that Maddie would never grasp the concept of an "inside voice." I should have known better than to show her the cake topper in a crowded diner. If the universe gave me a do-over, I'd go for something that stood a better chance of containing her excitement—maybe a fallout shelter.

"It's not a big deal." I shrugged. "I just used a mirror glaze for the inner labia."

Madison dismissed my modesty with a flick of her hand.

"It's not just that! It's the detail. I mean, look at the cute little—"

"It's just fondant," I put in hurriedly, desperate to head her off before her gushing became too anatomically specific.

"Seriously, Erin," she babbled. "You must have spent more time staring at pussy than I have. And that's—"

"You gals all set here?"

We looked up to find a plump woman in a pink waitress dress hovering politely by our table, wielding a coffee pot. By this point, my cheeks were on fire. I wondered whether my medium non-fat latte contained enough liquid to drown me. Madison was, as usual, completely unfazed.

"No, thanks," she chirped. "I think we're fine."

"Are you sure I can't get you a refill on your—"

The waitress's voice trailed off as her eyes fell on the open box. Madison just smiled brightly.

"Do you like it?" she asked innocently. "It's going to be the top tier of my wedding cake."

"Well, er," the woman faltered. "That's certainly an unusual choice. In my day, we just had the little people on top. What's the lucky feller's name, hon?"

Madison put her chin on her hand and eyed the waitress unblinkingly.

"Claudia," she said, not missing a beat.

The woman stiffened.

"Well, if that's all you need, I'd best be getting back to work," she clipped, all the warmth gone from her voice.

Madison rolled her eyes and gave the middle finger to the waitress's retreating back. I chuckled softly. For once, I didn't mind that Maddie had slipped into over-share mode. I'd watched her torpedo her way through a string of terrible relationships before she finally accepted herself for who she was. Now she was out and proud, and I was proud of her. When she met Claudia, she'd fallen head over heels. I'd never seen her happier. I'm not usually a weepy kind of girl, but I was genuinely choked up when they asked me to design their wedding cake. I just had to hope their families wouldn't want to flay me alive when they saw Madison's design.

Mentioning my job to people was always weird. "I design and craft erotically themed cakes and confectionery" tended to be a conversation stopper. Explaining how I got into it in the first place was even weirder. When I left college, I'd started out doing illustrations for anatomical textbooks. Name a body part and I've probably drawn at least one intricate diagram of it. Baking was a hobby, a way to unwind at the end of a long day hunched over my graphics tablet. It might never have occurred to me that my two worlds could combine if Madison hadn't thrown a Victoria's Secrets party. Several glasses of wine and a batch of cupcakes later and the conversation turned to themed snacks.

Like, "what if these cupcakes had cute little wieners poking out the top?"

Maddie's light-hearted suggestion had set the gears turning in my head and before I knew it, I was enthusiastically sculpting, amidst a mess of modeling chocolate and Rice Krispie treats. When those cupcakes were done, I felt a sense of artistic pride that I'd never experienced before. My drawings could be fulfilling, but there was always something flat and sterile about them. They were just work. By contrast, the cakes were fun, vibrant, and just a little irreverent. It was incredibly satisfying to create a 3D sculpture that could be enjoyed with every sense. From that moment I was hooked.

Of course, it wasn't without its challenges. To say my family was taken aback was putting it mildly. The term "erotic baker" confused them. Maddie was still snorting with laughter over the time my grandma anxiously asked me whether it was really a good idea to cook in the nude. Most of them came around as I got more successful. Turned out there was a surprisingly big market for raunchy sweets. Bachelor parties, coming out parties, anniversaries—even birthday parties and weddings.

Occasionally it created embarrassing situations. Being stopped by the cops and trying to explain the 4-foot chocolate penis in the back of my car wasn't an incident I was likely to forget. Let's just say, it taught me to be super vigilant about my taillights.

"So," said Madison, shooting a fond glance at her engagement ring. "I'm all set, but what are we going to do about your situation?"

I frowned.

"What situation?"

Madison looked me in the eye and donned her "I mean business" face.

"Three words, Erin," she said, counting them off on her fingers. "Work. Life. Balance. You don't have one."

"I do so!" I protested.

Maddie raised a skeptical eyebrow.

"Really? When's the last time you even went out?"

"Um..." I grasped for a few seconds and then my face lit up. Unfortunately, my best friend knew me too well.

"*Not* counting this brunch," she cut in.

I folded my arms huffily and stuck my tongue out at her.

"I'm serious, Erin," she scolded. "We've both read the Huff-Po horror stories. If you don't do the self-care thing, you might just... I don't know, flip out. One day you'll be perfectly fine then the next day you'll up sticks and move to Peru to raise llamas, and—and I don't wanna visit you in Peru. You know I don't do altitude well."

It was true. Madison could get a nosebleed standing on a chair.

"Fine!" I threw my hands up. "Self-care! Want me to light some scented candles and take a bubble bath?"

Maddie gave me a hard look.

"How about actually getting out and socializing occasionally? Work, sleep, repeat. That's all you do right now."

"You don't understand," I said wearily. "The bakery takes a lot of work, Mads. It's not just crafting and designing. There's cleaning and promotion and accounting and—"

"Well, maybe it's time to hire someone," Madison interrupted. "You're definitely doing enough business to justify it. Don't you think it might be time to trust someone else with your precious baby?"

My grip on my coffee cup tightened.

"Yeah," I bit out. "Because it went so well the last time I trusted someone."

Madison wrinkled her pretty nose.

"Let's not bring dick-face into this. I just ate. Listen, sweetie." Her voice softened, and she reached across the table to place a hand on my arm. "I know Stirling hurt you, but that doesn't mean you have to close yourself off forever."

I scowled at the last few inches of my coffee. That name still made my chest tighten and set something sour churning in my stomach.

"He did more than just hurt my feelings, Mad," I reminded her. "He nearly destroyed my whole career."

Madison grimaced sympathetically and squeezed my wrist harder.

"I know, sweetheart. But I worry about you. I don't want to get back from my honeymoon and discover you've turned into a hermit."

My face twisted into an ironic smirk.

"You trying to say you won't visit me in my hermit cave either? Ok, ok, you don't have to do 'the look'. I promise I will try to get out more, and I'll think about hiring someone else for the bakery. No dating though!" I resolved. "I'm done with that for now."

Frankly, after what had happened the last time I'd opened my heart, I was ready to hang up my dating hat forever. Men were nothing but trouble.

CHAPTER TWO

Nolan

Dear God, someone kill me now!

Maybe this is a dream, I thought. *Perhaps if I close my eyes and pinch myself really hard, I won't be standing in the middle of a crowded office, staring down my raving psycho of an ex-girlfriend.*

Take it from me: when a woman you've just dumped shows up at your workplace with a cardboard box and a mad glint in her eye, something very bad is about to go down.

I refused to give her the satisfaction of showing I was embarrassed. It's hard to feign nonchalance when your ass is clenching like a nutcracker, but I managed it.

"Heather!" I exclaimed in a tone that betrayed nothing more than mild surprise. "To what do I owe this—?"

The words died on my lips as Heather upended the box with a triumphant flourish. It was one of those weird occasions when events played themselves out in slow motion. I watched helplessly as a colorful cascade of dildos, fluffy handcuffs and flavored lube packets rained down around my feet.

There was a trick I'd used since I was a kid. Whenever anything embarrassing happened, I pretended I was just acting in a play. There was no need to blush because none of this was actually happening, and all the gawking onlookers were in on the joke. It worked when I'd wet my pants on that second-grade field trip, it worked that time I forgot my notes at a custody hearing, and it could work now. By putting on my mental blinkers and pretending this was nothing more than the set-up to a delightfully quirky rom-com, I kept myself together.

"Well, I know you said I could go fuck myself," I drawled, "but I didn't expect you to provide props."

Heather's mouth twisted into a sneer.

"Just thought I'd bring these back to you," she hissed. "You'll need them when you find someone else to fulfil all your nasty little perversions!"

My *little perversions?*

I was pretty sure I'd never seen half of the objects currently rolling around my ankles.

"Don't worry, sweetheart," I purred. "You were the nastiest of my perversions and I already sent you packing."

I was expecting the slap. The sound reverberated through the office like the crack of a whip. I imagined a big red hand-print blooming on my cheek.

You might expect that I'd be the center of attention by this point. In most offices, a vengeful she-hag summoning a rain of sex toys would turn some heads. The truth was my co-workers were used to it... used to me. They'd probably share the story over lunch, shake their heads and say, "Classic Nolan." In my professional life, I was a highly competent and successful attorney, but my personal life was a complete disaster. My sister claimed that when it came to women, I had the attention span of a spoiled toddler, and my aunt Norah would just shake her head and say I was my father's son through and through.

Looking back through the train wreck of my previous relationships, how could I say they were wrong? I was a whirling vortex of romantic destruction. Maybe that was why I kept falling into bed with women like Heather. As I left my 20s in the dust and cruised into my early 30s, I remained magnetically drawn to coke-sniffing party girls, trust-fund babies with daddy issues, and borderline sociopaths with a gift for making scenes. In short, people just as fucked up as I was. There was something weirdly safe about them. You can't fuck up someone's life if they're already doing it themselves.

I sighed and pinched the bridge of my nose.

"Heather," I said slowly. "You're making a scene."

Heather could never cope with people being reasonable. Her face paled and she seemed to swell like a bullfrog.

"Oh, I haven't even started yet," she promised.

"Nope. I think you're done."

Glancing over her shoulder, I was relieved to see a red-faced, sweating figure in a gray uniform. Mike from security was always a welcome sight. Short, fat, and balding—the sight of him didn't immediately suggest he was capable of heroic feats, but he had come to my rescue more times than I could count. A glance between me and Heather told him everything he needed to know, and we quickly fell into our usual routine.

"Everything alright, Mr. Reid?"

I smiled, swiftly smoothing any cracks in my professional veneer.

"Mike, this lady is very distressed. Would you be so good as to escort her downstairs and call her a cab?"

Mike took Heather's upper arm in a firm but gentle hold.

"Very good, Mr. Reid. Shall I put her on the, er—?"

He raised his free hand and mimed a squiggle with an invisible pen. Thanks to my chaotic romantic history, security had a list of women who were not to be admitted to the building under any circumstances. I'd never actually confirmed this, but apparently, a list of the names and the accompanying mugshots had been pasted in a prominent position on the breakroom wall. They'd need to update it now.

Heather looked daggers over her shoulder as she was

ushered politely, but insistently, from the office. I rubbed my hands over my face. I was impossibly tired, and it wasn't even lunchtime.

Before I had time to worry about how I was going to deal with the mess on the floor, I heard a familiar voice at my elbow.

"Gonna need to send our compliments to the guys in security. Their response time's improving."

"You called them?"

"Soon as she got here. Been workin' for you long enough to smell trouble when it walks in."

Alana Ramirez had materialized at my side at some point during the chaos. Now she was standing, tablet in hand, sucking delicately on the tip of her stylus as though nothing were amiss.

A lot of people were surprised when they met my PA, probably because she didn't look like one. People saw the asymmetric purple hair and the tattoos and jumped to conclusions—me included. When the agency first sent her to me, I thought it had to be some kind of joke. Turned out the joke was on me; she was the most efficient person I had ever worked with. She was only meant to be temping for a few days. That was five years ago, and now I wasn't sure how I'd ever gotten along without her. Not only was she brilliant at her job, but she was utterly unshockable. It was nice to have one person in the office who wasn't silently judging me. If I was an ass, she told me to my face.

She regarded the objects on the ground with cool detachment, as though she dealt with rogue dildos on a daily basis. Crouching down, she hooked a set of handcuffs on the end of her stylus and eyed them critically.

"Really, boss?" She held them at arm's length with an expression of distaste. "These are *pink*."

"They're not mine!" I protested, flushing hotly.

"And fluffy."

"Again, *not mine*!"

"Padded leather is the way to go if you want to—"

"Alana!"

She shrugged.

"Brought it on yourself, *jefe*. That's what you get when you dip your dick in crazy."

I scowled, wishing I could argue the point. She picked up a purple leather paddle with an embossed pink heart and began rubbing it gently over her palm.

"Don't get any ideas," I warned.

She raised a withering eyebrow.

"Relax, *querida*. You're not my type."

I raised a quizzical eyebrow—I was under the impression Alana didn't have a type.

"My heart is broken," I declared. "I was just waiting for you to notice me."

"I know better than to get involved with this mess."

She underscored her words by ruffling my hair affectionately. I made a half-hearted attempt to flap her hand away.

"You do remember I'm your boss, right?"

"Sorry, *jefe*. "

She gave me an ironic salute with the paddle hand. I rolled my eyes.

"Right now, I'm more concerned about *this* mess."

I took in the sordid jumble on the floor with a sweeping gesture. Alana picked up the empty box.

"I'll deal with 'em," she offered.

My mind couldn't help imagining the possibilities.

"Now who's getting ideas?" she teased. "Oh, by the way, Larry's lookin' for ya. Wants to go over the arrangements for Richard's party."

It took a moment for my brain to process the conversational gear-change, but when it caught up, I groaned. Organizing any kind of office party was a stressful, thankless task that somehow always landed on my plate.

"Come on!" Alana coaxed. "It's not every day a senior partner gets married."

"And who better to plan the bachelor party than the eternal bachelor?" I grumbled.

"If I were you, I'd see it as an opportunity," she mused. "Get this right and you're sure to be on his radar when promotion time comes around."

I guess there might be something in that.

Alana tapped at her tablet and consulted one of her many lists.

"As far as I can see, he just wants standard stuff. Free-flowing liquor, a lady in a cake. Nothing we can't handle."

I rubbed my forehead, feeling the approach of the headache from hell.

"Where am I supposed to go for a lady in a cake?"

I had barely finished speaking when an e-mail pinged on my phone. Alana looked at me with that little half-smile she always had when she was three steps ahead of me.

"Just sent you a list of the bakeries that can do you a stripper cake. I'm guessin' I don't need to tell you where you can find a stripper."

"Very funny."

"Personally, I'd go for the one at the top," she continued, ignoring my interruption.

I read the name aloud.

"Sticky Treats?"

"Yep. They did some themed cake pops for my cousin's baby shower. Tastiest nipples I've ever put my mouth around."

"What do nipples have to do with a baby shower?"

"I dunno. Breastfeeding?"

I'd met enough members of Alana's family to understand her strange immunity to my antics.

"Just trust me," she assured as she bent to gather the sex toys.

Ok then. Sticky Treats it is.

By the time I made it back to my desk, I was already composing the email.

CHAPTER THREE

Erin

"I need that final block."

The block of chilled cake was so large that Jayden needed both hands to lift it. He dropped it into the waiting tray with unnecessary force, making no effort to hide his petulant scowl.

Following my conversation with Maddie, I had finally caved and hired an assistant. Jayden was 19 and freshly graduated from catering school. On his first day, he'd shown up to my kitchen convinced I could teach him nothing and refusing to wear a hairnet over his lime green man-bun. I'd won the hairnet argument after showing him one of his Day-Glo hairs lying accusingly in a bowl of cream cheese frosting. The hair, combined with what came to be referred to as "the unfortunate incident with the ruby chocolate fountain," was enough to convince him that he had a lot to learn about the world of alternative confectionery.

After our rocky start, I'd concluded that he actually had potential. The cocky attitude and the tendency to believe he was God's gift to patisserie would inevitably be sandblasted away by a couple of years of experience. Beyond that, he was competent, creative, and quick to learn. After what had happened with Stirling, letting someone else into my life, even on a strictly professional basis, was terrifying. But I was starting to warm up to my teenage protégé. Of course, that wasn't to say we didn't frequently butt heads.

"Gonna trip over that lip," I warned.

I deftly sliced at the edges of the block with a sharp knife. I needed to carve it into the desired shape before it warmed up too much.

"I just think chiffon cake would be classier," he mumbled.

"I told you already." I sighed, carefully paring at a ragged edge. "This... monstrosity is going to be covered in decorated fondant. Chiffon cake would collapse. Besides," I added, stepping back to appraise my work. "Given what this cake is the wrapping for, I don't think classy really comes into it."

Not that I was kink-shaming. I'd just never seen the appeal of sequins, fake tits, and pasties. Maybe you had to be a horny drunk guy at a bachelor party.

"We could use buttercream instead," said Jayden mulishly.

"Too messy," I argued. "Transport alone would be an accident waiting to happen. You have to understand the needs of your client, Jayden. We're already pushing the envelope with this thing. Now," I slotted the final cake section into the base, "make yourself useful and go get the nipples from the blast chiller; they should've set by now."

With the sulky demeanor of a kid who'd just been grounded, Jayden stomped off to the blast chiller to get the raspberry Jell-O nipples.

Eyeing the six interlocking sections of cake, I rubbed the back of my neck anxiously. I hadn't been kidding when I'd said we were pushing the envelope. Most people are familiar with the concept of a scantily clad woman jumping out of a cake, but there is a surprising amount of confusion surrounding how this feat is achieved. Once I'd even been asked how I managed to bake the cake without hurting the stripper inside.

The most common method was a hollow structure made of cardboard or Styrofoam and covered in fondant. I'd decided a long time ago that this would not be good enough for me. I had a strict policy that my confections should all be 100% edible, and I was very proud of what I'd come up with this time.

The cake was a large, egg-shaped structure, consisting of blocks of cake built around a wire frame. The two halves were designed to open outwards, and the outer surface would be covered in decorations that could be pulled off and eaten. Cake pop boobs, tempered chocolate butts, and marshmallow penises were carefully arranged in a circular pattern, giving the appearance of an obscene Fabergé egg. It was my most ambitious piece to date. I always got excited when my clients had the budget to do something spectacular. Some fancy corporate law firm was throwing a bachelor party for a senior partner and money was no object. I couldn't wait to light up Instagram with this thing.

Maybe if I made enough of a splash, I'd finally feel like I'd erased the ugly smear Stirling had left on my reputation. Feeling a hot prickling under my eyelids, I hastily swallowed the angry lump in my throat. I couldn't afford to think about my ex right now—not when I had three huge batches of cake pops patiently waiting for their nipples.

As the deadline approached, the bakery was a flurry of activity. Jayden and I worked long hours, frosting, modeling, and sticking until we had six beautifully decorated pieces ready for transport. I was more thankful than ever that I'd gotten over my stubborn pride and hired someone. I could never have managed this on my own. We both stood admiring the finished product, and I put an arm around Jayden's shoulders.

"We did good, kid," I declared.

Calling him a kid would usually have made him grumpy, but on this occasion, he just beamed proudly. It was adorable. We had planned to close the shop early and deliver the cake to its destination so we could set up ahead of the party. I should have been basking in a job well done, but I could already feel the anxious weight of our next batch of orders creeping in. May and June were always crazy busy. Wedding season was no joke in the confectionery business. When Jayden came to me after lunch, I was eyebrow-deep in my graphics tablet, designing my next creation.

"Say, Erin," he ventured. "Why don't you let me deliver the cake?"

I put down my stylus and frowned.

"I don't know, Jayden. This is a huge order. If anything were to go wrong—"

"What could go wrong?" he protested. "We're slammed right now, and it's not like putting this cake together needs both of us."

I bit the inside of my cheek. He had a point. I hadn't even started making the profiteroles for the "suggestive croquembouche" Mrs. Gunderson had ordered for her daughter's bridal shower, and the Romance Writers Association wanted a life-sized chocolate boyfriend for their annual meet and greet.

Jayden cranked the puppy dog eyes to maximum.

"Sometimes I feel like you don't trust me to do anything important."

Manipulative little shit!

Still, he was itching to prove himself. Maybe after the work he'd put in over the last few days, he deserved that chance.

"Alright." I eyed him sternly. "I'll let you make the delivery, but there's to be no fooling around, and you're to follow my written instructions to the letter!"

"Yes!"

He grinned and punched the air.

"You won't regret this."

I regret it already.

I tried not to worry too much as I watched Jayden drive off

in the van. Instead, I focused my energy on profiteroles. By the time the last batch was cooling, I was exhausted. I leaned against the counter, flipping through my phone, not quite able to face the clean-up yet. I lingered over the Facebook invite that had pinged earlier. Several friends were planning an impromptu cocktail night and I had promised Maddie I'd try to socialize more. I hovered over the event for a few seconds before clicking decline. It had been a crazy few days. I deserved a night of "Netflix and chill."

I was gathering up my things to leave when my phone started buzzing. My heart sank when I saw Jayden's caller ID. I had already imagined six possible disaster scenarios by the time I answered the phone and heard his anxious voice.

"Erin. I think I fucked up."

"What do you mean you fucked up?!"

I tried to sound less hysterical than I felt. What had I been thinking, trusting a kid with a $3000 cake? I could already hear the rich liquid gurgle of my career trickling down the drain. Taking a deep breath, I tried to decipher Jayden's garbled explanation. Apparently, he'd set up the cake and everything seemed fine... until he got home with the van and found 3 dowels that had rolled under the seat. It could mean nothing, or it could mean the whole thing would collapse as soon as it was opened. Knowing my luck, it would be the latter.

I ran a hand down the side of my face and tried to think like a rational human being.

"It's ok," I said carefully. "I haven't left the bakery yet; I can swing by the party on my way home and check things out. There's probably nothing to worry about."

I wasn't sure whether I was telling myself or him.

"I'm really sorry, Erin."

He sounded so dejected that my anger evaporated. He'd tried his best. It was my fault, really; I should have known better than to leave things in someone else's hands.

"It's alright, Jayden," I soothed. "Accidents happen."

I tried to ignore the sense of overpowering exhaustion as I flopped into the driver's seat of my car and plugged the venue into the GPS.

So much for Netflix.

CHAPTER FOUR

Nolan

"Tell me, Nolan, are you ever planning to grow up?"

I winced and held the phone farther from my ear. My sister had been asking me this question for roughly a decade and somehow, she always managed to choose the worst time.

"Hello, Olivia," I snarked. "How are you? *I'm* fine, by the way. So sweet of you to ask."

"The hell you're fine," she snapped. "Nothing about your life is *fine.* What the hell happened with Heather at your office?"

My fist clenched and I felt the bite of my nails as they dug into my palm. Apparently, when your ex-girlfriend shows up at your office and starts scattering sex toys everywhere like a deranged dildo fairy, word gets around. Judging by my sister's tone, the whispers had even penetrated the cozy reaches of suburbia.

Phrasing!

"It was nothing!" I assured her. "Heather was a little... emotional. But it's all blown over now."

Olivia snorted.

"Sure! And what about Abby's party? You do remember it's next week."

"Of course."

My eyebrows knitted at the abrupt change in direction.

"You worried I'm not going to show? I'd never let my baby-girl down."

"Nolan!" I could feel my sister's exasperation oozing through the phone connection. "You've spent your whole adult life letting women down!"

Ouch!

The words sank to the bottom of my stomach like a rock. The heavy silence stretched on until it thickened into an awkward, sticky pause.

"Jesus, Nolan, I—I'm sorry. That was harsh."

All the anger had gone from Olivia's voice; now she just sounded tired.

"I'd never let my family down."

Abby's father had abandoned Olivia when she was eight months pregnant. My first impulse had been to track him down and break his legs, but in the end, I'd settled for filling the void. After watching our own parents' marriage dissolve in a storm of alcohol and resentment, I was determined that my niece would have a stable family, even if it only consisted of me, Olivia, and "Granny V."

"I know you wouldn't," said Olivia gently. "I just worry about you. Plus, I don't want one of your crazy ex-girlfriends showing up at my little girl's birthday party and dumping panties on the bouncy castle."

"Never gonna happen," I assured her. "Heather's taken care of. Trust me. Look, I have to go. I'm waiting on another call."

"Is that so?" Olivia teased. "Got the next girl lined up already?"

"Nope," I said breezily. "Just hiring a stripper."

"Aaand... we're done."

I rushed to qualify.

"Now, when I say *I'm* hiring a stripper, technically I'm—"

"You can definitely stop talking now," my sister cut me off firmly. "There are certain things I just don't need to know."

After ending the call, I ran a hand through my hair and stared at my phone screen. No messages.

The cake had shown up on schedule. Baking had never been my thing, but even I could tell that the workmanship was exquisite. I couldn't have been happier with the cake; it was set up in the backroom and ready to go. When I'd retreated in here to take my sister's call, I'd been struggling with the temptation to sample one of the cake pops. The problem was, there was no stripper to go inside it. I'd been exchanging increasingly irate messages with the agency for at least 30 minutes before my sister called. Apparently, the girl was "running late."

By this point, the bachelor party was in full swing; my phone conversation had been punctuated by bursts of raucous laughter. But as the minutes ticked by, I detected an increasingly restless edge to the noises, and I was starting to sweat.

I'd been pacing for about 10 minutes when the door opened, bringing in a louder swell of laughter and a pungent cloud of cigar smoke. Larry stuck his head through the gap and looked around the room as though he thought the stripper might be hiding in a corner. He was red faced and his tie swung loosely from his open shirt collar.

"Hey, Nolan!" he hissed. "What gives, man? The cake's right there, but I don't see the toy surprise."

His drunken whisper dissolved into a moist, wheezy chuckle. Clearly, he found himself hilarious.

"The girl's running late," I admitted. "Don't see what I can do."

"Well, you'd better do something," Larry urged. "The guys are ready to riot out here."

Perfect.

I clasped both hands behind my head and squeezed my eyes shut. I was on the point of calling Alana to see if she could somehow procure me an "emergency stripper," when I heard a soft but insistent knock. With a swooping feeling of relief in my chest, I hurried to open the door.

"Finally!"

The tirade I had prepared about professionalism and timekeeping instantly died in my throat. Whatever I'd been expecting, it wasn't a petite and slender brunette in chef's whites.

Unconventional, but I guess it ties in with the cake theme.

She was cute too. Full lips, doe eyes, perky tits. I certainly wasn't going to complain.

"Uhm... hi."

She raised her hand in an awkward little wave and I realized I'd been silently staring at her for a fraction too long.

"Sorry." I shook my head slightly. "It's been a long night. I'm really glad you're here, though."

Her pretty features creased into a frown.

"Is it that bad? I'd have gotten here sooner if—"

"You have no idea. "

I seized her by one of her delicate wrists and led her hurriedly through the passage and into the back room. The cake was standing open on the dolly, ready to be wheeled in. I'd hoped she'd immediately get into it, but she just stood there, head tilted to one side, examining it critically. When I heard the tinkling of broken glass from next door, my frayed nerves finally broke.

"Well, go on then!" I snapped, gesturing at the cake. "In you go!"

She raised an eyebrow.

"Just like that? You're not going to tell me—?"

"What would I need to tell you? Just get in there and do your thing; it's hardly rocket science."

She placed her hands on her hips and all at once she was five feet of fiery indignation.

"Nothing to it?" she bristled. "That's what men like you think, isn't it? It's nothing special; it's just what women do. On tap treats for entitled jerk-wads. No consideration at all to the work that goes into—"

"Woah, woah!" I raised my hands in a gesture of surrender. "You're right. I'm sorry, I was an ass. I'm sure that there's a lot of... skill that goes into what you do. But right now, I have 43 horny guys out there waiting for a show, so could you just get inside the cake and do what you do best... please?"

"Alright."

She sighed and pressed her hand to her forehead. I noticed the dark circles under her eyes for the first time. Stripping was obviously more demanding than I realized.

"I'm sorry too," she conceded. "It's just been... a day."

"Tell me about it."

We shared a small smile. She had a beautiful smile. Her eyes sparkled and it made the most adorable little crease in her cheek. There was a funny feeling in my stomach like I'd missed a step going downstairs.

"Uhm... yeah... well."

Clearing my throat awkwardly, I stepped aside and ushered her onto the platform. I needed to stop flirting with the stripper and let her do her job.

As soon as she was inside, I closed the cake with a click and began to wheel the dolly into the main room. Before we reached the noise and chaos of the party, I could have sworn I heard a squeak of protest, but I dismissed it as a wheel in need of oiling. Why would the stripper be screaming? This was what she was expecting to happen.

CHAPTER FIVE

Nolan

As soon as the cake was in place, I felt the overwhelming urge to retreat to the bar and collapse with a cold beer. The idea of Nolan Reid turning down a striptease would surprise most people, but by that point, I was far too stressed to appreciate the show.

It's a fact that people who plan parties don't get to enjoy them. I'd seen it with my sister at all of Abby's birthday parties. She was always so busy trying to create magical memories for each of her little girl's milestones that she ran herself ragged. At a certain point, she always made the transition from fairy godmother to Disney villainess—elbow-deep in paper and frosting, hissing at anyone who came near.

My mouth watered as the bartender popped the top on my beer. I had barely taken my first pull of frosty, foamy goodness when my phone buzzed.

I scanned the short message three times before its meaning penetrated the tired fog between my ears. The agency had contacted me to inform me that the stripper had unexpectedly canceled. They sent their sincerest apologies and offered to fully refund my deposit.

But then, who...?

"Shit!"

I slammed my beer down and launched myself into the function room. The cake was exactly where I had left it. It stood in the center of the room, sealed like a giant frosted clam and surrounded by drunk, indignant party guests. The remote that controlled the room's sound system was lying on a nearby table. I grabbed it and swiftly cut the music. Instantly, most of the men turned around, their outrage now directed at me.

"What the hell, Nolan?"

"What gives?"

Cursing and elbowing my way through the throng, I motioned at them to stand back. My usual trick of pretending none of this was real wasn't working this time. No play had ever been this embarrassing. I stood staring at the intricate pink shell, at a loss for what to do. Eventually, I approached the join between the two cake halves. I raised a hand to knock before I realized what I was doing and tried to turn the motion into a cough.

"Ahem... er, Miss?"

Silence.

Ignoring the snickers behind me, I raised my voice a little and tried again.

"Miss? Are you in there?"

"Nope."

I blinked. The voice was muffled and slightly echoey.

"Nope as in, nope, you're not in there?"

"Oh, I'm in here. I don't think I'm ever coming out though."

"Look..." The back of my neck was getting warm. When did my shirt collar get so snug? "Obviously there's been some sort of mix-up here," I reasoned. "But if you'll just step out of the cake, we can talk about this."

"What's going on here, Nolan?"

I winced at the sudden intrusion of Larry's piercing stage whisper at my elbow.

"This chick got stage fright?" Without waiting for a reply, he addressed the inside of the cake, raising his voice to a shout, "It's ok, sweetheart. Everyone here is very open-minded."

Not missing a beat, he turned back to me and continued in what he fondly imagined was a whisper.

"Not the end of the world if we've got a double-bagger on our hands; we can just dim the lights."

"She's not the stripper!" I exploded.

"She's also not deaf!"

The muffled retort made us both jump. Biting back a groan of mortification, I seized Larry by the shoulders and turned him back towards the party.

"Can you just let me handle this?" I pleaded.

"Ok." He shrugged. "Might wanna avoid antagonizing her, though. Sounds like she's riding the cotton camel."

Pinching the bridge of my nose, I took a deep breath and headed back into the breach.

"I can understand you not wanting to come out," I called gently. "But can I at least come in?"

There was a derisive snort. Tonight, I was learning that sound traveled surprisingly well through sponge cake.

"I just want to talk," I qualified. "I'm alone and unarmed, I promise."

She paused for so long that I assumed I was getting the silent treatment. I was on the point of opening my mouth to try a different tactic when she finally replied.

"You can stick your head in."

"That's what she said!"

I wasn't sure who'd shouted, but I stretched out an arm and flipped off the crowd at large. One side of the cake moved out, revealing a gradually expanding sliver of darkness. Once there was enough of a gap, I gingerly pushed my head and shoulders through, grimacing as something soft and creamy squished against the lapel of my jacket.

I inhaled deeply, caught off balance. I wasn't used to small dark spaces smelling this good. I could smell vanilla and caramel, mingling delightfully with a hint of floral shampoo. My mouth went dry, and my tongue felt too big. I opened my mouth and made the horrifying discovery that I had somehow forgotten every single word in the English language.

I couldn't see much, but the light filtering in from behind me was just enough to pick out the outline of a small, hunched figure. My instincts told me to gather her in my arms and hold her. Fortunately, there wasn't enough room, and I hadn't trusted a single instinct in my body since the onset of puberty.

"So," I managed eventually. "You're not the stripper then?"

"How many strippers have you met who wear chef's whites?" she hissed.

"Well, uniforms are actually quite a popular—"

I let my sentence trail off. I didn't need to see her face to feel the frosty glare. I went for a more direct approach.

"Who are you?" I asked.

"Who do you think?" she scoffed.

"Well, if the whites aren't a costume, I'm going to guess you're a... baker?"

"No, I'm not *a* baker. I'm *the* baker."

"Ohh!"

My mouth made a perfect circle as the penny dropped.

"You're not the kid who was here earlier."

"Nooo." Her words were delivered with the deliberation and patience of someone attempting to explain thermodynamics to a five-year-old. "That would be my assistant."

"So, you're the big boss, huh? I like that in a woman."

I had a bad habit of trying to turn on the charm when I was in an awkward situation. It didn't get much more awkward than negotiating with a woman you've just locked in a cake while trying to ignore the derisive hooting of your colleagues. Predictably, my efforts were not appreciated.

"Are you seriously flirting with me right now?" she squeaked.

"No, of course not." I shifted slightly and felt my thumb poke through the shiny surface of a chocolate buttock.

"But if I was trying to flirt, I'd ask you to guess where my thumb is right now."

I was lost. The verbal diarrhea had progressed to a raging case of dysentery. It could only be a matter of time before this woman slapped me.

"Come on, Nolan! We're ready to bust a nut out here."

I examined the shadowy figure, remembering the heart-shaped face and the deliciously tight ass. I couldn't stop myself.

"Don't suppose you want to earn an extra $500?"

I guess my mouth just wants women to slap me.

"What the fu—?"

"Sorry," I said hastily. "Joke. Bad joke. Terrible. But as you can see," I shrugged sheepishly, "I'm kind of up against it here."

"Well," she spat. "Maybe *you* should get up and dance. I'm sure it's not rocket science."

The call-back to my unfortunate words from earlier didn't go unnoticed. I reddened.

"Touché," I quipped. "If I do get up and dance, will you come out of the cake?"

"I don't know. Will I see anything worth looking at?"

Her voice had taken on a subtle edge. A tiny hint of husky flirtation that made my cock stir. I could hear the hint of a smirk creeping across her face. Seized by a sudden fevered madness, I licked my lips and spun to face the room. The guys had stopped clamoring and were now staring at me in slack-jawed amazement. I raised the remote and flicked the speakers on.

CHAPTER SIX

Erin

The opening strains of David Rose's "The Stripper" erupted from the speakers.

Why don't you get up and dance?

I hadn't expected him to take me at my word.

When the cake door had closed and I felt the movement underneath me, my first thought had been that this was some malicious prank of Stirling's. It fit his MO. The torrent of filth that had flooded onto my company website after our breakup all had a particular theme, and it hit a nerve. People tended to get the wrong idea about me when they found out what I did—now it seemed that they expected me to jump out of the cakes as well as bake them.

The shouts and catcalls began soon after the movement stopped, and I couldn't bring myself to go out and face them. I hunched miserably in the dark, wondering how long it would take me to die of embarrassment. Certainly not before I'd need to go to the bathroom. There wasn't enough space to stand up, and after a couple of minutes my thighs began cramping. I felt a pang of sympathy for the woman who was supposed to have been in here. Running a hand over the wire mesh, I started to ponder how I could make the next one roomier.

Maddie would have laughed at me for thinking about work at a time like this. If she were here, she'd probably be halfway through the striptease. She'd always been a much more comfortable passenger on the insanity train than I was. I could see a weird irony to this situation. At our last lunch, she'd accused me of being buried in work; now, here I was, encased in one of my own confections.

By the time *he* made his attempt to persuade me out, panic was setting in. My chest had tightened, and the stuffy, vanilla-scented darkness was closing in on me.

How much air was even in this thing?

Even so, I wasn't in the mood to deal with the jerk who'd put me here in the first place. Yet, as we talked, something about him threw me off balance. It was like turning the handle on a gumball machine, only to find your candy pouring from a completely unexpected hole on the other side. When I caught myself responding to his flirting, I chalked it up to oxygen deprivation.

I was ready to write him off as a jerk-stuffed jerk with a crunchy jerk coating. But then he ruined everything in his disarming willingness to completely humiliate himself. I told myself I wouldn't look, but I couldn't help it. I leaned forward and peered through the gap. This guy might have been a jerk, but I couldn't deny that he was also a snack. I'd noticed as soon as I'd arrived. He had thick, reddish-brown hair that tumbled over his head in copper waves. The even growth of scruff on his strong jaw and chin was an even deeper red and I couldn't help but imagine how it would feel, scratching over my cheek. His beautiful green eyes sat beneath thick lashes and sparkled with a permanent devilish twinkle. He was tall and broad-shouldered, and I could see the enticing play of muscles beneath his well-tailored suit.

My vantage point from inside the cake meant that I was

eye level with his gyrating ass—and what an ass. Those buttocks had been hand-sculpted by Satan himself. I wanted to reach out and cup them. I imagined the feel of the taut muscles clenching and shifting under the smooth fabric of his pants. My breath hitched and I felt something twitch low in my belly. Fighting temptation, I crossed my arms over my stomach and clenched my fists into tight balls.

Not today, Satan!

Before my resolve could be tested any further, he slunk out of reach. The temporary silence of the crowd had given way to confused shouting and I couldn't contain my curiosity any longer. It was time to leave my frosted fortress.

Pins and needles shot up my legs as I eased myself from my crouch and slipped out of the cake. No one noticed me. All eyes were fixed on my... I honestly wasn't sure if he was my captor or my rescuer at this point. He was down to his shirt-sleeves by now. I scanned the crowd and noticed one of the men clutching a familiar jacket uncomfortably. Locking eyes with someone in the front row, my mystery man loosened his tie and dropped it coyly in his unfortunate victim's lap.

He was throwing himself into the performance with enthusiasm and I was riveted by the graceful undulation of his hips. Our eyes met when he spun around, and he held my gaze as he slowly unbuttoned his shirt. I blushed hotly but I was unable to look away. Before I realized what I was doing, my tongue had darted out to moisten my lips. The gesture only seemed to encourage him further and he threw his head back as he shrugged the shirt from his shoulders and discarded it behind him.

My eyes traveled along the smooth, hard contours of his pecs and traced the subtle outline of his six-pack. By this point, he was glistening with exertion, and I could almost taste the salty sweat on my lips. He ran his hands down his stomach, pausing to unbutton his fly. I stood frozen as he eased his pants over his hips, and I forced my eyes away from the obvious bulge in his black boxers. It felt like the rest of the room had fallen away and he was dancing just for me.

My hand flew to my mouth as he slipped his thumbs into the waistband of his underwear and waggled his eyebrows suggestively. My cheeks were red, I was sure, and I could feel a molten throbbing between my legs. I knew I should look away, but I was enthralled by the power of his—

"Enough!"

"Seriously, Nolan! Come on!"

"Someone pass the brain bleach!"

The loud, disgusted protests brought me back to earth with a bump. Judging by the look on his face, Mr. Universe had forgotten about the other members of the audience as well. He grinned like a naughty school kid, giving me a helpless half shrug before turning around and taking a bow. Some of the audience laughed, one or two hurled beer nuts and wasabi peas at him.

"What gives?" one man groused. "We were promised a stripper and we get your hairy ass?!"

Nolan was quick with his retort.

"Just thought you might like a taste of what I gave your wife last night."

The man's face reddened amidst the burst of raucous laughter. By the time we were interrupted by a knock at the door, a few people had even started calling for an encore. It turned out the gods had delivered a distraction in the form of a massive order of sushi and most of the party trooped into the next room to line their stomachs.

"Phew!" Nolan shot me a roguish grin and passed a hand over his forehead. "Saved by the bell!"

Now that we were alone, I fumbled for words. Attempting to ease the tension, I moved amongst the abandoned chairs, helping him retrieve his scattered clothes. Blushing as I handed him his pants, I realized that I had only made things worse. We were going through the motions of the awkward morning after without actually having had the sex.

"I assume you know my name by now. Do I get yours?"

I looked up reluctantly. I had been stubbornly absorbed in hunting down a stray sock. He was shrugging on his jacket, but his shirt remained unbuttoned. There was an enticing slice of toned washboard staring out at me from the crisp white folds. Now that he was standing closer, I could see that his stomach was coated in a fine down of golden hair. I could imagine how soft it would be, like moleskin.

"Erin. Erin Donovan. You have cake pop on your—"

I gestured at the pink and white smear on his lapel.

"Shit."

He glanced down at the stain and colored.

"Well, this is embarrassing." He grimaced. "It's tempting to make an innuendo about getting my hands on your boobs at this point, but I expect you get those all the time."

"Lil bit," I admitted, allowing my face to relax into a smile.

"Jesus. I'm—I'm really fucking sorry about the mix-up. The stripper was late and then you—"

I held up my hand. Ten minutes ago, I'd been ready to slap him, but any anger that hadn't been thawed by the striptease was dissolving under the influence of his obvious remorse.

"It's ok," I reassured him. "No harm done."

"Look. Can I buy you a drink?"

Uh-oh.

It was tempting to say yes. I was supposed to be socializing, and what could be more sociable than accepting a drink from a tall, handsome stranger with disconcertingly beautiful nipples? Still, something held me back. After Stirling, I'd pledged to avoid unnecessary drama at all costs. However cute and enticing this guy might have been, was he worth the risk? Anyone who tries to resolve an awkward social situation with an impromptu striptease should probably be raising some red flags in the drama department. I threw Nolan an apologetic half-smile.

"Maybe some other time."

"Are you sure?" he coaxed. "I can be very good company when I'm not imprisoning people in cakes."

He stuck his lip out a little and gave me a pleading look from under his lashes.

Damn it! You're not making this easy!

"I'm sure. Besides, I have a ton of work on right now."

He relented with a good-natured shrug.

"Ok. But at least let me send some business your way. Sticky Treats, yes?"

"That's the one!"

I gave him a little wave and turned on my heel. I could feel him watching me as I walked away, but I was determined not to look back. I knew I shouldn't read too much into it. He was a gorgeous lawyer at a bachelor party. He would have moved on to the next girl before the night was over. The chances of seeing or hearing from him again were practically zero.

CHAPTER SEVEN

Nolan

"You should ask her out."

"Who?"

I stabbed viciously at the buttons on the vending machine. My fingers drummed against the glowing plastic as a thin trickle of coffee filled the paper cup. Alana rolled her eyes.

"Who do you think? Cake woman! It's obvious she got to you."

I took a mouthful of coffee and wrinkled my nose.

"We have to stop at Starbucks. This stuff is disgusting."

I threw the half-full cup into the trash and headed for the elevator. Alana remained glued to my elbow.

"Quit changin' the subject," she chided.

I sucked in a heavy breath and bit the inside of my cheek.

"Keep this up and I might decide I can take my own notes at the lunch meeting," I warned her. "I'm not above sentencing you to cafeteria food."

Undaunted, she followed me into the waiting elevator.

"Right there, you just proved my point. Never seen you this cranky."

Scowling, I pressed the button for the basement parking lot and the elevator began its slow descent.

"Is it surprising I'm cranky?" I grumbled. "I accused an innocent woman of being a stripper and trapped her inside a cake."

I ignored Alana's snort. Apparently, this story didn't get any less funny on the third retelling.

"And then, because I'm somehow incapable of backing down from a challenge, I make a total ass of myself in front of her and half my colleagues."

Alana jabbed her phone with a stylus. In the time it had taken the elevator to descend she'd probably sent six e-mails and rearranged my appointment diary for the next month.

"You're still makin' my point for me," she murmured, frowning at her screen. "You make an ass of yourself all the time. Why is it suddenly a big deal?"

"The cafeteria line is calling you, Alana. Can you feel it?"

She pocketed her phone and held out her hands in surrender.

"Hey, chill! I'm just saying, this has to be way less embarrassing than that thing with Heather last week. You shook that off quick enough."

Groaning, I rested my head on the cool metal wall of the car.

"I know. It's just that this party was supposed to help advance my career. I'm not sure that stripping in front of a large group of the senior partners is the best way to convince them that I'm promotion material."

The elevator slowed to a stop and the doors swished open. No matter how warm it was outside, the basement parking lot always felt cold and damp. I shivered and groped in my pocket for the keys to my Lexus. Alana yawned and ran a hand over the shorn hairs at the nape of her neck.

"Surely they won't hold it against you. Isn't that part of the 'bro code'? What happens at the bachelor party stays at the bachelor party."

I chuckled mirthlessly.

"I wish it had stayed at the bachelor party. All morning I've had people humming 'The Stripper' and sticking dollar bills in my back pocket."

Alana winced sympathetically.

"Now, that's just unfair," she consoled.

"Thank you!"

"You're worth a five at least."

I was gearing up to be angry but one look at her impish grin disarmed me. My shoulders relaxed and I allowed myself to smile.

"Seriously though." She punched me gently on the arm. "That stuff's never gotten to you before. You'd just laugh it off. I think this girl got in your head."

I gave an exasperated growl.

"Enough, woman! The only thing in my head right now is this very important lunch meeting and since we're already la—"

When I caught sight of my Lexus, I froze in mute horror. The sleek silver finish was covered in giant splashes of neon pink paint, and the word 'prick' had been daubed in dripping letters on the windshield. The scene hit me like a punch to the stomach. There was a faint clink as the keys dropped from my limp hand. My head slumped forwards and I closed my eyes.

"Alana," I said numbly.

"Yep?"

"Please tell me I'm hallucinating."

"Afraid not, *jefe*."

This day just gets better and better.

I took a deep, shuddering breath and shook myself like a wet dog.

"Ok," I said, somehow tapping my inner reservoir of calm. "Reschedule that meeting."

"On it."

She was too. I could already hear the rhythmic tapping of her stylus on the phone screen.

"And while you're at it, get on to security. Ask them to pull their thumbs from their asses and grab the security tapes from this morning."

Immediate business taken care of, I sank down on the hood of my ravaged car and put my head in my hands. A few seconds later, Alana sat down next to me and squeezed my shoulder.

"Hey!" she soothed. "It's just paint. We'll send her to Carlos, and she'll be good as new in no time."

Three years ago, I'd dated a backing dancer who'd wound up keying my car. Alana introduced me to her cousin Carlos. He was a mechanic who specialized in custom bodywork. After my car came back within 24 hours looking better than new, I'd never trusted my baby with anybody else. One day, some enterprising car company would come up with an insurance plan that covered "acts of ex-girlfriend." Until then, Carlos and his "friends and family" discount would have to do.

"Think this was Heather?" Alana asked, running her finger over a lumpy pink splotch.

"Oh, definitely. She always dots her i's with those stupid hearts."

I scrubbed a hand over my face wearily.

"Why do they always go for the car?"

Alana leaned back on her elbows.

"You hurt her," she stated. "When it comes to revenge, women are brutal. Precision strikes at the things you love most. We're good at that shit. I knew a guy once. Cheated on his girl. She found out and she poured bleach in his tropical fish tank."

I raised an eyebrow.

"Is that a euphemism?"

"No. This was an actual tank, y'know, with fish? He had lots of 'em too: butterflyfish and angelfish and those orange ones from *Finding Nemo*."

"Clownfish," I said absently. Abby had gone through a phase of being obsessed with that movie.

I shuddered.

"You know," I mused. "I'm suddenly glad you talked me out of that iguana."

Alana grimaced.

"Yeah. That could have been ugly."

"She turned me down."

Alana turned to face me.

"This the cake woman?"

"Yeah," I sighed. "Erin."

Alana's eyebrows shot up.

"So you did ask her out."

I nodded.

"Offered to buy her a drink, but unsurprisingly—"

I shook my head.

"Probably a good thing too. I got the impression she didn't deserve to have her life ruined."

Alana looked at me with her head on one side.

"Does it always have to end like that?"

I gestured at the pink explosion where my car used to be.

"Apparently, yes. It's the Reid family curse. Can't keep it in our pants! I said I'd send her some business, though, and I plan to keep my word. She deserves it."

In an instant, my prodigy of an assistant was scrolling through her phone again.

"Doesn't look like we have any birthdays or bachelor parties coming up, and if you eat too many chocolate wangs your stripping days will be over."

I just smiled smugly.

"As it happens, I've already thought of something."

"You have?"

"Yep. Abby's birthday party is next week and the bakery my sister ordered from just canceled."

For a few moments, Alana stared at me, mouth agape. I placed a finger under her chin and gently pushed it closed.

"You can't be serious?" she demanded eventually.

"What?"

"Ok." Alana rubbed a hand over her forehead. "Here's a sentence I never thought I'd use. You probably shouldn't order your niece's sixth birthday cake from an erotic bakery."

I gestured dismissively.

"I'm sure she can do other kinds of cakes. It's going to be super simple. The kiddo wants themed cupcakes instead of a birthday cake. You've seen the pictures of the cake from the bachelor party. If she can do something like that, I'm sure she can handle cupcakes with cat faces."

Alana pursed her lips.

"Plus, she might deliver the cakes herself, giving you the perfect excuse to see her again."

"Yeah, that's pr— No! That has nothing to do with it. I'm just doing her a favor. Stop grinning at me like that! Go ring Carlos. See if he can pick up the car this afternoon."

I didn't care what Alana said. I had no ulterior motive. Maybe a part of me did want to see Erin again, but so what. It would be nice to have the chance to make amends properly. Besides, it wasn't as if anything could ever happen. It was hard to think of any setting less romantic than a kid's birthday party.

CHAPTER EIGHT

Erin

"I don't understand how this happened. I told you a thousand times, you need to use LED spotlights."

Using my cheek to cradle the phone against my shoulder, I rummaged through my desk drawers irritably. I'd long been convinced that my office was inhabited by a race of light-fingered, pen-obsessed gnomes.

"No, Ma'am. The tempering process only protects the sculpture at room temperature. Under the conditions you've described, I'm not surprised that he's a little less... enthusiastic than he was when I delivered him."

Out of the corner of my eye, I saw that Jayden had appeared in the office doorway. He was frowning at a notepad and scratching his head.

"Look, calm down." I held up a finger and mouthed to Jayden to wait.

"I might be able to do something with fans and some dry ice. Just turn those lights off and hang tight. I'll be there soon."

As soon as the call disconnected, I leaned back in my chair and covered my face with my hands. After a moment, Jayden cleared his throat pointedly.

"Don't tell me," I deadpanned. "Those religious protestors are back, and the kitchen is on fire?"

Jayden looked bemused.

"Nope. Not yet anyway. Can we do 'kitty' cupcakes?"

My brow furrowed.

"Kitty?"

"S'what the guy said. Do you think he meant, like... pussy?"

I made a mental inventory of the possibilities.

"Technically, I guess that is a term used for... Jayden, what exactly did the customer say?"

"Uhm."

Jayden bit his lip and looked at the ceiling.

"He said his baby-girl was having a birthday and he wants three dozen cupcakes with kitties on them."

"Oh!" I'd heard that one before. "It's one of those age-play things."

"One of those what now?"

"You know." I gestured vaguely. "Bigs and Littles. Daddy-doms and their 'little princesses.'"

"Oh yeah." He wrinkled his nose. "That stuff's creepy as fuck."

"Hey!" I said sternly. "No kink-shaming! That's company policy. How consenting adults spend their free time is none of our business. It should be easy enough in any case. I can use a scaled-down version of the design I used for Maddie's wedding cake."

I got up from my desk and retrieved my purse from the hook on the wall.

"Can you hold down the fort here? I have to go to the Romance Writers Association thing and fluff up the 'Penis di Milo.'"

Jayden grinned and gave me a jaunty salute.

"Aye-aye, Captain. Ah!" He clapped his hand to his forehead. "One other thing. The kitties all need to be pink."

I stopped rifling through my purse for my car keys and raised an eyebrow.

"What other color would they be?"

He shrugged.

"I dunno. Black? Brown? Flesh-light blue? It's called diversity, Erin."

His face suddenly lit up.

"We could use those edible silver balls and give some of them little piercings!"

I bit my lip and frowned.

"I like your thinking, but I prefer all our decorative elements to be genuinely edible. Those balls are a root canal waiting to happen."

———

The cakes did turn out to be as simple as I'd hoped. The design I'd used for Madison's wedding cake scaled down to cupcakes extremely well. The trick with the mirror glaze really had been a stroke of inspiration. Jayden got his wish, and a random selection was pierced. We'd ended up using tiny balls of fondant and silver powder so, hopefully, everyone would escape with their fillings intact.

I didn't need the van for such a small delivery, so I simply secured the three boxes in the front seat of my car.

Almost as soon as I pulled up to the cozy suburban address, I got the feeling that something was wrong. The balloons on the gate weren't, in themselves, a cause for concern. Even the banner on the front of the house reading "Happy 6th Birthday" didn't immediately set alarm bells ringing. What *was* worrying was the large number of actual children milling around the yard and being chaperoned to the door by parents. Something about this was starting to feel extremely inappropriate.

I took the top box from the pile and carried it up the path.

It felt hot in my hands, like I was carrying an unexploded bomb. Or more aptly, as if I were a teenage boy sneaking dirty magazines into school in my backpack. I clutched the (mercifully opaque) cardboard box in my sweating hands and rang the bell with my elbow. The door opened almost immediately, and I nearly dropped the box when I was confronted by a familiar face.

"Erin!"

Nolan was leaning against the doorframe. He looked very different than he had at our last meeting. He had exchanged his expensive suit for rumpled jeans and a soft flannel shirt, rolled up to the elbows. My mind threatened to wander off-track when I began to wonder if he was also wearing the same style of pleasingly snug boxer briefs. I could hear Disney music blaring from inside the house, punctuated by suspiciously high-pitched squeals and giggles.

What the hell is happening?

By now, it wasn't just my hands that were sweaty; I could feel it trickling down my spine and across my shoulders, sticking my shirt to my back.

"Nolan! What are you doing here?"

He continued smiling but his brow furrowed slightly.

"I'd be a pretty lousy uncle if I missed my niece's birthday. I didn't know if it would be you doing the delivery, but I hoped it might be. Abby's so psyched about these."

So this is how it feels to stand in the path of an oncoming truck.

The air had thickened like Jell-O and it felt like his voice was coming from far away. I'd heard each of the words that came out of his mouth, but I was unable to translate them into a coherent sentence.

"I—"

My mouth opened and closed, goldfish style.

"Uncle... you... niece. *Six?!*"

I knew I was babbling nonsense, but thinking and speaking

at the same time is difficult when you're in a state of blind panic. Nolan, on the other hand, looked perfectly at ease.

"I did say I'd send some business your way."

He was smiling proudly, like a cat that had just dumped a headless mouse on the carpet and is waiting for praise.

"Are those my cakes, Uncle Nolan?"

The shrill little voice caused us to look down. An angelic redhead in a silky blue princess dress was looking up at us with an excited gleam in her eye. A massive red badge with a yellow six was pinned to her breast and her pink cheeks were smeared with sticky traces of chocolate. Nolan's smile widened and he scooped her up in his arms, prompting a bout of adorable squeaky giggles.

"They sure are, baby-girl. This nice lady made them especially for you."

A bright, unnatural smile stretched across my face until my cheeks began to ache. The little girl seized the front of Nolan's shirt in her chubby hands.

"Can I see them?" she demanded.

If my smile stretched any wider, I was pretty sure my face would come apart. I was in so much trouble.

CHAPTER NINE

Erin

"Can I speak with you privately for a moment?"

My smile remained fixed, but my eyes were sending frantic distress signals. Nolan held my gaze for a second before turning back to his niece with a conspiratorial smile.

"You know what, baby-girl? I think someone might have hidden an extra present for you in the den. Bet you can't find it!"

"Bet I can!"

The little girl shrieked with delight and scrambled to get down. Mad as I was, I couldn't help melting a little when I saw them together. It was obvious she adored him and that the feeling was more than mutual. Once Abby was out of earshot, he followed me towards my car. I put the box on the roof and rested my forehead on the sun-warmed metal.

"What's up?"

He sounded so casual that I instantly shot from a four to an eight on the Richter scale of irritation.

"What's up?!" I hissed, whipping round to face him. "Everything is up! Things have never been more... up."

I gestured vaguely in the direction of the sky. At this stage, letting Nolan feel the full force of my anger was more important than making any kind of sense. He frowned and scratched the back of his head.

"Ok," he admitted. "You've completely lost me."

I closed my eyes and took a deep breath.

"You do know that Sticky Treats is an *erotic* bakery, yes? We don't usually cater first-grade birthday parties."

He blinked.

"So, what's the issue? I saw how talented you were and I figured you could do other things. I only asked for cats."

"No! No, no, no."

I shook my head emphatically.

"You did not say cats. You said *kitties.* You telephoned a bakery well known for specializing in erotic confections, and asked for 'kitty' cupcakes for your 'baby-girl's' birthday."

"Oh... crap!"

I watched him turn green as realization dawned. But, by this point, my rage had gathered momentum and I was not taking prisoners.

"Why does this happen every time I meet you?"

"Erin..."

"I'm just a woman trying to run a business, but the universe doesn't seem to want that. Instead, it keeps sending me men hellbent on complicating my life."

I began to pace restlessly, my voice steadily rising.

"I never tried to—"

He had made the fatal mistake of opening his mouth to defend himself. I turned on him mercilessly.

"Really?" I demanded shrilly. "So it's just a coincidence that every time I meet you, I end up stripping or bringing edible pornography to a children's birthday party?!"

I'd forgotten to keep my voice down. A little old lady walking her dog nearly plowed into a streetlamp as she eagerly rubbernecked. I groaned and covered my face with my hands.

"Pornography? Are they really that bad?"

Wordlessly, I took the box from the car roof and cracked the lid so he could peek in.

"Wow!" He tilted his head and peered at the cakes. "These are really good. You've even made them look—"

"Yep. Mirror-glaze," I snapped.

"Nice touch with the piercings, by the way."

"I'll tell Jayden," I said wearily. "It'll make his day. Especially after I rip him a new one for mangling a simple phone order."

"No, it was my fuck-up."

Nolan was standing with his hands in his pockets, shoulders slumped. He looked so dejected that my anger deflated.

"My monumental fuck-up, as usual."

He kicked disconsolately at a tuft of grass.

"Now my sister is going to kill me, and I've ruined my niece's birthday. You know, I always prided myself on doing right by my family; no matter how many times I messed up in other areas of my life, I never let them down. First time for everything, I guess."

I'd gone from wanting to throttle him to wanting to hug him. He looked so furious with himself that I wanted to take his stupid handsome face in my hands and kiss the furrows from his brow.

Did I seriously just think that?

"What's going on?"

A pretty woman in jeans and a fluffy pink sweater was walking down the path towards us. She had wavy red hair and when she got a little closer, I noticed her vivid green eyes. The family resemblance was striking. This had to be Abby's mom. Nolan flushed guiltily as soon as he saw her.

"Sis. I—"

I cut across him hastily.

"Hi. I'm Erin. Nolan made an order with my bakery for your daughter's birthday."

The woman's face cleared, and she smiled warmly.

"Oh, the cat cupcakes! Abby's so excited to see them. Can I take a peek?"

"No!"

I clamped my hand over the lid of the box. A second later, Nolan stepped forward and clasped his sister's hand.

"Listen, Olivia. I'm gonna need you to hear me out," he coaxed. "Something's gone a little awry."

Her expression darkened in an instant and she pulled her hand from his grip.

"You have got to be kidding me," she snarled. "Ugh! I'm such an idiot! Why did I trust you with this?"

Nolan looked as though he'd been punched in the gut. I couldn't stand to watch any more.

"Actually, Nolan's covering for me."

Their heads snapped towards me in unison.

What now, genius?

"He knows what a perfectionist I am," I babbled. "Your cakes are right here."

"Ok," said Olivia uncertainly. "Then why can't I—?"

"They don't have their whiskers."

I had no idea where I was going with this, but my brain got the memo that I wanted a steady stream of word vomit and the drivel kept flowing.

"I use extra fine licorice bootlaces and if you put them on too early, they tend to roll up like... roll-ups."

I squirmed under Olivia's penetrating gaze.

"Well," she reasoned. "If that's all that's missing then surely I can—"

"No!"

Nolan had finally climbed aboard my train of thought. I appreciated the gesture, even if we were on course to go careening off a bridge.

"Erin is an artist, sis. She gets very uncomfortable when people view her unfinished work."

"Nolan didn't want to bother you because he knows how

stressed you are," I embellished. "We were just discussing your kitchen facilities. I was hoping I could slip inside and add my little finishing touches."

Olivia folded her arms and narrowed her eyes.

"This is... very unusual."

"I did say that this was a fancy bakery, Liv." Nolan put an arm around his sister and began to steer her back towards the house. "They refuse to deliver anything but perfection. Erin and I actually discussed on-site whisker application when I made the order."

We did?

He definitely had a talent for bullshit. Even I almost believed him. Olivia was looking understandably befuddled by this point, but she gestured towards the house.

"The kitchen's round the back. I've ordered the kids some pizza so that should give you all the time you need."

I doubt that very much.

I turned around to grab the box from the top of the car, and I jumped when I heard Nolan's voice in my ear. It was a deep, pleasant rumble that made me want to lean back into him.

"Why did you do that?" he asked.

"I don't know," I admitted, handing him the first box. "I must be out of my mind."

"Luckily for me."

He gave me a gentle smile that caused something to melt in my stomach.

Hurriedly, I turned my back on him and opened the car to grab the second box of cakes. Squeezing my eyes shut for a second, I puffed out a breath and switched into what Madison always described as my "kitchen voice."

"Right," I said decisively. "I need a palette knife, a quiet place to work, and all the candy you can lay your hands on."

"Anything else?" he asked.

"Yes. Above all, I need you to stall."

CHAPTER TEN

Nolan

"Shit!"

I swore under my breath as brightly colored food packets rained down on me from the open pantry.

How can a house that contains a six-year-old have so little candy?

I'd turned the store cupboard upside down, and all I had managed to find was a packet of those mini marshmallows that go in hot cocoa. Rubbing my forehead, I consulted the hastily scrawled list that Erin had pressed into my hand. I needed help.

"Hello?"

Alana picked up on the fifth ring. She sounded distinctly groggy.

"Alana, hey! I need a favor."

"It's Saturday," she grumbled. "I believe my contract specifies that Saturday-Nolan's needs are not my problem."

"C'mon, please," I wheedled. "I'll make it worth your while."

She sighed and I heard the click of her lighter.

"Do you have any idea how many men have said that to me?"

"You gonna make me beg?" I groaned.

"Hmm, that could be fun. But no. Fortunately for you, I'm a sap."

"Alana, you're a saint!"

"I know," she said airily.

"I promise, when you get to work on Monday, they'll be an extra-large hazelnut latte and maple glazed yum-yums waiting on your desk."

"That'll do for a start," she purred. "What do you need?"

"I need licorice laces."

"Are you trying bondage again? Because we've discussed this."

"What do you mean again?" I hissed. "I told you, I've never... Ugh, never mind. This is a thing for Abby's birthday."

"Shoulda just opened with that. Did she like my present?"

"Yep," I confirmed. "Your Tamagotchi triggered the most piercing shriek I've ever heard. How do you always know?"

I swear, I could hear her smirk from the other end of the phone.

"I do my research. So, you gonna tell me what's goin' on?"

I took a deep breath.

"Remember when you told me not to order the birthday cupcakes from the erotic bakery?"

"Yes."

"I ordered the birthday cupcakes from the erotic bakery."

"Oof! How bad is it?"

I told her in as few words as I could, wincing every time a set of young, impressionable ears ran past. By the time I had finished, Alana was breathless with laughter.

"That's fuckin' priceless," she gasped.

"Yeah, side-splitting," I deadpanned. "Aren't you going to say 'I told you so'?"

"Ah-ah! Don't rush me," she protested. "Moments like this need to be savored."

"Your latte just got downgraded to a large."

"Nah! Even you'd never stoop that low. Did your girl make

the delivery in person?"

"She's not my girl," I snapped. "And yes, she did. She's hidden away in the kitchen now, trying to turn—"

"Pussies into cats?" Alana offered. "That's some impressive dedication to cleaning up your mess. Treats is always busy this time of year."

I smiled for the first time since I had picked up the phone.

"She's actually pretty amazing," I enthused. "She totally covered for me with Liv and now she's just rolling up her sleeves and making the best of things. I've never seen someone so professional and dedicated. Talented too. I wish I'd taken a picture of the cakes before she started to dismantle them. They were so—"

"Stop!" Alana pleaded. "Much more of this mushy gush-fest and you'll make me barf. Just hang tight. I'll be there soon. Is there anything else you need?"

"Uh, yeah." I looked at the list again. "M&Ms, Lucky Charms, and Fruit Roll-ups. Red ones."

"Your wish is my command!"

After hanging up the phone, I bent down to pick up the food packets that had jumped out of the cupboard.

"Last time I caught you rooting around in the pantry, I spanked your butt."

I looked up and found my grandmother staring down at me.

My grandmother had been the one stabilizing influence in a crappy childhood. All the times that our parents had dropped the ball, she was there to step in. In the end, she practically raised us herself. Her name was Veronica, but everyone called her Granny V—and when I say everyone, I mean *everyone.* Me, Olivia, all our friends, the neighborhood kids, the mailman. Every waif or stray that floated onto her radar was swiftly adopted into her massive brood.

At 79, she was as energetic as she had been at 50. Her personal mantra was: "Growing older is inevitable, growing up is optional." It became obvious that she'd taken this wisdom to heart two years ago. She surprised us all by turning up to a family lunch with Russ, her 65-year-old "toy boy."

"All his own teeth, a full head of hair, and you'd better believe you won't find any blue pills on *our* nightstand, dearies."

We could forgive her disturbing moments like that, as her happy glow was infectious. After everything she had done for us, she deserved to be happy. Plus, they'd announced their engagement two months ago, so Russ was clearly doing something right. I hoped he knew what he was letting himself in for. Among her many talents, Granny V was a lie detector on legs. At that moment she was standing with her hands on her hips, staring down at me suspiciously.

"Nolan Reid, it's your niece's sixth birthday and you're skulking around in the pantry like a hypo-glycemic burglar and feeding your poor sister some cockamamie story about on-site whisker application."

"Look, Granny, I—"

"Don't Granny me," she warned sternly. "After 32 years, I know one of your ridiculous lies when I hear it. Now, what is going on?"

I struggled painfully to my feet and leaned on the pantry door.

"Ok," I admitted. "There has been a minor hiccup with the cakes, but we're fixing it."

"We?"

"Me and Erin."

"Ah!" Her eyes took on a triumphant twinkle. "I wondered who that pretty young lady was. I saw you talking to her through the living room window."

"Granny!" I groaned.

I knew that look only too well. My grandmother's dearest ambition was to have her grandchildren follow her down the aisle while she was still around to see it. She already fancied herself as something of a matchmaker and now that wedding bells were on her mind, she was relentless.

I got the brunt of this. She was confident that Olivia could take care of herself, but after years of romantic disasters, she was keen to see me "all settled down with a *nice* girl." Now that Erin was in Granny V's crosshairs, we were both doomed.

"Would this be the same young lady you've been prattling on about for the past week?" she said archly. "The one who made the stripper cake."

I nodded. Olivia might have stuck her fingers in her ears when I said the word "stripper," but Granny V was less squeamish. I had sent her a picture of the cake on Facebook. She'd thought it was "an absolute hoot" and proceeded to share it with all her friends.

"And you couldn't wait to see her again, hm?"

"It's not like that," I insisted. "This is strictly professional. She's very talented and I just wanted to send her some business."

"Because clearly you saw her portfolio and thought how appropriate it would be for a six-year-old's birthday party."

I flushed. It was becoming obvious that nobody was planning to let that go. Granny V gave me a knowing look.

"The kids are settled with their pizza," she said conversationally. "And I have a feeling that Abby is about to request a dinner-time screening of *Frozen*, so you have plenty of time on your hands. Why don't you head back to the kitchen and check on how she's doing?"

The woman was incorrigible... but maybe she had a point.

When I re-entered the kitchen, Erin was absorbed in destroying her beautiful works of culinary art. With one stroke of a palette knife, the exquisitely sculpted frosting was flattened to a marbled pink swirl. There was something so graceful and hypnotic about the way she wielded that knife that I just stood there, staring at her. A shaft of sunlight was falling on her dark hair, burnishing it a deep red, and she had the most adorable expression of concentration on her face. Watching her repeatedly erase what must have been massive investments of time and energy created a squirming feeling of guilt in my belly. I didn't understand why she would come to my rescue like that.

After a moment she put down the palette knife, yawned, and stretched. I could see the delicately shifting of muscles in her back. Her movement caused the fabric of her top to ride up at the waist, exposing half an inch of creamy skin. I imagined how soft it would feel. I wanted to reach out and touch it. My palms began to sweat, and I could feel the flutter of butterflies in my stomach. Suddenly feeling like a perv, I cleared my throat, drawing attention to my presence. She jumped and spun around.

"You scared me," she breathed.

"Sorry."

"Any luck on the candy?"

"I got marshmallows."

I held up the crumpled bag feebly.

"It's ok, though," I added hastily, observing the panic that crept onto her face. "My assistant's coming to the rescue. She should be here soon."

I hope.

Erin smiled.

"You're surprisingly good in a crisis, Mr. Reid."

"Some crises," I admitted. "Missing candy, I can definitely handle."

"Don't forget stripping," she teased.

I cringed at the awkward barking laugh that emerged from my throat.

"Yes, well, you'll be relieved to hear that my clothes will be staying on today. And it's Nolan, by the way. People who've seen my underwear get to use my first name."

Two spots of color rose in her cheeks, and she bit her lip. I felt something stir within me.

"Is everything alright?" she asked, peering at me with sudden concern.

No. No, I'm not all right. I'm going to hell. I want to take you right now, over this kitchen counter. I want to make love to you on the squashed and mangled remains of my niece's birthday cupcakes.

"Yes, everything's fine."

I cleared my throat hurriedly, tearing my gaze away from her face and onto the kitchen counter.

"Seems a pity, really," I said, gesturing at the disassembled cakes.

"I'll preserve you an original specimen." She chuckled. "Want a pierced one?"

"Silly question."

She shrugged.

"Seriously, though. It's not the project I imagined, but I still think these will look great. Buttercream can give you a really good fur texture if you use a cocktail stick, like this."

She bent over and started to demonstrate, and I leaned over her shoulder. I could feel her small body pressed against mine and she smelled far too good. Burnt caramel with a hint of rose and just a touch of that strange, fresh smell that lingers in the air before it rains. I bit my lip and thought very hard about baseball. At one point, she brought a hand up to brush a strand of hair from her face, leaving a tiny smear of frosting on her cheek.

"Look at me for a second."

She turned her head. Her caramel-colored eyes looked huge and bright, and her lips were slightly parted.

"You've got a little—"

I reached out with my thumb wiped away the buttercream. At that point, I should have taken my hand away, but I didn't. My fingers splayed out to cup her cheek. The pink tip of her tongue came out to moisten her lips and her breaths were coming shallow and fast. Moving as if in a dream, I let my head tilt forward to capture her lips.

CHAPTER ELEVEN

Nolan

My heart was pounding in my throat. We were so close that I could smell something minty on her breath. If either one of us moved, even a fraction of an inch, our lips would—

"Oof! Someone leave the oven on in here? Things are heatin' up!"

Erin and I jumped apart as though someone had sprayed us with a fire hose. I could hear Erin panting and I swear you could have roasted a marshmallow on my face. Gathering up the tattered shreds of my dignity, I shot a scowl at my smirking PA. It was tempting to throttle her, but she was saved by the bulging paper bag she dumped on the counter.

"Got your candy, Casanova."

My features stretched into a strained smile.

"Alana," I gritted. "This is Erin, from Sticky Treats. Erin, this is Alana. She used to be my PA, until about five seconds ago when I fired her."

Alana ignored me, beaming at Erin as they shook hands.

"Hi," she gushed. "I'm a huge fan of your work. I haven't been able to stop thinking about your boobs since my cousin's baby shower."

My brain ground to a screeching halt. I was suddenly

picturing the two women in several heated scenarios that had absolutely nothing to do with cake. I shuffled to the side, seeking the protective cover of the kitchen counter.

I was about to launch into a flurry of apologies for my shameless assistant when I realized that Erin wasn't blushing. She was smiling at Alana and looking utterly relaxed.

"The cake pops, right? I'm so glad you liked them. It took me ages to get the contouring right. It would be easy to just stick two blobs together, but it's important to me that my creations have an element of realism. Not to mention the nightmare I had getting the nipples to set."

Before I knew it, I was hanging on her every word. When she was talking about her craft, she was so passionate and knowledgeable. It was sexy.

Alana leaned on the counter and examined the unmodified cupcakes. Her eyes lit up when she spotted one of the pierced ones.

"Ooh! I have that one!" she enthused, pointing at an uncomfortable-looking fondant barbell. "Points for realism."

Again overwhelmed by the feeling of not knowing where to look, I cleared my throat nervously. However, to my amazement, Erin still looked unfazed. You'd think they were discussing the weather. This woman was getting more intriguing by the second.

"I have to give my assistant credit for that one," she admitted. "He threw himself into the research with surprising enthusiasm."

They shared a laugh, but Alana's face immediately fell when she caught sight of the most recent victims of the palette knife.

"Yeesh! This is just vandalism," she said, shaking her head in disgust. "These things are works of art."

I'd thought the same thing myself a few minutes ago, but I didn't like the idea of Erin being made to feel bad about what she was doing. Time for some top-tier mansplaining.

"Well, actually, Alana. I think you'll be amazed at the fur effect Erin can achieve with textured buttercream."

Erin turned to me, blinking in surprise.

"Wow," she marveled. "You were really paying attention."

She gave me such a sunny, gratified smile that I wasn't sure what to do with myself. I felt like I had eight limbs and didn't know what to do with any of them. I settled for stretching, followed by leaning on the counter with exaggerated nonchalance.

"Well," I breezed, hoping that no one would notice I had my elbow in a stick of butter. "I'm not much of a baker, but it's interesting when you talk about it."

"Wow, thanks."

She blushed and tucked some loose hair behind her ear. Out of the corner of my eye, I could see Alana making dramatic gagging motions.

"Ooh! Have I interrupted a secret meeting?"

I whipped round in time to see my grandmother bustling into the kitchen with a tray of empty juice glasses.

Alana smiled fondly. Despite claiming that the problems of "Saturday-Nolan" were none of her business, Alana had ended up at my family gatherings with enough frequency that she'd now been adopted. She adored my grandmother as much as the rest of us did.

"Couldn't have a secret meeting without you, Granny V."

My grandmother's smile widened.

"Alana, dear! I didn't know you were coming."

"Wasn't planning on it," Alana admitted. "Saving his ass, as usual."

She jerked a thumb in my direction.

"*He* is standing right here, and *he* is still your boss," I muttered.

My grandmother swatted at me like I was an irritating fly and continued talking to Alana. I noticed Erin subtly slide the paper candy bag in front of the un-doctored cakes.

"How's that lovely boyfriend of yours? Is he still dating that handsome young doctor?"

Alana nodded.

"Yeah. Coming up on a year now. The four of us are going out for an anniversary dinner next week."

"Oh, how nice," my grandmother cooed. "Maybe he'll finally decide to get his act together and make an honest man of him."

"Granny!" I hissed furiously.

"What?" she protested. "Just because Alana refuses to choose between her girlfriend and her boyfriend, there's no reason someone shouldn't get the tax breaks."

I pinched the bridge of my nose. I'd finally been having a conversation with Erin that wasn't utterly mortifying and now my family and friends seemed to have made it their mission to be as embarrassing as possible.

"Ok," I groaned. "I'm going to step outside this kitchen for a second and when I come back in, you're both going to be normal!"

Suddenly I heard laughter. I looked up, startled. I had expected Erin to be horribly uncomfortable; instead, she was standing there, giggling at me. She had a lovely laugh, bubbly, musical, and utterly adorable. I instantly wanted her to do it again.

"You're being very rude, Nolan."

"Huh?"

I was pulled from my trance by my grandmother slapping me on the arm.

"You haven't introduced me to your friend," she scolded.

I sighed wearily.

"Granny, this is Erin. Erin, this is my grandmother Veronica."

My grandmother stepped around the counter and took Erin by the hand.

"You can call me Granny V, dear," she said. "You don't have

to, of course, but you might feel a bit left out if you don't. You know," she said confidentially, "Nolan has been talking about you *endlessly.* All week it's been Erin this and Erin that. I've never seen him so taken with a young lady."

Why me?

"She's exaggerating," I put in hastily. "Not that I wouldn't. I mean you're very—"

"You wanna watch it with this knuckle-head, Erin," Alana drawled. "He's trouble."

"I think he's nice," Erin declared, patting my hand.

I swallowed.

"I don't know," Alana snickered. "Some guy locks me in a cake, he's getting a right hook, no matter how good his striptease is."

"What's this, Nolan?"

My grandmother's gaze flicked between me and Alana like a curious bird's.

I think I'll just put my head in the oven now.

Resigned to my humiliating fate, I started to tell the story of the ill-fated bachelor party, but Erin interrupted.

"Actually, Nolan rescued me. There was a mix-up with the cake, and I ended up shut inside it. One thing led to another, and Nolan performed the striptease himself to divert attention from me. It was very gallant."

She was generously glossing over the fact that it was me who'd trapped her in there in the first place. Alana snorted but my grandmother's face took on a misty-eyed smile.

"He's always been like that," she remarked.

Uh-oh. It's the one-stop express to memory lane, with a brief layover in embarrassing story-ville.

"Last year, we all went to the carnival. Little Abby let go of her balloon and Nolan climbed on top of a ring-toss booth chasing it. We told him to let it go, but..."

Her expression froze.

"Mercy me! I've just remembered," she gasped. "I'd come in to tell you they're at that bit in the movie when Esther—"

"Elsa," I corrected.

"Yes, her. Anyway, they're at that bit where she has a tantrum and builds that snow palace. You'd better get a move on."

I looked at everything we still needed to do, and panic took hold. We were never going to make it.

"Alright, people, we can do this, but I need all hands on deck."

Erin had clapped her hands and addressed us all in a clear, confident voice. Just like that, all my fears evaporated, and I was ready to leap into action. Within minutes, Alana was color-sorting M&Ms and Granny V was picking the pink hearts out of the Lucky Charms. As I separated licorice laces, I watched Erin's palette knife flying across the cakes and my stomach twisted. She really was wonderful.

CHAPTER TWELVE

Erin

As I frantically arranged licorice whiskers on the last few cupcakes, I could feel Nolan watching me. My professional façade was cracking under the soft gaze of those green eyes, and I was all thumbs.

Just like the bachelor party, this whole experience had been a crazy roller-coaster. The mix-up with the cakes, the scramble to fix things, and that moment when we had almost...

The memory of his lips, less than an inch from mine, made my heart race. I felt both terrified and exhilarated.

I stared at my impromptu kitchen crew, resisting the urge to ask one of them to pinch me. This had all the hallmarks of a crazy fever dream. For the past six months, I had avoided anything that risked complicating my life; now here I was, in a stranger's kitchen, surrounded by utter chaos.

The funny thing was, I didn't mind. I was experiencing none of the usual chest-constricting panic—just a strange, warm feeling. I felt as though I belonged.

Maybe chaos wasn't always a bad thing. I chanced a glance at Nolan, and he gave me a shy smile. My stomach somersaulted.

In the end, we got the cakes ready in time. I was reasonably happy with them, and they sent the little girl into transports of delight. By the time everyone was happily munching the sugary treats, Olivia was already talking about booking me for next year's birthday.

When the party wound down, I stayed to help with the clean-up. I was in the middle of stuffing wrapping paper into garbage bags when Granny V pulled me to one side.

"So," she began conspiratorially. "What were those cakes before they were cats?"

"How did you—?"

She arched a knowing eyebrow.

"Nolan showed me some of your previous work, dear. And I know re-textured buttercream when I see it."

"I... Uhm..."

How exactly do you tell a sweet little old lady that you brought a box of vaginas to her granddaughter's birthday party? Seeing my struggle, Granny V took the garbage bag from my limp fingers and patted my arm gently.

"I've been on this earth for 79 years, honey. You won't surprise me."

Sighing, I glanced furtively around the room, before bringing up Instagram on my phone. I always took pictures of my finished projects before delivering them to clients. Granny V pondered the picture for a moment, whilst I squirmed.

"Do you happen to have any business cards with you?"

"Any— What?"

It took a moment to process what she had said. I'd been too busy mentally preparing a defense for my calorific smut.

"Business cards, dear."

"Oh, sure." I fumbled awkwardly in my pocket for the silver card case and gave her one. I wasn't sure why I was feeling embarrassed. Perhaps it was the fact that I was still surrounded by the innocent trappings of a kid's birthday party. That had to be it. I had absolutely no other reason in the world to feel bashful.

"What are you up to, Granny?"

Nolan had crept up behind us and was eyeing his grandmother with mock severity.

Nope. No other reason at all!

"Just having a little chat with Erin, dear. Although," she looked at him significantly, "I should probably go and see if your sister needs any help in the kitchen."

When we were left alone, Nolan rolled his eyes and chuckled.

"Sorry about her. She's... Well, she means well."

"Don't apologize," I protested. "I think she's a gem."

He grinned, giving me a flash of his even, white teeth.

"She has her moments," he admitted. "Look, I was wondering. If you're not doing anything right now, I thought you might like to go out for a bite to eat. To say thank you, I mean, for today."

By the time his rambling sentence came to an end, he was bright pink.

"I—"

There were a million reasons to say no. I had a mountain of work to get back to. I'd left Jayden alone in the bakery all afternoon. I was supposed to be avoiding romantic entanglements. I'd destroy my career. I'd get my heart broken. Toads would rain from the heavens and the sky would fall in. There was no way I could accept this invitation.

"Sure, that sounds nice."

My mouth was a treacherous troublemaker.

The universe was determined to bring my cloistered existence to an end. When we pulled up outside a Vietnamese noodle bar and Nolan told me to prepare for the best pho I had ever eaten, it looked like further proof that the stars had aligned. Give me a steaming bowl of noodles in delicious bone broth and I'm in comfort food heaven. I needed him to chew with his mouth open, pick his nose, fart at the table, anything. If he continued being perfect, there was no way I was getting out of this alive.

While we waited for our food, he reached across the table and put his hand over mine.

"You were fantastic today."

The excited little flutters in my chest were almost painful. I tried to swallow around my dry mouth, and I could feel the onset of panic. I extricated my hand and folded my arms protectively across my chest.

"Just doing my job," I said airily.

"Oh."

He cleared his throat and drew his hand back. The brief look of hurt that flashed across his face was swiftly quashed and he continued in a falsely jovial tone.

"Well, whether it's pussies or cats, you nail it." He raised his glass of ginger ale with an air of ceremony. "To Erin, the Pussy-Master."

I burst out laughing; I couldn't help it. He joined in and the weird tension dissipated. We were attracting pointed looks from a few of the other diners, but for once, I didn't care. When I had recovered myself a little, I shook my head incredulously.

"You know, it's funny," I mused. "After that bachelor party, I never thought I'd hear from you again. You were the last person I was expecting to be on the other side of that door."

He frowned.

"How come? I said I'd send some business your way."

I fiddled with my glass of water, staring at the bobbing ice cubes.

"I guess I'm not used to men who keep their promises," I admitted.

"Ouch! Sounds like there's a story there."

I shrugged and looked at the tablecloth.

"There is, but I don't want to unload on you like that."

"Come on, Erin." Nolan sat back and placed his hands on his chest. "These broad shoulders can take it. Besides, you came to my rescue twice today. You don't know my sister. She'd be wearing my balls as earrings by now. Plus, disappointing Abby would eat me up inside."

For a moment he looked pained, and I wanted to reach across the table and hold his hand. Then he blinked and seemed to shake himself out of it.

"Enough about me! C'mon, unload!"

I let out a shaky breath.

"Starting up Sticky Treats was a dream come true. The first few months went great. Way better than I expected, and when I started dating the handsome, charming guy who designed my webpage, it felt like the cherry on the cake."

I paused. I rarely spoke about any of this. Exposing it to the light after holding on to it for so long felt raw and terrifying. All the same, something compelled me to keep going. For his part, Nolan seemed to instinctively know what I needed. He didn't press; he just sat there and let me talk.

"At first, Stirling seemed like the perfect guy. He was so caring and supportive. And he'd helped me build the digital side of my business, so I thought he understood my dream."

"What changed?"

I took a sip of water. When I put the glass down on the table, I noticed that my hands were trembling slightly.

"Sticky Treats was a runaway success, but it was just me doing everything, and any business has teething troubles in its first year. It took up a lot of my time and Stirling started to get resentful. He said I was becoming self-absorbed, that I wasn't interested in his needs. And I felt bad, you know? So, I—"

I pushed a hand through my hair and leaned my elbow on the table.

"Well, according to Madison, I started letting him walk all over me. Make all my decisions for me. Where I went, who I saw—even what I wore. He said I shouldn't wear anything too provocative because people were already going to look at what I did and get the wrong idea."

Nolan scowled.

"I don't know who Madison is, but I think they had the right idea about this guy. He sounds like a grade-A shithead."

By this point, our pho had arrived, and he punctuated his speech by digging viciously through his noodles.

"He definitely had some issues with insecurity," I conceded.

"Bullies usually do."

I broke the membrane on my egg yolk with the end of my chopstick and watched the bright yellow liquid seep into the surrounding broth.

"Things came to a head when he started getting jealous of the customers."

It was so much easier to pretend that I was confiding this to my soup rather than another human.

"Some of the stuff I do is very... intimate. If one of a couple wants a cake or sculpture dedicated to their partner, it sometimes requires explicit photos or even body casts. Strictly professional, of course!"

My mind had wandered unbidden to Nolan's sculpted torso with its perfect perky nipples and that suggestive bulge in his boxers. I took a hurried gulp of water, resisting the urge to press the cold glass against my burning cheeks.

"Anyway," I continued hurriedly. "Unless someone's really comfortable, I usually just leave the casting kit with them. Stirling wasn't happy with that side of things, though. He'd claim I was blowing him off to spend the evening staring at another guy's junk. One time, a woman wanted a chocolate sculpture of her husband for their anniversary and Stirling actually showed up at the guy's house to warn him off me. I ended up losing the contract."

"Jesus!" Nolan exclaimed. "That's messed up."

"Yeah, it was."

I was surprised at the effect of hearing this from someone else. It slapped me harshly in the face. At the same time, it also made me feel better and like I hadn't been over-reacting.

"I'd had enough after that. I broke up with him."

"Good for you!" said Nolan warmly.

I managed a shaky smile. I was getting to the worst part of my story, and I was determined to get everything out.

"He said I'd made a fool of him, and I'd be sorry. The next morning, I woke up and my website and social media had been completely trashed. There were all these horrible pictures and videos. He'd done something with Photoshop so it looked like I—"

My throat wouldn't let me get the words out anymore. Realizing that my cheeks were wet, I hastily reached up to swipe at my eyes.

"What did you say this guy's last name was?"

I looked up to find Nolan furiously typing on his phone.

"I didn't," I mumbled, sniffing away the last of my tears. "Why? What are you planning to do?"

"Nothing he doesn't deserve."

"Are you going to track him down and defend my honor?" I joked.

"No," he declared. "I'm going to do better than that. I'm going to litigate the crap out of him."

"That's sweet, but you don't have to—"

"I mean it!" he insisted. "Say the word and I'll shove so much paperwork up his ass he'll be choking on the pulp. Seriously, Erin, you should have applied for a restraining order."

Part of me knew he was right. It was just that, after it happened, I was more preoccupied with crawling into my shame hole and never coming out again. I'd been humiliated enough without having my dirty laundry aired in a courtroom. As if reading my thoughts, Nolan reached across the table and grabbed my hand again. A lump instantly rose in my throat, but this time, I didn't pull away.

"Before I switched to corporate litigation, I worked in family law," Nolan revealed. "I met lots of people in your situation, and you know what they had in common?"

I shook my head.

"They were all convinced they were somehow to blame or that they had something to be ashamed of. They didn't, and neither do you."

I was so moved that I didn't trust myself to speak. He ran his thumb gently over the back of my hand and a thrill went through me.

"Nolan, I—"

For the second time that day, I found myself leaning towards him tentatively, lips parted in expectation.

CHAPTER THIRTEEN

Erin

"You conniving, lecherous bastard!"

Our perfect moment was shattered when the entire contents of an ice bucket cascaded into Nolan's lap. As he doubled over with a pained gasp, I looked up to see where the attack had come from. A tall woman with wavy blonde hair was standing over us, holding the empty bucket triumphantly aloft. She had enormous blue eyes, a cupid's bow mouth, and expertly applied make-up. She would have been extremely pretty if her face hadn't been contorted with rage. She was breathing heavily and there was a manic glint in her eye.

"I thought the car would get my message across," she panted. "I mean, you showed more love to that hunk of metal than you ever showed to me. But then I realized, if I actually wanted to get your attention, I should go after the thing that does all your thinking."

Wincing, Nolan staggered to his feet. I could hear the soft rustle of ice chips pouring to the floor. He stared at the woman with an expression that was equal parts anger and confusion.

"What are you even... Did you follow me here?"

The woman's shoulders slumped, and her tone shifted from gasping anger to wheedling petulance.

"Well, what choice did you give me?" she whined. "You ignore my messages, you won't take my calls, and you had me removed from your office like a common criminal!"

Her speech was slurred, and when she attempted to point an accusing finger, she staggered slightly. This hadn't escaped Nolan either. He stared at her impassively.

"Heather," he said flatly. "You're drunk. You need to go home."

I marveled at his ability to block out the fact that we were the focus of every pair of eyes in the restaurant. Despite not being the target of the tirade, I desperately wished I were small enough to hide under the table. Unfortunately, Nolan's eerie calm only seemed to enrage Heather further.

"Yes!" she shrieked. "Yes, I'm drunk! What's the matter, Nolan? Worried it'll loosen my tongue? That I'll tell everyone here what a shit stain you are?"

She turned from the table and spoke to the room at large.

"Hey!" she yelled. "Hey, restaurant people. Stop eating and listen! Including you, old man. Put down those crackers! This man," she flung her arm wildly at Nolan, "this man is a cheater and a liar. I opened my soul to him, like a precious delicate flower, and he used and discarded me like a cheap whore."

By this point, she was crying. Her speech had dissolved into gulping sobs. Even when her makeup had run in long streaks down her face, and her shoulders were heaving, Nolan continued to stare at her coldly. I was surprised at him; he'd seemed like such a compassionate person. I couldn't watch her distress any longer. It had to be so humiliating for her, with everyone watching and whispering. Reaching out with the same caution I'd use to approach an ill-tempered cobra, I tried to pat her on the arm.

"Here. You should sit down and have a glass of water."

She whipped around as though I'd struck her and stared at me with wild, red-rimmed eyes.

"Get away from me, you two-faced bitch," she hissed.

I took an instinctive step back, but I wasn't quick enough. Heather made a grab for the first object on the table. As luck would have it, it was a brimming dish of sweet chili sauce. Now my cream sweater was decorated with an angry red streak from boob to hip. I continued backing up as Heather advanced on me, still clutching the empty dish.

"Does it make you feel good about yourself to steal someone else's man?" she raged.

"I—I didn't."

Could it be true? Did Nolan really have a girlfriend? Did Nolan really have *this* girlfriend? The thought had never occurred to me. It had seemed like he truly—

"Don't give me that bullshit," she snarled. "You can sit there all innocent with your big doe eyes and your fluffy... blurry sweater. But you're just a man-stealing slut. Y—You're a WHORE!"

I felt sick. The word hit me like a slap. Was she right? She'd called me out. She'd even branded me. The red stain was there on my breast for all to see. My skin prickled hotly, and my chest tightened. Suddenly, I wasn't looking at Heather anymore. I could see the word "WHORE" in red block capitals all over my website and Facebook. I could practically feel the dreaded buzz of my phone in my pocket as I remembered the disgusting, tasteless messages mounting up. The accusing eyes in the restaurant multiplied a thousandfold. In my head, they were all chanting it. "WHORE! WHORE! WHORE!" The noise was deafening, and the room started to spin.

"Heather, that's enough! Now, I wasn't going to call the police—I don't want to do that to you—but if you continue to—"

I could hear Nolan's voice, but it sounded like it was coming from far away. How could he do this to me? I trusted him. I was just starting to think about letting him in and now here I was, at the center of another drama. Vilified and publicly humiliated. I couldn't do this.

I grabbed my coat from the back of my chair and ran from the restaurant. I could hear Nolan shouting my name behind me, but I didn't stop. I paid no attention to where I was going, I just ran, blinded by tears.

Eventually I didn't have the breath to run anymore and I wound up slumped against a cold brick wall in a lonely alleyway. Sagging down, I gave vent to my tears, huddled behind a dumpster, where no one could see. When I had cried myself out, I fumbled in my pocket for my phone to call a cab and saw that I had five unread messages. Four of them were Nolan, wanting to know if I was ok and begging for the chance to explain himself. I deleted them all without responding. It would be much less painful for all concerned if I just cut him out of my life. After deleting the final message from Nolan, the fifth message popped up on my screen. When I saw who sent it, I nearly passed out for the second time that evening.

Stirling: I don't much like the look of your new boy toy, Erin.

CHAPTER FOURTEEN

Nolan

"You didn't try to go after her?"

Steam rose from my cup as Olivia poured the hot cocoa. I rolled my eyes when she insisted on scattering a handful of marshmallows on the surface. The only illumination in the kitchen was the dim glow of the lights nestled into the underside of the cupboards. After the chaos of the party, everything felt eerily quiet.

I was huddling miserably on a stool at the breakfast bar while my sister and grandmother helped me pick through the wreckage of the disastrous dinner.

"I tried, but I couldn't find her. She got quite a start on me, though. I couldn't chase her immediately; Heather still had her tentacles wrapped around my neck."

"So I see." Olivia's eyes narrowed as she inspected the long, red scratches under my jaw. "How did you get rid of her in the end?"

I sighed wearily.

"The restaurant manager called the police. I guess it was the only option at that point. The cops talked her down, then took her home in a patrol car."

"They should have taken her to a cell," Olivia growled.

"I didn't press charges."

"Nolan!"

"I can handle her myself! Besides, Heather might be cuckoo for cocoa puffs, but it's not all her fault. I'm at least partly to blame."

"Well, I'm not going to argue with that," Olivia conceded. "But you're still my baby brother. I'd like to give her a piece of my mind."

Despite my gloomy mood, I gave her a watery smile. She had that same look she'd gotten that time we were at the beach and an older kid had stomped my sandcastle. He was bigger than both of us, but that hadn't stopped Liv chasing him down and kicking him in the nuts.

"I always found something off with that woman!" Granny V mused.

Olivia chuckled indulgently.

"You say that about all of Nolan's exes, Granny."

"Well, it's always true," she protested. "Honestly, Nolan. I've never understood this. You're such a *nice* boy."

My sister raised a skeptical eyebrow.

"You do remember he's a corporate lawyer, right?"

Granny V shook her head and tutted.

"Now, Olivia, stop it! We both know that he's got a big soft heart under that suit." She paused to poke me in the chest. "He just needs to stop throwing it away on—"

"Unsuitable women?" Olivia suggested.

"Put it that way if you want to, dear. I was just going to call them skanks."

"Granny!"

Olivia's eyes widened. I was shocked too. Granny V was usually the first person to stick up for someone everybody else was condemning. She truly believed anger and aggression should be met with an equal force of compassion. My great-aunt had been known to waspishly remark that "If Satan himself showed up on Veronica's kitchen doorstep, she'd try to redeem him with a cookie and a hug." She didn't look in a cookies-and-hugs frame of mind now, though. Her mouth was a thin line of disapproval.

"When you get to my age, you can spot a trashy woman a mile away. 'Pretty is as pretty does,' as my mother used to say."

She looked at me with a pained expression that made me feel guilty.

"I just want to see you settled with a nice girl. Someone who deserves you. And," her expression became stern, "someone who can keep you in line."

"I don't think I'm meant for a nice girl," I brooded. "I'd just mess things up."

Olivia leaned forward and topped up my cocoa.

"Did you try calling Erin?" she asked gently.

At least five times.

"No. I'm not going to call her."

"But she liked you," Granny V pleaded. "Anyone could see that. And she was such a sweetheart."

"And that's exactly why I'm not going to call," I said firmly. "She's been through enough, and she deserves better than me."

I'd expected them to press me, but, to their credit, they appeared to accept my feelings on the subject. Nearly two weeks went by without either of them mentioning it. I would have been suspicious if I hadn't known that Granny V was swamped with wedding preparations. Under normal circumstances, my grandmother was a practical, frugal person. But, when it came to this wedding, she'd been possessed by the spirit of a Disney princess. Four-tiered cake, horse-drawn carriage, a dress that looked like it shared a fair amount of DNA with an exploded meringue. She was getting the whole shebang.

My parents had griped on the subject continually and made dark insinuations that Russ was a gold digger. I suspected my father was simply worried she was blowing his inheritance on a fairy-tale wedding. On the other hand, Olivia and I liked Russ.

It was obvious he and Granny V made each other happy. As far as we were concerned, it was her money. She'd worked hard for it, and she deserved to spend it on whatever she liked.

While the preparations swirled around me like a white lace carousel, I buried my head in work, determined to leave Erin alone.

However, there was one thing I found myself unable to leave alone. The boyfriend. *Stirling.* Even the name left a bad taste in my mouth. I didn't need a last name to find him. He advertised his web-design business extensively, and it wasn't as though Stirling was a common name. I spent every spare moment hunting down every detail I could find on this slimy fuck. This led to Alana breezing into my office on Friday lunchtime and finding me glaring at the obnoxiously grinning picture on his LinkedIn profile.

She stood behind me, regarding the photo with her head on one side.

"Now, that's what I like to call a 'punchable' face," she quipped. "What do you need a web designer for?"

"I don't," I murmured. "That's Erin's ex-boyfriend."

Quick as lightning, Alana snatched the latest copy of the *Wall Street Journal* from my desk, rolled it into a tube, and smacked me over the head.

"No!" It sounded like she was chastising a puppy that had just chewed her slippers. "If you start goin' full cyber-stalker on me, I'm withdrawing your internet privileges," she warned.

I swiveled my chair to face her.

"Ok, number one: this is not what it looks like. Number two: we have discussed, at some length, my feelings about you bonking me in public."

"Care to rephrase that?" She smirked.

When I simply scowled in response, she pulled up the chair on the other side of the desk.

"Ok," she said with a probing glare that would have had a CIA agent sweating. "You've been moping over this woman for the past two weeks. If this isn't you goin' off the deep end, then what's going on?"

I slumped back in my chair, took a deep breath, and launched into the story of Erin's ex. By the time I had finished, Alana's face was scrunched in an expression of disgust.

"What a shit-heel!"

"Yep," I agreed. "I've been trying to work out what sort of legal ground she'd be on if she wanted to take action against him. Looking into his background, there are some definite red flags."

"Like what?"

I knuckled at my eyes and stifled a yawn. Sleep had been something that happened to other people lately.

"Numerous incidents with previous girlfriends, but the charges were dropped every time."

Alana inspected her perfectly manicured nails.

"We could just drop him off a bridge," she suggested casually.

I put my head on one side and pretended to consider.

"Tempting, but I think that might put *us* on shaky legal ground. I told her she should have taken out a restraining order the first time he acted up."

Alana rested her chin on her hand and gave me a long look.

"Ever consider takin' your own advice on that one?"

I swiveled my chair again so I didn't have to meet her gaze."

"This is going to be about Heather, isn't it?"

"Well, I know for a fact she's still calling you a thousand times a day. And I gotta tell you, security did not appreciate the glitter bomb."

I winced.

"Yeah." Alana sucked in air through her teeth. "You might wanna send Mike a nice bottle of something. Three showers later and he's still faintly... iridescent. I'm fond of the guy, but I don't think he can pull off the Edward Cullen look. This whole business is getting out of hand."

Suddenly feeling restless, I jumped up from my chair and walked over to the window.

"I can handle Heather myself," I growled.

"Wow," Alana exclaimed. "I always knew you were an idiot, but I never had you down as a sexist douchebag too."

"Excuse me?"

I spun around and glared at her indignantly. Alana was unfazed. She drew herself up to her full height (which still put her a head shorter than me) and raised her chin defiantly.

"You think because you're a big strong man, you don't need legal help? Think harassment doesn't happen to men? If a female client came in and said her ex was showing up at her workplace, constantly calling her, following her when she went on dates—you'd tell her to handle that herself?"

I opened and closed my mouth like an inarticulate goldfish. Sensing my hesitance, Alana steam-rollered on. She was usually cool and unflappable, but this had her riled up.

"If you won't do it for yourself, how about protecting the other people in your life? Think she's above showing up on Olivia and Abby's doorstep?"

I passed a hand slowly down my face. That mental image hit me like a punch to the gut.

"You're right. I'm an idiot."

Alana came over, wound her arms around my waist, and gave me a hard squeeze.

"Yeah, you are. But you're my idiot. Now," she stepped back, suddenly all brisk again, "get your coat and come buy me lunch. That always cheers you up, right?"

I smiled and rolled my eyes.

"I have a couple of things to finish up here. Meet me at the car in five minutes?"

"Aye-aye, *jefe.*"

I was just packing up to leave when my phone buzzed with

a text from Olivia. I groaned out loud when I read the words on the screen.

> *Olivia:* Been going over wedding plans with Granny. You'll never guess who she wants to do the cake. I tried to talk her out of it, but you know what she's like. Gotta take Abby to karate now. Talk later.

CHAPTER FIFTEEN

Erin

"Earth to Erin!"

"Huh?!"

My stylus fell to the floor as I woke up with a violent twitch. For the third time that week, I had nodded off at my desk and Jayden had started to notice that something was up. As I bent to retrieve my pen, still shaking with adrenaline, he stood on the other side of the desk, examining me critically.

"You should get more sleep," he declared. "Those bags under your eyes are not couture."

"You're so sweet," I deadpanned.

All the same, he wasn't wrong. I'd been sleeping terribly ever since that disastrous dinner with Nolan. I'd felt something—a spark of potential that I hadn't felt in a long while. When that woman stormed in, the rug had slipped from under my feet. It had completely blindsided me. Then afterward...

Stirling had sent two more messages since that night. The first was an incoherent plea to take him back. When I ignored it, he followed up with a vile string of abuse. The thing that disturbed me most was the question of how he had known about Nolan. He had to have been following me; there was no other way. This created an endless string of terrifying questions. How long had he been following me? How was he doing it? Was he watching my house? My work? It had gotten to the point where I didn't feel safe anywhere. I always had the feeling I was being watched.

My first impulse had been to call Nolan. I still wanted to call him. Not just because he was a lawyer, but because, somehow, he made me feel safe. I knew I couldn't. He wasn't good for me. Every time I met him, something crazy happened, and I didn't know how much more insanity I could take. Besides, he obviously had more than enough problems of his own.

I rubbed my eyes and looked at Jayden blearily.

"Did you want something or are you just here to boost my self-esteem?"

"Some old lady just came into the bakery. She asked for you specifically."

I took a deep breath and pinched the bridge of my nose.

"We've been over this, Jayden," I said patiently. "Our valued customers are not 'some old lady' or 'a sweaty leather daddy with a gross neckbeard.'"

He wrinkled his nose.

"Are you saying I should've—?"

"Asked them their name?" I suggested. "Yeah, that might have been a good start."

When I stepped out into the bakery and saw who was waiting for me, my heart sank to my toes. Nolan's grandmother was standing by the window, admiring my latest chocolate diorama. Steeling every last ounce of resolve, I approached awkwardly.

"Hello, Gra—Ver—Mrs. Reid."

I wasn't sure what I should call her anymore. She didn't appear to notice my discomfort. When she heard my stammered greeting, she spun around, beaming all over her apple-cheeked face.

"I told you, dear, it's Granny V! It's so lovely to see you again. We haven't heard a thing from you in two weeks."

"Well, I—"

Despite having only met this woman once, I was oddly chastened by her gentle scolding. I felt like a careless grandchild who never bothered to write.

"You're looking tired, dear."

Granny V was looking at me closely, face creased with concern.

"Have you been working too hard?"

"N—no," I faltered. "I've—"

"You're so much like my Nolan it's uncanny," she burbled. "I keep telling him he's going to work himself into an early grave. Poor boy needs someone to take care of him."

She gave me a meaningful look. For a moment, I was unable to muster a reply. The mention of his name had caused a dull ache to gnaw at my stomach. Gritting my teeth, I forced a bright smile onto my face and tried to steer the conversation into less treacherous waters.

"I'm sorry. I wasn't expecting you. My assistant... Well, more like my apprentice, really..."

I smiled serenely as Jayden looked daggers at me from behind the counter.

"He didn't have the good manners or common sense to ask you for your name."

"That's alright, dear." Granny V chuckled. "I was just admiring these adorable little bunny rabbits."

I flushed. The scene in question *was* adorable, at least at first glance. It was a flower-covered hillside, sprinkled with a prolific family of white chocolate rabbits. A keen-eyed observer would also have seen that some of the larger rabbits were enthusiastically... making more rabbits. I wasn't sure if Granny V had noticed, but she didn't seem to disapprove.

"Abby has not stopped talking about her birthday cupcakes," she prattled. "She insisted we save one and put it in the freezer. Your sweets truly are amazing. I've never seen anything so clever."

The glow in my cheeks came from a different source this time.

"Thank you. I really—"

"That's why I want you to do my wedding cake."

My jaw hit the floor. For a moment I just stood there, staring at her stupidly. I was flattered, but under the circumstances, it was impossible.

"I'm not sure that's such a good idea," I began.

"Why ever not, dear?"

Because it would virtually guarantee I'd see Nolan again and I'm not sure I'd have the resolve to push him away a second time.

"You do wedding cakes, don't you?" Granny V persisted.

"Yes," I said carefully. "But not in the conventional sense."

Granny V waved a hand dismissively.

"Who wants conventional? I have something much more fun in mind. I have some delightful mischief planned with my wedding cake, and I can't think of anyone more capable of doing it justice."

She paused to cast another eye over "bunny hill."

"I'm just relieved to see you can do good old-fashioned sugar paste flowers."

"Of course I can," I said, trying not to sound insulted. "But—"

Deaf to my protests, she rummaged in her purse and came up with a folded piece of paper.

"Here's my concept," she said proudly. "Take a look and see what you think."

Helpless in the face of her good-natured enthusiasm, I took the paper and unfolded it.

"Wow," I murmured.

It was nothing like I was expecting. It was beautiful and complex, and the more you looked at it, the filthier it got. Despite my better judgment, I loved it. This commission was becoming harder to turn down by the second. If all my decisions were made by little cartoon people who lived in my brain, the artist would just have joined forces with the romantic idiot. When I looked up from the drawing and caught Granny V's eye, she smiled softly.

"One thing I've always tried to instill in my children—and my grandchildren for that matter—is 'never judge a book by its cover.' Look beneath the surface of something and wonderful things can happen. That's the theme of this cake. Really, it's the theme of this whole wedding. Look at me," she proclaimed. "I met the love of my life at 79 years old. Isn't it a good thing he didn't just look at me and see, 'some old lady'?"

I smirked to myself. I could feel Jayden blushing from the other side of the room. Granny V took hold of my arm, and her smile became impish.

"Who knows? If you decide to make my cake, maybe wonderful things will happen for you."

A lump had formed in my throat. Whether she had intended it or not, Granny V's speech had made me quite emotional. All of my misgivings were still cruising the waters of my mind like hungry sharks, but was it humanly possible to tell this woman "No"?

CHAPTER SIXTEEN

Nolan

I was furious. My grandmother had meddled in my love life before, but using her wedding cake to try and force me and Erin together was taking things too far. She had to be stopped.

I decided on a face-to-face confrontation. My grandmother was relatively techno-literate, but she still typed all her messages with one finger, which could get frustrating. Also, she wasn't quite fluent in the language of emoticons. This had led to some truly surreal moments. I didn't like the idea of a serious talk being undercut by the sudden appearance of a rainbow turd... again.

Fortunately, my sister had decided we all needed a break from wedding prep and had scheduled a family dinner. Driving over after work, I mentally rehearsed what I would say to my grandmother. I couldn't get much further than, "I know you mean well, but." Part of what made this so hard was that I was desperate to see Erin again. The thought made me feel like there was an expanding bubble in my chest. Then I remembered the fear and betrayal on her face as she literally fled from me and the bubble burst. She didn't deserve to have me thrust at her by the reincarnated spirit of Yente the Matchmaker.

I never needed to knock on Olivia's door; I had a key. While this was convenient, it sometimes meant that there was no one to protect me from the playful whims of my niece. When I entered the house, I heard the familiar sounds of my sister bustling around the kitchen. However, before I could go and say hi, I was accosted by an excited six-year-old and dragged into the living room.

Abby had taken most of her dolls and stuffed animals and seated them in orderly rows facing the fireplace. This strange meeting was being presided over by Olaf the snowman, who had been placed front and center. I gazed around, trying to decipher the scene. My first guess was a cult meeting. Abby took both of my hands and gave me her patented sunshine smile.

"Uncle Nolan, will you marry me?"

Ok, not what I was expecting. Trust me, kiddo, you can do better.

I crouched down to her level and put my hands on her shoulders.

"Sorry, princess. You'll always be my number one girl, but uncles can't marry their nieces. Besides, you told me you were going to marry Olaf when you grow up."

I cast a glance at the grubby snowman, now more gray than white. He'd definitely seen a lot of love. Abby giggled.

"I don't want to forever marry you, Uncle Nolan. I just want to marry you *now*."

She gestured at the tableau behind us and understanding dawned.

"Alright," I agreed. "There should be time before dinner. We'll just have to make sure we get a quickie divorce before dessert."

She bit her lip and frowned.

"Why before dessert?"

I arranged my face into the most solemn expression I could manage.

"Well, baby-girl, I'm afraid, under state law, I'll be entitled to half of your baked alaska."

Abby folded her arms and smiled.

"Not if I get a prenup," she said smugly.

"Who told you about those?" I demanded.

"Alana."

Who else?

"She said if I ever get married when I grow up, I'll need one."

I pursed my lips.

"Well, as a lawyer, I'm inclined to agree. As your future husband, I'm not so sure."

She giggled and grabbed at a piece of lace netting lying in a discarded heap on the floor.

"This is the veil," she informed me, thrusting it into my hands.

I leaned forward to place it over her fiery curls, but she took a step back and stuck out her lip.

"No," she insisted. "I was the bride this morning. I want to be the groom."

"But I can't be the bride," I protested. "I'm a boy."

I realized my mistake as soon as the words left my mouth. Olivia's voice floated in from the kitchen.

"What have I told you about warping my child's mind with heteronormative stereotyping?"

Curse her bat-like ears!

"Come on!" I pleaded.

"Put the damn veil on, Nolan!"

Abby grinned up at me triumphantly. I reluctantly reached up and perched the lace on my head.

I had been through three marriage ceremonies and agreed to a series of increasingly incomprehensible vows before Olivia rescued me. I flipped the veil from my face and flopped onto the couch with a groan. My sister handed me a mug of coffee and poked my calf with her foot.

"Wipe that scowl off your face," she chided. "This is supposed to be the happiest day of your life."

I frowned at my coffee.

"The happiest day of my life will be the day all this wedding stuff is over."

Olivia raised her eyebrows.

"Someone got out of bed on the wrong side and pulled on their cranky pants," she observed. "I thought you were happy for Granny."

"I am." I sighed. "It's just this cake thing."

"Hm."

Olivia paused for a sip of coffee.

"She claims to have no ulterior motive."

"You believe her?"

"Partly. I know she was thinking about it. I think you might have made up her mind, though. No way she'll budge now. You know very well you can't stop her."

"No," I conceded. "But I can try to reason with her."

"Just keep a lid on your temper," she warned. "I take pride in my baked alaska. Don't want any of it getting thrown. Dad RSVP'd, by the way."

I blinked.

"To the wedding? I thought he was adamant he was going to boycott the whole thing."

Olivia shrugged.

"Changed his mind. He's flying in in two weeks."

I grimaced.

"What the hell is he up to?"

Ten years ago, my parents had finally given up on their train wreck of a marriage. Soon after the divorce was finalized, my father's company relocated to Dubai, and he'd been living there ever since. The weird thing was, once the pressure of marriage and fidelity had been lifted, my parents' relationship had improved. My mother frequently visited him in Dubai, and they were on more than cordial terms. This might sound good on paper, but it was a mixed blessing. When they actually presented a united front on something—like their hatred of Russ—they were a two-headed monster.

"What about Mom?" I asked.

"Nothing yet." She gave me a warning dig in the ribs. "Granny's really happy though. Don't ruin it for her."

I crossed my arms defensively. I loved my grandmother dearly, but this had to be one of her more frustrating blind spots. Her refusal to accept the fact that her son was a piece of human trash.

Granny V and Russ arrived soon after that. I waited until we were settled, and Russ had carved the ham, before launching my attack.

"Granny, about this cake," I began.

"It's all sorted, dear," Granny V breezed. "I dropped my design off at Erin's bakery this afternoon."

I was taken aback. I hadn't expected her to move this quickly.

"Are you telling me she agreed to do it?"

Hope flared treacherously in my chest. Granny V spread her napkin on her lap and smiled demurely to herself.

"Not yet, but I think she was quite taken with my design. And, if you ask me, that's not all she's taken with."

I put my elbows on the table and rested my head in my hands.

"Granny," I groaned. "You know how things ended with me and Erin. This isn't going to—"

"I know, dear. I'm not trying to meddle. This is all, as you would put it, strictly professional. Oh, Sugar Bear." She turned to Russ. "Did you telephone the country club to make sure they had an extra room?"

I choked on a piece of ham.

"An extra room?!" I croaked, eyes streaming. "She'll be there for the whole weekend?"

Olivia poured a glass of water and placed it in front of me.

"I seem to remember someone telling me this is a fancy bakery," she teased. "Cake assembly and onsite whisker application included in the service."

I balled up my napkin and pitched it across the table at her. She caught it nimbly and stuck her tongue out.

"Is Erin making kitty cakes again?" Abby piped up.

"Not this time, pumpkin," said Granny V. "Kitty cakes were *your* special treat. Granny has something else in mind."

"What exactly is this cake going to be?" Olivia asked.

"Good luck with that," Russ chuckled. "She wouldn't even let me see the design."

A whole weekend with Erin at a country club? There was nothing for it; I'd just have to avoid her. Still, a *whole* weekend. Anything could happen.

The conversation moved on to other matters after that. I bit my tongue while Granny V enthused over my father's change of heart, and I listened to Abby's attempts to charm Russ into being her next bride.

By the time dessert came around, I was feeling calmer. Nothing was set in stone. Erin hadn't even accepted the commission yet. After the debacle with Heather at the restaurant, there had to be a good chance she'd turn it down. After all, guys like me didn't get second chances.

CHAPTER SEVENTEEN

Erin

"You aren't seriously considering turning this down?"

I didn't answer immediately. I was too busy staring apprehensively at the garish blue cocktail my best friend had placed in front of me. It looked more like an elaborately adorned fishbowl than a drink. I bit my lip.

"Yes. I mean, no. Perhaps. You think I shouldn't?"

Maddie gave me a withering look.

"You know, I've always admired how decisive you are."

"Hey!" I reached across the table and jabbed her with a cocktail stirrer. "I agreed to come out for drinks. I didn't sign up for a visit from the sarcasm fairy."

Madison fished a gummi shark from her glass and popped it into her mouth with an unrepentant smirk.

"You were invited by the legitimately concerned friend fairy," she pointed out. "You should know by now that the sarcasm fairy always comes along for the ride."

I folded my arms and flopped back against the leather seat of the booth.

"Concerned about what?" I huffed.

"You, turning down commissions for a guy... again."

I winced.

"You have it all wrong," I said. "This is nothing like what happened with—"

My throat constricted. With everything that had happened in the last couple of weeks, I found it hard to say Stirling's name out loud. Part of me knew it was irrational, but I couldn't escape the idea that he could hear me. He had become this evil omniscient presence. I swallowed around the lump in my throat.

"This isn't the same as what happened with You Know Who. This is just me thinking that it might be a little awkward if I make a wedding cake for the grandmother of the guy I've just—"

"The guy you've what?" Maddie demanded. "Things seem to have gotten pretty intense for a guy you've never even had a proper date with."

"We had pho!" I insisted. "And there, in the kitchen, there was... We had a moment."

I gestured lamely and took a sip of my drink. It was sweet, fruity, and didn't taste all that alcoholic. Experience told me this meant it was probably lethal.

"You had a moment... at his niece's sixth birthday party? You still haven't explained why you were there."

Madison had only recently returned from her honeymoon, and she had received a rather fragmented account of the recent developments in my life. I rolled my eyes and recounted the debacle of the "kitty" cupcakes.

"It's not funny!"

Once she was able to breathe again, Maddie looked at me skeptically.

"Ok, it is a little funny, but at the time it was mortifying."

"So let me get this right," said Madison, leaning forward and resting her chin on her hand. "Not only did you fix the cupcakes and cover for him with his family, but you also stayed for the party and helped with the clean-up?"

I blushed and looked away.

"That's true love if I ever heard it. Kiddie birthday parties belong in the ninth circle of hell."

"It is not," I objected. "I mean yeah, he's good-looking and kind and really smart... but that's not the point!"

"Come on, Erin! I know you better than that. Every time this guy's name gets mentioned—which has been a lot, just sayin'—you blush."

"I do not!"

She fixed me with a hard stare.

"Nolan."

She enunciated his name slowly, placing a heavy stress on both syllables.

"Now you're just being silly."

Madison sat back and stirred her fishbowl.

"Ok," she said. "This guy seems like Mr. Perfect. What went wrong? We *should* be having this conversation by text right now because you're too busy licking chocolate from his exquisite nipples."

I narrowed my eyes.

"Sometimes I think I overshare with you," I grumbled.

"Not possible. Now, dish."

I sighed.

"We were having dinner, it was all going great, and then—this woman showed up. I think she was his ex. She started yelling and screaming and she made this whole big scene. It was awful."

Maddie's eyes widened and she placed one hand dramatically over her breast.

"You don't mean to tell me," she gasped, "that he's had... a relationship before. Thank God you got out. This could have been the thin end of the wedge; he might have had more than one!"

I raised an eyebrow.

"Are you done?" I inquired dryly. "Because I think the sarcasm fairy is abusing her privileges at this point."

"You might have a point," she conceded. "But I'm serious. You can't always judge someone by their ex. You should know that better than anyone. What if Stirling had shown up and started yelling all those things he posted on your website? Would you want someone using that to form their opinion of you?"

Ouch! This girl does not pull punches.

"Perhaps not," I said, feeling a little ashamed. "But it's not just his ex. I told you about the stripper cake and the cupcakes. Every time I meet this guy, something crazy happens."

She grinned wickedly.

"Sounds like a lot of fun to me."

"I'm not like you, though," I pointed out. "You met Claudia at a bar one night and the next day you're both at a bed and breakfast in San Francisco. I don't hear from you for three days and then I get a selfie from the freakin' pier, and a message saying, 'Can't wait to introduce you to the love of my life.' And yeah, maybe that's worked out great for you, but I've never been as good at... going with the flow. Especially not after what happened with *him*."

She reached out and took my hand.

"Calm down, sweetie. I know you're not great at embracing insanity, but you have to loosen up a little. Sure, your business is going great now, but you need to have a life outside work. It doesn't feel like you're living. You're just existing."

"I think that's a little harsh," I objected. "I need to do this in baby steps, ok? What happened at the restaurant was extremely humiliating, and I've had enough public humiliation for one lifetime. I took some of your advice, though."

"True," she sighed. "You have left the house, and you hired that obnoxious teenaged gremlin."

I laughed. The first meeting between Jayden and Maddie had not gone well. I'm not sure she'd ever been called a "boomer" before. In his defense, she had insulted his hair. I'd been forced to spend the rest of the afternoon reassuring him that he *didn't* look like the Joker's effeminate younger brother.

"Here's a thought," Maddie said. "You make the cake and let the clown prince of crime deal with the family. He has to learn sometime, right?"

"Hmm."

It wasn't such a terrible idea. Leaving aside the disaster with the bachelor party, Jayden had demonstrated a lot of growth. Maybe I could trust him with this.

"Seriously," Madison urged. "Don't turn it down. That would just be dumb. I can tell you're really excited about this design. Plus, you never know. Maybe you and Nolan could still—"

"Don't finish that sentence," I warned. "Never going to happen. You might be right about the cake, but I'm right about this. If everything goes according to plan, I can fulfill this commission without ever having to see Nolan. I mean it. Romance is off the table!"

"But—"

"Nope." I raised a finger and eyed her sternly. "I'm going to refresh our drinks and then you are going to tell me about your honeymoon."

"But you know what I'm like once I get going," Maddie warned. "I'll talk your ear off all evening."

"Good," I said firmly. "I like hearing about you and Claudia. It gives me hope. Same again?"

By this point in the evening, the bar was crowded. I stood on my tiptoes and craned my neck, trying to see a way through. It was at times like this that I cursed my unreasonable shortness. Fortunately, like many tiny people, I had developed pointy elbows to compensate. I nudged my way through the throng and finally made it to the bar. It took a while to get served; I'd never been known for my assertiveness. When I managed to attract the attention of a bartender, I opened my mouth to give my order, and nothing came out.

Frozen with terror, I stared across the bar at a familiar face in the crowd. It was only the briefest glimpse. I blinked and he was gone. Had I imagined it? Perhaps I was losing my mind.

"Hey, are you gonna order or—?"

I mentally shook myself.

"Sorry. Zoned out."

Luckily, when I got back to the table, I'd composed myself enough that Madison didn't notice anything. The rest of the evening was spent discussing her honeymoon in what most of the civilized world would consider to be unseemly detail.

By the time we were leaving, I'd convinced myself I had imagined seeing Stirling. It would be easy to mistake a face in a crowded and dimly lit bar.

I wasn't wasted, but I was definitely too drunk to drive. Maddie called for an Uber while I ran to retrieve my gloves and scarf from the front of my car. I was just about to lock up and head back to my friend when I spotted something lying on the back seat. My heart sank. It was a sleek, black, oblong box with a silver bouquet embossed on the front. I glanced around nervously, but the parking lot was as silent and empty as it had been when I'd arrived.

What were you expecting, a skulking figure in a black cloak and opera hat?

Heart pounding, I opened the car door and slid onto the seat, next to the box. My hands trembled as I lifted the lid. The box was lined with black silk, and it contained two dozen red roses and a card. My throat constricted with panic as I read the familiar handwriting.

It was nice to see you enjoying an evening out, but you know I don't approve of that friend of yours. Thinking of you every moment.

CHAPTER EIGHTEEN

Erin

Madison freaked out when I told her about the roses. I'd planned to keep it to myself, but I was still shaking when I rejoined her outside the bar. Finally, I cracked under her interrogation and showed her the phone messages as well. She insisted we go straight to the police.

I didn't want to. The thought of telling a stranger about all the horrible things Stirling had said and done made me feel as though something was squirming in my stomach.

The reception area at the police station was a harsh, bleak room. Cologne and stale coffee hung thickly in the air, and I could hear the faint buzzing of the neon strip lights. A desk sergeant with a drooping mustache and big belly lounged behind the counter eating noodles from a takeout carton and watching a small TV set. There was an unshaven man asleep on one of the orange plastic benches but other than that, the place was empty. This had obviously been a slow night.

I hung back when we approached the counter, still feeling horribly embarrassed; Maddie on the other hand stepped forward and cleared her throat pointedly. Sighing, the sergeant put down his noodles and killed the volume on the TV.

"Can I help you, ladies?" he grunted.

"Yes," Maddie clipped, with a condescending glance at the blob of sriracha on his tie. "We'd like to report a serious crime."

He swiveled his chair through 90 degrees and jabbed at the keyboard on his desk. The computer monitor flickered into life, casting an eerie blue light on his jowly face.

"Oh yeah?" he said disinterestedly. "What's the problem?"

Maddie took me by the elbow and ushered me forwards.

"Go on, Erin," she coaxed.

"I—I. The thing is, it's my boyfriend. Well, my ex-boyfriend, actually. He—"

The sergeant leaned back and folded his hands over his stomach.

"So you're here to report a domestic situation?"

I clenched my fists and my nails dug into my sweaty palms.

"Y—yes. Well, no, actually. H—he doesn't—"

"This boyfriend beat you up?" he demanded, clearly scanning me for visible injures.

"No! Nothing like that."

"Then what?"

My eyes filled with tears. I was starting to feel like I was the criminal. As usual, my best friend came to my rescue.

"He's been stalking her," she snapped. "He's been following her around, sending creepy phone messages and leaving little tokens of his affection in her car. Is that clear enough, or did I use too many complicated words?"

The sergeant reddened and seemed to swell inside his uniform. This was quite a feat, given he was already filling it to capacity.

"Listen, honey," he growled. "I don't have time to—"

Maddie cut him off.

"You look like you have all the time in the world from where I'm standing," she said crisply. "Now, if you don't want to deal with us, that's fine. You can continue to sit on your donut-munching ass while I draft this strongly worded complaint to the chief of police."

She made a show of jabbing at her phone.

"Erin, how do you spell 'belligerent little man with condiment stains on his tie'?"

She was brutal when she got into her stride. I almost felt sorry for the sergeant at this point.

"Alright, alright!" He threw up his hands in surrender. "Don't get your panties in a bunch. I'll take some initial details and then I'll get someone down to take a statement."

He raised an eyebrow when he looked at my business address.

"Sticky Treats?" he asked.

I flushed. Something about the way he looked at me made me feel naked.

"I—It's a bakery," I gabbled. "I bake cakes."

"Mmhmm."

He gave me the once over and looked back at the screen. I could hear Stirling's voice echoing in my mind.

People are already going to look at what you do and get the wrong idea. You don't need to add fuel to the fire.

I pulled my coat more tightly around me.

After giving my details, I perched nervously on one of the plastic benches and waited. Madison found a vending machine down the corridor and procured two paper cups of truly foul coffee. This whole night was beginning to feel very surreal.

We were on our second cup of Colombian paint thinner when another uniformed police officer came down to fetch us. We were taken to an interview room, and I gave my statement. I tried my best. I gave them "the entire history of my interactions with this individual," and the officer wrote everything down. I didn't really feel like he took me seriously. He said there wasn't enough evidence for them to take action at this stage, but I should keep a diary of any future incidents and report the situation to them if things escalated.

"What the hell did that even mean?" Maddie fumed.

She had insisted on seeing me to my front door. She'd wanted me to go and stay with her. It was a sweet offer, but she and Claudia had only just got married; I didn't want to impose on them.

"I mean..." She leaned against the door breathing heavily. "It sounded a hell of a lot like 'sorry, can't help you right now, but be sure to let us know if he strangles you in your sleep.'"

I winced and she instantly looked repentant.

"I'm sorry, sweetie," she said, pulling me into a hug. "My stupid mouth ran away with me. I'm sure it won't come to that, but you call me immediately if that creep contacts you again."

"Ok."

She held me by the shoulders and studied my face closely.

"You promise?"

"I promise."

Thankfully, he didn't contact me again. The next day I had new locks fitted on my door, which gave me some level of comfort. Even if he had held on to his key, it wouldn't work anymore.

Granny V was delighted when I accepted her commission and, for my part, I had never had a better rapport with a client. It turned out she had been a children's illustrator when she was younger, so she understood the artistic process. It also explained her stunningly beautiful design, rendered in delicate watercolor. I was tempted to have it framed and hang it on the wall of the bakery.

The design for her cake would definitely not have been appropriate for a children's book. At first glance, it looked very much like a traditional wedding cake. It was a four-tiered structure with a spray of sugar paste flowers cascading down one side. The twist was that the flowers had all been designed to exploit the natural tendency of flowers to look like... other things. The blossoms were blushing pink and deep crimson and there were plenty of suggestive curves and tumescent stamens. Some of the flowers also contained tiny fairy couples, who graphically demonstrated what the flowers merely suggested.

I wasn't surprised that Granny V was in and out of the shop on an almost daily basis. She was excited about the cake, and she seemed to find the whole bakery fascinating. What did surprise me was the fact that she and Jayden got on like a house on fire. She made a good first impression when she complimented his tattoos and asked how he'd managed to achieve such a vibrant color on his hair. When she heard about Madison's Joker comment, she said he should own it and get a purple suit for Halloween.

I often came down to the bakery to find them gossiping and giggling together. He made several suggested additions to the cake design which she eagerly accepted, and he even persuaded her to let us do chocolate bunny centerpieces for all the tables. Granny V loved the idea, but I didn't want to picture Olivia's face when she had to explain to little Abby why all the bunnies were playing leapfrog. When Granny V pinched Jayden's cheek and called him a "clever boy" I held my breath for the scowl, but he just blushed and grinned. Apparently, no one could get mad at Granny V.

I knew Jayden was looking forward to going to the wedding. I didn't blame him. An all-expenses-paid weekend at a 5-star country club was nothing to be sneezed at. Officially, he was there to assemble the cake and take care of any emergency repairs, but the chances of anything going wrong were minimal. At any other time, I would have been jealous. Getting away for a bit of pampering was just what I needed. This wedding on the other hand... A whole weekend at a country club with Nolan did not sound relaxing. It sounded dangerous. I was already working myself up imagining how hot he would look in formal wear. There was just something about a man in coattails.

The night before the wedding party was due to leave, I was getting ready to go to dinner with Maddie and Claudia when my phone buzzed. I cradled it to my ear as I wrestled myself into my heels.

"Hi, Jayden. Do you need me t— What do you mean, you're sick?"

CHAPTER NINETEEN

Nolan

"I spy with my little eye something beginning with 'g'."

"Hmm."

I stared out of the car window at the drab and featureless landscape. The five-hour drive to the wedding venue had taken us through some picturesque landscape, but this was a low point. For the past 15 miles, we'd been driving through onion fields.

"Grass," I guessed, finally.

"No."

"Er... gearshift?"

"Nope."

"Abby," I said patiently. "We've been through this. It has to be something I can see, either in the car or from the window. Remember our trip to Niagara Falls, when it took Mommy and me three hours to figure out that it was 't' for Triceratops?"

Sometimes I regretted getting her hooked on the Discovery Channel. Personally, I found I spy to be one of the worst car games ever invented, but we didn't have many other options. Playing 20 questions with Abby was unwise unless your Hello Kitty and dinosaur trivia were both on point.

"It *is* something I can see, Uncle Nolan," Abby insisted. "It's in the car."

"Glove compartment?"

"No."

"Ok, I give up."

"Grump!" she announced, pointing at me through the rear-view mirror and smiling triumphantly.

"Kiddo has a point." Olivia chuckled. "You've had a face that would curdle milk ever since we left home."

I grimaced.

"I've been getting a lot of that lately."

"Well," she suggested, "maybe that should tell you something."

Abby fiddled with the hair on her Olaf stuffie.

"You look like you're mad with the road," she observed.

I glanced at myself in the driver's side mirror. Abby was right. My brow was deeply furrowed and the muscles in my jaw and forehead were aching.

"I'm not mad with the road, baby."

"Then what are you mad with?" she asked innocently.

Where do you want me to start?

I had a lot on my mind at that moment. Taking legal action against Heather had proven to be just as much of a headache as I had anticipated. Shortly after I submitted my application, I received papers from her lawyer informing me that his client had a countersuit. Miss Heather Grabowski was seeking punitive damages for the "prolonged emotional abuse" I had inflicted on her during our relationship.

"What relationship?" I had yelled, clutching the paper in my shaking fist. "We were only seeing each other for a few weeks, and if anyone suffered abuse in that time, it was *me*."

I wasn't worried about the outcome of the case. I had nothing to hide, and she had no evidence. It was almost guaranteed to be thrown out. What I objected to was the soul-sucking waste of my time. Endless paperwork, hours spent in court. Not that I minded those things so much, it's just that I was used to getting paid for them. I knew what she was trying to do. It was pure, petty-minded spite. Heather was making it clear that, if I wanted to get rid of her, it was going to be a long, painful, and costly procedure. Like pulling very expensive teeth.

To add to my stress, my father had arrived last night, and he hadn't been alone. Rather than bothering to RSVP herself, my mother had simply shown up as my father's plus-one. The two of them had spent the entire evening making not-so-subtle digs at Russ. My father was head of an accounting firm, and he had an endless supply of "completely incidental anecdotes" illustrating the "awful" things that could happen if families failed to manage the financial affairs of their elderly relatives, and how vulnerable older women were to exploitation by "grasping" men. If Russ had been a less reasonable guy, I think I would have had to pull them apart by the end of the evening.

My mother pursued a different, but equally irritating, tactic by commenting loudly and repeatedly on the extravagance of the wedding preparations. What really got to me was the way my grandmother had defended them afterward, saying things like "I'm sure they didn't mean anything by it." I knew exactly what they meant by it, and it made me want to throw them out on their asses. I only hoped we could get through the weekend without one or both of them making a scene.

At least I didn't have to worry about bumping into Erin. She was sending her assistant to manage the cake. I'd met him before, at the ill-fated bachelor party. He seemed like a nice enough kid. Although, as Granny V had been threatening to let him dye her hair for the wedding, I hoped that she didn't share his aesthetics. I doubted acid green would be her color.

Granny V had been suspiciously quiet on the subject of Erin. I knew she'd been stopping in at the bakery almost daily, so I had expected a constant stream of information and hints, calculated to entice my interest. In reality, she'd been extremely tight-lipped about everything that had been happening there. I should have been pleased. Instead, I was uneasy.

I think you mean disappointed.

I scowled. My inner voice could be a jerk sometimes.

We arrived at Green Acres country club around mid-afternoon. My first impression was of a luxurious Mediterranean villa, incongruously dumped in the middle of an evergreen forest. The buildings were white with deep red roofs and everywhere you looked there were elaborate fountains and sparkling turquoise pools. Grateful to stretch my legs, I stepped out and took a deep breath. The air was sharpened by the fresh scent of pine.

As I was unloading our bags, I saw a familiar van pull into the parking lot. The sight of the Sticky Treats logo caused a sharp pang in my chest, and I forced myself to look away. I knew she wasn't in there, but I couldn't help picturing her; her sweet face, that lovely smile. I wondered what she was doing right now.

"You're here!"

I looked up from the trunk and spotted Granny V and Russ striding towards us. For a moment, I couldn't speak. I stared at my grandmother with my mouth hanging open. She had actually done it. She had followed through with her threat and allowed Jayden to dye her hair. It wasn't lime green; it was shocking pink. She looked like she was wearing a candy floss clown wig.

"Y—Your hair," I stuttered.

It seemed I was the only person to notice anything amiss. Olivia didn't pass comment and Abby squealed with delight. Granny V just beamed at me.

"Fun, isn't it?" she said.

"That's... one word for it. Why pink?"

"It's Abby's favorite color," she said, as though this was a silly question.

She ruffled her granddaughter's hair and Abby gave her a gap-toothed grin.

"Now," she paused to fuss at my lapels and tuck my trouser pocket back in, "give me a kiss and finish unloading. When you're all settled in, we can go exploring. The facilities here are unbelievable."

Shaking my head, I kissed my grandmother and shook Russ by the hand. I was just about to stick my head back in the trunk when Granny V touched me on the arm.

"Nolan, I see that the bakery van's just arrived. Go and see if they need a hand, darling."

Sighing, I left Olivia and Abby with the bags and trudged over to the van. The back doors were open, and I could hear movement inside.

"Jayden." I stepped around the side of the vehicle. "Granny sent me over to—"

My words caught in my throat. If someone had sauntered by wielding a feather, they would have had no difficulty in knocking me over. I stood in the back door of the van staring stupidly. A familiar pair of beautiful brown eyes stared nervously back at me.

"Erin?"

CHAPTER TWENTY

Erin

I should call him, or at least send a message. No, I absolutely should not do that. What is wrong with me?

This internal argument had been my only company for the five hours and 15 minutes it had taken to drive to the wedding venue. What would I say if I did message him?

"Hi. Sorry I ran out on you in that restaurant and then ignored you for three weeks. Now we need to spend the entire weekend together, so let's try not to make this awkward, 'kay?"

Or...

"Did you bring that psycho-woman with you? I only ask because I'd rather not have to get this dress dry-cleaned."

I drummed my fingers on the steering wheel as I crawled along behind a combine harvester. Perhaps I was being unfair. He probably hadn't brought her. It wasn't as though he'd seemed overly pleased to see her when she showed up at dinner. Maddie was right; I shouldn't judge someone based on the behavior of their ex. I knew that better than anyone. The farm vehicle turned off the road into a field, and I lowered my foot onto the accelerator with a grateful sigh.

Still, Stirling was another reason to leave things as they were with Nolan. I shouldn't be going after a new boyfriend while I was still trying to get rid of the old one. Especially not one who seemed as talented at finding trouble as I was. I needed to keep in mind that I was attending this wedding as a professional. I was here for the cake. I shouldn't even be thinking about Nolan.

My friends had been no help whatsoever. I was unconvinced by Jayden's claim that he had "suddenly come down with stomach flu." He painted an unnecessarily graphic picture of his symptoms, with lots of references to upside-down volcanoes. This was followed by a firm assurance that Granny V would be fine with the change of plans and an instruction not to wear yellow because it would make me look "sallow." I guessed what he was trying to do, and it was very sweet, but it had also put me in an awkward position. Maddie was no better.

"Oh, poor Joker Junior! I guess you'll have to go now. Isn't it a good thing my stylist has an open slot tomorrow morning, so we can get your hair done?"

I detected the strong whiff of a conspiracy. Everyone was convinced they knew what was best for me. I took an angry bite of Butterfinger. I had been stress eating since this morning.

My mood lifted a little when I arrived at the country club. I slumped back in my seat and took a moment to breathe in the opulence.

There might be an upside to Jayden's imaginary stomach flu.

I hadn't had time to check out the facilities in advance but I suspected there would be hot tubs, many hot tubs. Every tired muscle in my body ached in anticipation. A lot of people don't realize that baking can be hard physical work. I would never have to worry about bat wings.

Jumping down from the cab, I headed straight to the back of the van to check that all the boxes of cake had survived. I hated transporting large projects. Every bump and pothole had me making deals with God.

After a quick inspection, I released the breath I had been holding for five hours. Everything looked good.

I was about to climb out when I heard footsteps crunching across the gravel. His voice floated in from outside, slightly muffled but still unmistakably him.

"Jayden. Granny sent me over to—"

I froze in a ridiculous half-crouch. I briefly considered hiding behind the boxes, but I rejected the plan on the basis that it was ridiculous, infantile... and there wasn't enough room.

He was standing in the doorway of the van, the shock clearly written on his pale face. Maybe I really should have sent that message. I'd assumed someone else would tell him.

"Nolan—"

I could see the muscles in his jaw working, and his mouth was opening and closing without making a sound. Eventually, he managed to stutter.

"H—How are—? You look... How've you been?"

"Not bad," I lied. I gestured at the boxes behind me. "Been busy mostly. How about you?"

"Same. You know how it is."

This was starting to get uncomfortable, and I wasn't just thinking of the soul-crushing awkwardness of our forced small talk. The half squat I was forced into by the low roof of the van was making my thighs burn. My discomfort must have shown on my face because Nolan reached out to help me down. I took his hand automatically and jumped to the ground. As soon as our fingers touched, I felt a sharp, electric pulse of desire coursing through me, and my heart sped up.

"Listen," he said softly. "About what happened with—"

I pulled my hand away.

"Can we not?" I pleaded. "Not now anyway. I—I can't. I think we should just leave things as they are."

He took a step back.

"Sure," he said.

He was trying to sound casual, but I could see the hurt in his eyes. I could also hear Maddie's voice in my head, scolding me.

At least hear the poor guy out.

I felt like a bitch, but I couldn't afford to come apart. Granny V needed her cake. I swatted inner Maddie away and attempted to harden my heart to Nolan's puppy dog eyes. For a few seconds, we both stood there, groping for something to say.

"Lot of boxes in there," Nolan managed eventually. "How many tiers does this cake have?"

"Just four," I assured him, grateful for the change of topic. "It's not all cake. A lot of this is the bunny centerpieces."

"Sounds... sweet," he said suspiciously. "What is my grandmother up to?"

"Nuh-uh. I'm sworn to secrecy."

"Let me help you with all this," he offered.

I flapped my hand dismissively.

"No. You should go be with your family. You don't need to be humping boxes with the help."

"You're not the help, Erin," he insisted gently. "Not to insult your talent in any way but I'm fairly sure the main reason my grandmother hired you for the cake was to make sure you'd be here."

My cheeks began to heat up and I could feel something gnawing behind my navel.

"She's sweet," I mumbled, crossing my arms over my chest. "Very silly, but sweet."

"I know someone else like that," he murmured.

Our eyes met. We'd been staring at each other for way longer than was appropriate before I managed to drag my gaze away.

"You'd better be getting back," I said briskly. "They'll

wonder where you've got to. Could you tell front desk I'm here? They can send some kitchen porters down to help me with the boxes."

He nodded and I turned back to the van. I could feel his longing look burning into the back of my neck long after his footsteps had faded away.

Once the cake was squared away and the centerpieces were chilling in the walk-in fridge, I was more than ready for those hot tubs. The kitchen porters were helpful and efficient, but a couple of them were a little heavier-handed than I'd have liked. I did another quick check of the boxes to make sure the bunnies still had all their appendages. By the time I was satisfied, my teeth were chattering. I decided to check in and then immediately go for a soak.

I was leaning against the counter, waiting to receive my key, when I heard a voice behind me.

"Ah, it's the woman of the hour."

"Excuse me?"

I turned around to face the speaker. It was an older guy. He was still handsome, but his face was lined, and his chestnut hair was gray at the temples. I recognized his vivid green eyes immediately. Nolan's... father?

"The cake woman," he drawled. "My mother hasn't stopped singing your praises."

He stepped forward and held out his hand.

"Gabriel Reid."

"Erin."

I accepted his hand politely, but I let go as soon as I could. I wasn't sure why. He stood next to me, leaning one elbow on the reception desk.

"Mom showed me some of your work," he said, smiling thinly. "Interesting little niche you've found. How did you fall into it?"

I blushed hotly.

"I—I don't know really. I just—"

"Don't be embarrassed," he murmured. "I like a woman with a healthy interest in the earthier side of things."

His gaze roamed languidly over my body. I stiffened my shoulders and wrapped a protective arm around my chest.

"I don't know what you mean," I said, forcing a sweet and confused smile onto my face.

He just smirked coldly and leaned in closer.

"I noticed that my son wasted no time getting his foot in the door. Nolan takes after his old man."

I sincerely hope not.

His breath tickled my ear and I shuddered. He didn't miss the flinch, but he obviously misinterpreted it. He chuckled softly.

"If you get tired of waiting for him to get his act together, I'm in room 203," he purred, giving me a lazy wink.

My mouth fell open as I stared up at him, certain I must have misheard. I was still trying to frame my reply when Granny V called to us from across the lobby.

"There you are, Gabriel. We were about to send out a search party. Is that Erin with you?"

Gabriel turned around when he heard his mother's voice. I took my chance and fled from the lobby, practically running for the safety of my room.

CHAPTER TWENTY-ONE

Nolan

As I stormed towards reception after my awkward encounter with Erin, I reflected that I had never been more furious with my grandmother. How could she not tell me about this? Did she think I'd enjoy being blindsided like that? I scowled as I recalled her innocent request that I go and help unload the cake. I'd tolerated her interference until now, but this was too much. It wasn't fair on me or Erin.

I experienced a pang of guilt as I surveyed the empty parking lot. Olivia and Abby must have gone on ahead with the bags.

When I got to reception, I found them all waiting for me in a little cluster. My parents were there too.

Great! Just what I needed to make this day absolutely perfect.

Remembering my errand, I shot my family a surly wave and approached the front desk. The poor receptionist must have wondered what she'd done. I could feel my intense irritation bleeding into my voice as I asked them to send someone to help with the cake.

I swiftly realized that confronting my grandmother at that moment would be uncomfortable for everyone. Abby was more than sharp enough to pick up on any fighting, and she hated it. Upsetting my baby-girl was one of my least favorite things to do—alongside getting my balls crushed by my furious sister. I took a deep breath and bit my tongue, forcing myself to smile as Granny V and Russ gave us a tour of the spa facilities.

There were pools, saunas, Turkish baths, steam rooms, and ice showers. In fact, it looked like they could offer water at any temperature and consistency you wanted. I eyed the hot tubs longingly. It had been a long, tense drive and my shoulders were aching. I made a mental note to come back later for a soak. As the tour progressed, I was shown treatments and facilities I'd never heard of. I'd barely got through wondering what an "experience shower" was before I was presented with the "Kneipp walk."

The designated children's area was a rainbow/pastel paradise with a vast ball pit and stuffies so big *I* could have slept on them. Liv had to physically restrain a drooling Abby. There seemed to be something for everyone. Even my father was impressed. I caught him looking out of the window and giving the enormous golf course an approving nod. Strolling in front of my parents, I heard my mother murmur in my father's ear.

"No need to wonder who chose this place. Casanova clearly has a taste for the finer things."

My hands balled into fists. I knew for a fact that it had been my grandmother who chose the wedding venue. I think what finally swayed her was all the extra facilities they offered for children. She wanted Olivia to be able to relax and enjoy the day without worrying about Abby getting bored and wreaking havoc. I could have corrected them, but I was too angry. I didn't trust myself to do it politely.

After we'd finished exploring the country club, my parents retreated to their rooms to take a shower and Olivia went to put Abby down for a nap. I pounced on the chance to corner my grandmother.

"Is there something you forgot to tell me?" I demanded, struggling to keep my voice level.

My grandmother eyed me innocently.

"I don't know what you mean, dear," she said, fanning herself with a brochure. She turned to Russ. "Sugar-bear, I think I'm having one of my tropical moments. Could you fetch me an iced tea?"

Once Russ had obediently trotted to the bar, I folded my arms and eyed her sternly.

"You told me Jayden would be chaperoning the cake."

"Oh, of course. I'm sorry, darling. It slipped my mind."

I raised an eyebrow.

"Slipped your mind, huh?"

"Yes, well, it was all very last minute," she said, slipping her arm disarmingly through mine and steering me towards the bar. "Jayden, poor boy. He came down with terrible stomach flu last night. Fortunately, Erin was still available." She eyed me slyly. "Maybe this is the universe throwing you a bone."

I knew my grandmother too well to let myself be derailed. I disengaged my arm and put my hands on my hips.

"No," I corrected. "This is my grandmother throwing me a curveball."

"You can't honestly claim you're not pleased."

I started. Somehow my sister had snuck up behind us.

"Yeah," I spat. "I was delighted. I love awkwardness."

"Hello, sweetheart," Granny V beamed, diving on the distraction. "Did Abby go down ok?"

"Like an angel." Olivia yawned. "She was exhausted after that drive. To be honest, it was tempting to join her."

"Maybe you should," my grandmother suggested. "You could all do with some R&R before dinner tonight."

She smoothed her hands over the front of my jacket and brushed some imaginary lint from my shoulder.

"You've had a long drive. Why don't you head down to the

spa for a little pampering? I saw you eyeing those hot tubs," she coaxed.

"Maybe," I grumbled, not yet willing to be placated.

"Unless you'd rather stay," Olivia smirked. "I believe we're supposed to be meeting up with Mom and Dad for afternoon tea."

"If they ever show their faces again," said my grandmother, looking at her watch. "Go and see if your mother is still in her room, Olivia. I'll look for your father."

I took the opportunity to retreat. The prospect of afternoon tea with my parents was not enticing. When I reached the sanctuary of my room, I made an immediate beeline for the minibar. Sipping on a ludicrously overpriced double scotch soothed my nerves a little. Once the alcohol had taken the edge from my irritation, I could see the merits of my grandmother's suggestion. A few minutes later, I emerged from my room dressed in my swim shorts and a robe.

The spa was quiet at this time of day, and I had most of the facilities to myself. I padded across the tiles in my hotel flip-flops, skin already prickling in the hot, moist air.

There was one other person in the hot tub room. Excitement and dread bubbled under my ribcage as I stared at the petite, dark-haired woman lounging in the water. I did start to wonder if the universe was toying with me. Even my grandmother couldn't have engineered things this perfectly.

Erin was sitting in the tub with her arms spread out, an expression of total relaxation on her face. Her lips were slightly parted, and her eyes were closed. She looked positively sybaritic. The heat of the water had given her creamy skin a rosy flush and she was covered in a light sheen of sweat. I knew she hadn't seen me yet and I felt like an intruder, but I couldn't tear my gaze away. My eyes traveled slowly over the contours of her wet, near-naked body, and my cock stirred. Her breasts bobbed as she shifted in the water, and I bit back a groan. By this point, I was tenting out the front of my shorts. I had to move. I knew that she could open her eyes at any moment and find me leering at her like a pervert. Holding my breath, I backed silently out of the room, wrapping the robe around me to conceal my straining bulge. Relaxation would now be impossible until I had "taken matters in hand."

My grandmother insisted that Erin join the wedding party for dinner, and I couldn't help noticing that she seated herself as far away from me as possible. I don't think I tasted anything I ate; I was too busy stealing glances at her. I don't know which was worse—the disappointment when I failed to catch her eye, or the exquisite agony of my heart leaping into my throat when I caught her looking back. To add to my predicament, I knew what she looked like under her clothes now, and that image wasn't going away any time soon. I started wishing for several extra napkins to place across my lap.

Throughout the meal, my father was oddly quiet. I enjoyed it at first, but then I began to grow suspicious. On several occasions I caught him looking at Erin, and I didn't like the expression on his face. It gave me the irrational urge to flip the table and punch him in his smirking face. My mother didn't appear to have noticed his distraction; she was too busy trying to charm Abby. My baby-girl had never warmed to either of her grandparents, and to my mother's consternation, she refused to call her Granny. Children are often exceptional judges of character.

CHAPTER TWENTY-TWO

Erin

I don't usually get emotional at weddings, but there was something about this one. It was a gorgeous day; the sun streamed down from the cloudless blue sky, giving the already picturesque surroundings a vibrant, freshly minted look.

The ceremony was going to be held outside. White chairs had been arranged on the front lawn, facing an ornate archway wreathed in white roses.

I wasn't surprised when I saw the size of the guest list. People like Granny V rolled through life gathering an ever-expanding mass of friends like a giant *Katamari* ball. I didn't recognize many people, but I did see Alana, and she sent me a friendly wave. When I spotted her, she was standing off to the side with two men and a woman. I got the impression that an invitation bearing a "plus one" would always create an awkward situation in Alana's household.

When Granny V walked down the aisle, arm in arm with her scowling son, she looked amazing. I'd had some reservations when she'd asked Jayden to dye her hair. The idea of shocking pink hair with a crystal white wedding dress conjured up images of the fluffiest unicorn from *Despicable Me*. She should have looked ridiculous, but she was as beautiful as any bride on her wedding day. The pink hair was the perfect representation of her unbridled joy. She seemed 20 years younger. Abby was adorable as a flower girl. Somehow, she grew even more adorable when I spotted the toy Pterodactyl nestling in her basket of rose petals.

And then, of course, there was Nolan. My expectations of how good he would look in formal wear were not disappointed. He was wearing a three-piece suit with a forest green waistcoat that brought out the mossy hues in his eyes. He looked edible. At certain points during the ceremony, I caught myself staring at him longingly. I imagined what he'd look like standing at the altar, turning to catch a first glimpse of me walking down the aisle in my white dress. The forbidden image brought a lump to my throat. Fortunately, weddings provide the perfect cover for a discrete sniffle, so I wasn't horribly embarrassed.

I convinced myself that my emotional outburst was mostly the product of stress and exhaustion. Seeing Nolan again had been hard, and the unwanted attention of his father was making me seriously uncomfortable. To add to my problems, I'd received another message from Stirling last night, warning me that it would be "unwise to ignore him." I nearly called Maddie, but it felt too late to disturb her. She was a married woman now; it was only fair to let her enjoy her domestic bliss.

Before Granny V threw the bouquet, she glanced over her shoulder and caught my eye. I could practically hear the bleep of targeting scanners as her "totally random" throw sent her bouquet sailing into my arms. I blushed as everyone turned around to look at me. I think my attempt at a gracious smile had more of an "insane grimace" vibe. I didn't dare look towards Nolan, but I knew he was watching me. I got the feeling his father was watching me too, and this gave me a different, more unpleasant feeling in my stomach. I'd sensed it the previous night at dinner. I'd skipped the mints and coffee to make sure of securing my escape after the meal.

While everyone else gathered for photographs, I headed back to the main house to assemble the cake. It was a relief to escape the crowds and lose myself in work for a while. It wasn't my largest creation to date, but I suspected it was the most complex. Once all four tiers were safely unpacked and the flowers and fairies had been arranged, I walked around it, taking pictures from various angles.

"Impressive."

I'd been so absorbed that I hadn't heard Olivia approach.

"Thanks," I said awkwardly.

Of all Nolan's family, I was the most nervous around Olivia. Our first meeting had been chaotic and stressful, and I still felt bad for lying to her.

"Are they done with the pictures?"

"Not quite," she murmured, stepping closer to admire the flowers. "Abby had to go to the bathroom."

"Ah."

I fidgeted with my hands as she examined the cake. After a moment, she stood up and leveled her piercing, green gaze at me.

"He really likes you."

"Who?"

It was a stupid question, but she'd thrown me off balance and my brain hadn't caught up with my mouth.

"I think you know who," she said severely. "My thick-skulled brother. I've never seen him like this over anyone."

I opened my mouth to reply, but she cut me off.

"Look, I don't blame you. If I'd crossed paths with someone like Heather on a first date, I'd probably have run the other way too."

"It wasn't just that," I protested.

"Then, what?"

I shrugged. My teeth began worrying at the skin around my pinkie nail. Olivia sighed heavily.

"Nolan does an excellent impression of a hot mess—and

most of the time he is. He's arrogant, impulsive, and irresponsible."

I gave her a sidelong glance.

"I think your sales pitch might need a little work."

"I mean it," she insisted. "He's all those things and more, but that's just the surface stuff. He's like... you know when you toast a marshmallow and you leave it in the flame for too long? It doesn't look too good anymore, but underneath all that crusty, sticky crap, there's still—"

"An ooey-gooey center?" I ventured.

"Exactly." She chuckled. "When it comes to the stuff that matters, he's a good guy—for a lawyer, anyway." She stepped around the cake to stand next to me and her tone became serious again. "He's also my brother, and I've spent years watching him make bad decisions. I've honestly been tempted to wring his big, dumb neck on more than one occasion. But now—now he seems to have found someone worth hanging on to."

I pressed my lips together tightly. Olivia's approval touched me more than it logically should have, and I could feel the tears welling up.

"And you like him too," she asserted. "I'm not wrong, am I?"

I looked at her silently. I suspected that my face told her everything she needed to know.

"Just promise me you'll think about it. Give him a chance. And don't let my grandmother or anyone else make the decision for you. Just go with your gut."

I didn't know what to say. I was moved. She obviously loved her brother a lot and it somehow made me feel closer to her. I wanted to hug her, but I was afraid of bursting into tears. Instead, I just nodded.

"Thanks, Olivia," I muttered.

"No problem." She smiled.

"Mommy!"

The excited squeak caused both of us to turn around. Abby was standing in the doorway, looking considerably less immaculate than she had during the ceremony. Her flower crown sat crookedly on her red curls, her shoes were scuffed, and her dinosaur bounced around in the little basket, deprived of its comfy bed of petals. When she saw the cake, her eyes widened, and her mouth formed an 'o'.

"Look with your eyes, baby," Olivia warned.

Abby tiptoed closer and her eyes stretched even wider.

"Look at the cute fairies," she cooed.

I squirmed.

For I am Erin. Purveyor of filth and corrupter of innocent children.

After she had spent a moment examining the cake, Abby turned back to her mother.

"Mommy, there are chocolate bunnies on all the tables," she announced. "Can we sit at the table with the pink ones?"

"I hope you're talking about tables in the bathroom," said Olivia sternly, "because that's the only place you should have been."

"I went to the bathroom," the little girl chirped. "Then I peeked into the big room with the tables on my way back."

Her mother rolled her eyes.

"Of course you did."

"I think the bunnies got married too," Abby prattled.

"Why do you think that, sweetheart?"

"Because they're making babies," Abby announced.

I think I just heard crickets chirping. Thanks, Jayden. Thanks bunches.

"Oh, Jesus!"

I brought my hand up to cover my face. Olivia raised her eyebrows.

"Not my suggestion," I assured her.

"Oh, I'm sure." Olivia smirked. "I know my grandmother. She's quite capable of making mischief by herself. I'm just glad we got Abby that book about mommies and daddies and 'special hugs.' I wanted something a little less heteronormative, but I had to work with what I could find."

"When's Granny going to make a baby?" Abby piped up.

I stifled a giggle. Now it was Olivia's turn to look flummoxed.

"Um— What makes you think Granny's going to make a baby, honey?"

"Well, she's married now," Abby reasoned as if this were obvious. "That's what happens."

Olivia frowned.

"I've let you watch too many Disney movies," she said darkly.

Bending down, she scooped her daughter up and lifted her onto her hip.

"Granny doesn't need to have any babies," she explained. "She's already had her babies and her grandbabies." She paused to poke Abby in the chest. "She even has a great-grandbaby."

"That's me!"

Abby grinned proudly, before laying her head on her mother's shoulder. I smiled warmly. She was just too adorable.

"Time to trawl the book section of Amazon again," Olivia drawled. "Find a six-year-old's guide to menopause."

Abby's sharp ears pricked up.

"What's menopause?"

"Hey!" I interrupted, with a conspiratorial smile. "I think if we go now, we can sneak into the dining room and switch that pink bunny to your table!"

Abby's face lit up and she squirmed down from her mother's arms. Olivia shot me a grateful smile.

The wedding reception went just as smoothly as the ceremony. Everybody was bowled over by the cake. It was amusing to watch the shifting of their expressions as realization dawned. A few looked shocked but most people dissolved into laughs. Alana raised her glass and winked at me approvingly. It wasn't often that I got to see people enjoying my work. I usually delivered the goods and then left. It was nice to bask in the professional glow of a job well done. I held my breath when Nolan went up to look. He caught my eye and gave me such a warm smile that I swear my stomach melted.

As the evening progressed, I found myself looking at Nolan and thinking about what Olivia had said. I watched him scoop his niece into his arms and kiss his grandmother. I watched him fuss over an elderly woman I presumed to be his aunt, fetching her food and drink, and sitting patiently while she scolded him. He *was* a sweet guy.

When the lights dimmed and the dancing started, I retreated farther into the shadows. I never wanted anyone to find out about my two left feet. Leaning against the wall, nursing a glass of champagne, I continued to watch Nolan. He'd spun Abby around while she shrieked and giggled, and then he had danced with his grandmother. It was so wholesome that I couldn't help but smile. I was brought out of my reverie by a voice at my elbow.

"Tut! Tut! This is unacceptable!"

My heart sank. Nolan's father had materialized next to me. It sank even further when I noticed that his speech was slightly slurred.

"What sort of gentleman would I be if I let the prettiest girl in the room stand all by herself?"

I scanned the room frantically, hoping to catch someone's eye. Unfortunately, I'd chosen my discreet corner well.

"Come, dance with me!" he demanded, gesturing effusively at the center of the room.

"No, thank you," I mumbled, shrinking farther back. "I don't really like dancing."

"It's a wedding!" he cried, seizing my arm. "You have to dance at a wedding."

I suppressed a shudder and tried to extract my arm from his grip.

"Seriously, you don't want to dance with me," I protested. "I'm terrible; I'd probably tread on your toes."

He leaned forward and whispered in my ear.

"Trust me, sweetheart, with tits like yours pressed against me, I won't care what your feet are doing."

Eww.

The feeling of his hot, moist breath on my cheek made my skin crawl and I tugged my arm harder.

"Mr. Reid," I said firmly. "I really don't want to dance. Now, let me go!"

With a grunt, he yanked hard on my arm, pulling me against him.

"Enough of this nonsense," he growled. "The shy girl act may work on everyone else, but I'm a man of the world. I know what women want."

"Erin! What are you doing? You promised *me* the next dance."

I had never been happier to hear Nolan's voice. Gabriel released me instantly and turned to face his son.

"Oh! I didn't realize you'd already marked her card," he quipped. "I thought I taught you better than that, Nolan. You shouldn't leave a tasty morsel unattended or someone else will make a grab for your plate."

"So I see," said Nolan, eyeing his father coldly. He extended a hand towards me. "Come on, Erin."

Hurrying past Gabriel, I took Nolan's proffered hand and allowed him to lead me towards the dance floor.

CHAPTER TWENTY-THREE

Erin

As Nolan led me onto the dance floor, the lights dimmed, and I heard the opening chords of an alarmingly slow song. A mirror ball covered the entire dance floor with moving dots of light, so it felt like we were standing on a field of stars. Nolan was still holding my right hand in his left and I tried not to think about how sweaty my palm must be. I managed not to gasp as he slid his right arm tentatively around my waist, but there was nothing I could do about the blushing. It was like being in a dream where you discover you're in a play but you don't know any of your lines.

In an attempt to calm my racing heart, I glanced around at the other couples on the dance floor. Granny V and Russ were dancing, as were the two men who had shown up with Alana. They were wrapped very tightly around one another and looked achingly adorable. Abby had taken a break from dancing and was industriously working her way through an enormous slice of cake. Olivia was sat next to her, surreptitiously scraping some of the frosting off. I was startled from my observations by Nolan's quiet murmur.

"Are you ok?"

"Yeah," I said, managing a lopsided smile. "Thanks for the

rescue back there."

"No problem." He glowered at an unseen point over my shoulder. "My dad can be an ass when he's drunk... and when he's sober, come to think of it. Let's just say, he's an ass."

He gave a forced laugh.

"Now you know where I get it from."

"No," I insisted quietly. "You're nothing like him."

I watched the convulsive movement of his Adam's apple as he swallowed.

"I always hoped not to be. It's nice to hear it from you, though."

There was a moment of silence. Granny V caught my eye over Russ's shoulder and gave me an ecstatic thumbs-up. I sighed; she really was incorrigible. Nolan sent a cursory glance around the room.

"Well, I don't see him around anymore, but," he wrinkled his nose mischievously, "we should probably finish this dance, just to keep up appearances."

It was my turn to swallow.

This was not fair! How was he so fucking cute?

"I don't know," I said, biting my lip.

"Don't trust me?"

"More like I don't trust *me*." I chuckled. "I wasn't kidding when I told your dad I couldn't dance."

As if on cue, I stepped heavily on Nolan's foot. He couldn't entirely suppress the wince, but he managed to keep a stoic smile on his face.

"Maybe I should unleash you on Dad," he joked. "You might put him out of action for the rest of the evening. Ow!" he protested as I stomped on his toes again. "Now you're doing it on purpose."

"I don't know what you mean," I said, smiling innocently.

His hand splayed on my back, and he pulled me closer. My breath caught.

"I'd challenge anybody to dance when they're this tense,"

he exclaimed. "Just relax and let me lead."

"I've never been very good at relaxing," I admitted.

"How come?"

I shrugged.

"Lately, it's felt like every time I let my guard down, something terrible happens."

He looked at me thoughtfully.

"I bet I can get you to relax," he asserted. "I know exactly what you need."

The soothing warmth of your strong and manly embrace?

"A little pampering!" he said. "And we're in the perfect place too. We've got five-star spa facilities and free-flowing champagne."

I made a face.

"Getting drunk alone at a wedding? Isn't that a little tragic?"

"You could get drunk with me," he offered.

The music stopped and the lights turned on. Cold reality began to sink in, and I took a step back.

"I—I don't think—"

"Just as friends," he stated. "I promise, I have no ulterior motive."

Give me enough champagne and you won't need one.

He snagged two flutes from a passing tray and held one out to me. I stared at it, wavering. My shoulder devil was filling my ear with an endless stream of wonderful, awful ideas. The angel must have been stuck in traffic. What's the worst that could happen? I reasoned. We were at a resort in the middle of nowhere. A surprise cameo by an irate ex-girlfriend seemed unlikely. As I accepted the glass, Nolan's face relaxed into a broad grin that made something clench in my chest. He truly was heart-stoppingly gorgeous.

"Why are you going to all this trouble for me?" I asked, taking a sip of champagne. "I ran out on you after that meal, and we haven't even talked since then."

"Well," he said, linking his arm through mine and walking me towards the cake table. "It just so happens that I offer a comprehensive knight in shining armor package. I can't just pluck you from the grasp of the swamp monster and then ride off into the sunset. I refuse to consider you rescued until you relax and enjoy yourself."

I couldn't suppress the giggle. It gurgled up from my throat, tickling like champagne bubbles.

"There you go!" he encouraged. "That's a start. You've been working hard. You should relax. Seriously, that cake is incredible."

"I can't take any credit for the design. That was all your grandmother."

"Yes, but you brought it to life," he enthused. "The funniest thing is," he leaned in closer, smirking conspiratorially, "I don't think Aunt Norah's noticed anything yet."

I followed the direction of his gaze and saw the fussy older woman who had been scolding him earlier. She was deep in conversation with the person next to her, oblivious to the fondant fairy three-way taking place on her slice of cake.

I put my hand over my mouth to stifle a laugh, but then I made the mistake of catching Nolan's eye. Before long we were both doubled over.

"Oh my God," I panted. "I think that champagne's gone to my head already."

"Then you should definitely have more!"

"No," I protested. "No. Bad idea."

"I would if I were you," he warned. "I intend to have you back on the dancefloor before the evening's out."

He made good on his threat. I hadn't danced to "The Birdie Song" since I was in elementary school, but somehow, all the moves came back to me. This DJ knew what he was doing. He played a steady stream of golden oldies that acted like a siren's call on the slightly tipsy. After a long bout of hustles, hokey-pokeys, and conga lines, I was red-faced and sweating, but I had an enormous grin plastered across my face.

"Right!" Nolan declared, stumbling slightly. "Now, it's hot tub time."

"Hot tub?" I said blearily, my head still reverberating with the irresistible beat of the "Macarena." "Are we sure that's a good idea?"

There was a naughty drunken fairy cavorting in my brain that informed me it was an excellent idea. The image of Nolan's moist, glistening body created an insistent throb between my legs.

"It's a very good idea," he said confidently. "It's all part of the science of relaxation, you see? I loosened up your muscles on the dancefloor and now the hot tub is going to finish the job."

"The science of relaxation?"

"'S a real thing, scout's honor."

He raised three fingers in a vague salute.

"You were a boy scout?"

"Maybe," he murmured shiftily. "There might even be photographic evidence."

"Show me!" I demanded, seizing him by the front of his jacket and bouncing on my heels like an excited child.

"Ah-ah." He held up a hand. "Hot tub first."

I chewed my lip.

"We're pretty wasted," I mumbled. The floor had developed an annoying habit of shifting under my feet when I wasn't looking. "Shouldn't we wait 30 minutes or something?"

"You're thinking of eating," he assured me. "Besides, 's fine. I got my lifesaving badge in the scouts."

He grinned disarmingly and offered me his arm.

"Well..." I chuckled. "If you can't trust a boy scout, whom can you trust?"

The last thing I saw as we staggered from the room was Alana's suggestive wink.

CHAPTER TWENTY-FOUR

Nolan

To access the spa, we had to go through separate changing rooms. As I watched Erin stumble off, I felt a twinge of apprehension. She was drunker than I'd realized; hell, *I* was drunker than I'd realized. But it had been so nice to watch her let go.

All weekend, I'd been trying to leave her alone, trying to avoid even looking at her. All the same, I'd been constantly aware of her. It was like the urge to poke your tongue into the tender gum after a lost tooth.

It turned out to be a good thing that I'd unconsciously kept my eye on her. Thinking about my father's hands on her made anger well up inside me and I clenched my jaw. I'd honestly intended just to rescue her from Dad and retreat. Then I'd felt the mass of tension impossibly coiled within that tiny body and I'd wanted to take it all away.

I knew what it felt like to carry that sort of tension. My job was stressful, even without the occasional catastrophic incursion of my personal life. I expended a lot of energy maintaining a calm exterior even though I was screaming on the inside. If I hadn't had Alana to field things for me, I'd probably have gone crazy. Erin didn't have an Alana of her own, but maybe I could be the one to take some of the burden from her, even if it was only for a few hours. I'd meant it when I said I had no ulterior motive. I just wanted to make her feel good. It gave me a warm, happy feeling that had nothing to do with champagne.

Erin was so cute when she was tipsy. Fluffy and giggly, like an inebriated bunny. She'd been so much fun to dance with. And then, somewhere between the "Hokey Pokey" and the "Macarena," I'd been struck by a bolt of inspiration. I needed to take her to the one place I'd seen her truly relaxed—the hot tubs. It was a genius plan with no possible drawbacks.

I stripped down to my underwear in the humid fog of the changing rooms, my head swimming from the heat and the booze. I remembered seeing Erin in the tub yesterday, all moist and flushed. This time I wouldn't be hiding in the shadows. I'd be in the tub with her, close enough to count the beads of sweat that formed on the gentle slope of each perfect breast.

I felt a stirring at my crotch and looked down in dismay. The outline of my straining erection was clearly visible through the clinging fabric of my boxer briefs. I groaned, palming myself through my underwear. This would not do. I strode to the showers and turned the nozzle to cold. The icy jets of water did an excellent job of sobering me up, but they did nothing for the anaconda in my shorts. There was only one thing for it. Glancing around furtively, I headed into one of the bathroom stalls.

On the one hand, I hated myself. Whacking it in a public bathroom like some pathetic teenager. It felt so sordid. On the other hand, the thought of touching myself in such a public place with Erin so close by was weirdly... stimulating. Besides, this had to be better than sitting in the hot tub with my stiff cock bobbing indiscreetly between us. That was bound to make her uncomfortable. I was also 90% certain it was a felony.

After making sure that the door to the stall was locked, I

pulled the waistband of my boxers away from my belly and eased them over my hips. I sighed with relief as my aching dick sprang free of its confines. I was so hard that my member slapped against my stomach, a tiny drop of pre already glistening at the tip. This wouldn't take long.

I was settled in the hot, bubbling water by the time she emerged. She walked with hesitant, stumbling steps, clutching a big, white towel around herself. When she saw me watching, her cheeks reddened, and she tightened her grip on the towel. Despite my precautions, the mere thought of what lay beneath that fluffy barrier was enough to make my cock twitch. I crossed my legs, grateful for the camouflage of the churning water.

"Aren't you going to get in?" I asked.

She chewed her lip and shifted her weight onto one foot.

"I—I don't want you to see me," she mumbled, eyes downcast.

"Would it help if I close my eyes while you get in?" I offered.

She paused.

"Maybe."

"Ok."

I screwed my eyes shut, resisting the temptation to peep. The water shifted as she slid in beside me. I caught the scent of strawberries, with a subtle hint of rose. Had she shampooed her hair? She smelled like summer.

We sat in silence for a while. I closed my eyes and let my head loll back, allowing the water to boil the tension away from my muscles. All the same, I was acutely aware of Erin's presence. It stirred something primal within me that curled and twisted in my belly like a restless beast, preventing me from fully unwinding. I opened an eye and glanced at her. She was perched on the very edge of the shelf around the edge of the tub, hands in her lap, shoulders stiff. I sighed.

"You're still not relaxed."

"I am!"

"You are not. Here," I got out of the tub and perched on the side, shivering at the sudden temperature shift. "Come and sit in front of me."

She pressed her lips together, turning her mouth into a thin line. Her huge doe eyes flickered from side to side. I could sense an internal struggle going on.

"I'm just going to rub your shoulders," I assured her. "It's no big deal. I do it for my sister all the time."

She hesitated for a moment more, before sliding across the bench to sit between my feet. This was the closest we'd been since getting into the hot tub and my heart was hammering. Rubbing my hands together to warm them, I carefully gripped her shoulders.

Because of the way she'd been sitting, her shoulders were mostly dry, and her skin felt warm and satiny. I massaged her gently, tracing the delicate shapes of the bones and enjoying the movement of muscle under the skin. She held herself stiffly at first, but after a while, she surrendered to my ministrations with a little sigh of contentment. As she yielded, I felt myself thicken again and I was glad that my crotch was out of her line of sight.

Digging in with my fingers and circling my thumbs, I gradually loosened the knotted muscle in her shoulders. Her noises of appreciation were getting steadily louder and more suggestive. It would have been easy for someone listening at the door to come away with the wrong idea. Nolan Junior definitely had the wrong idea. He was positively quivering with anticipation.

"Mm. You're turning me into a puddle," she groaned.

Her head fell back against the side of the tub. She opened her eyes and gave me a dreamy, upside-down smile. In any other situation, I might have made a flirty quip, but my heart was pounding, and my head was swimming. Between the heat of the tub, my intense arousal, and the champagne, my brain had ceased to function. I chuckled and tapped her on the nose.

"Good. That was the idea," I pointed out.

"You're very pretty," she murmured. "Even when your face is upside-down."

For the first time, I noticed the flushing of her chest and the black pits of her pupils engulfing her irises. Was she just drunk, or was this little massage session affecting her as much as me?

"You're very pretty too," I said fondly. "Even when you're shit-faced."

Her mouth opened wide in silent outrage.

"I am not fit-shaced," she spluttered indignantly. "I was about to express my professional admiration for your nipples, but now, I don't think I will."

I blinked.

"My nipples?"

"Yes," she declared emphatically, reaching up and sloppily twirling her finger in the air as if to trace them.

I imagined the feeling of her wet fingertip gently running around my areola and over the sensitive bud of my nipple. I gulped.

"Every time I see them," she continued. "I wish I had my casting kit. They're so pert and shapely and... fuzzy."

"Wait... fuzzy?"

She clapped a hand to her forehead.

"No... head fuzzy," she mumbled. I watched in alarm as her eyes rolled back. "Think I'm gonna—"

"Oh no you don't."

Moving swiftly, I seized her under the arms and hauled her out of the tub. Her face and neck were very pink. She tried to lie down but I pulled her up and sat her on the edge of a lounger.

"Here," I said, gently but firmly pushing her head between

her knees. "It's alright, you just got a bit overheated. You stay here and I'll get you a nice cold drink of water."

"No," she whimpered.

As soon as I made to get up, she clutched at my hand.

"Don't leave me, Nolan."

She sounded so pitiful that another piece of my heart melted. I put an arm around her shoulders and squeezed.

"It's alright," I soothed. "I'm just going to that vending machine over there. I'll be right back, I promise. You trust me?"

"Yes." She sniffled.

I wish I could trust that you'd say that sober.

When I got back, she rested her head against my chest, and I kept encouraging her to take small sips of water. I gave an internal sigh of relief as the fog cleared from her eyes and her color returned to normal. She slumped forward and put her head in her hands.

"Jesus, I'm so fucking embarrassed," she mumbled.

"Don't be." I rubbed my hand across her back. "I'm the one who fed you champagne and then forced you into a hot tub. If anything, this was my fault."

She smiled at me softly.

"I didn't take much persuading," she admitted. "Thanks for taking care of me, Nolan."

She snuggled back into me, laying her head on my shoulder and nestling it under my chin.

"Anytime," I croaked.

I felt like there was something stuck in my throat. We sat like that for a while. I wondered if she could hear my heart beating. It felt like it should be deafening. The odd thing was that I was incredibly excited, but also extremely relaxed and peaceful. Something about this just felt right.

"I'm sorry I ran out on you in that restaurant."

It was barely more than a whisper and I had to strain to hear her.

I blinked. I hadn't been expecting that.

"Erin, no. I don't blame you for that. You'd just been assaulted by a condiment-flinging harpy. Most people would've run away."

She laughed, causing her to vibrate ticklishly against me.

"Well, I guess that's true," she conceded. "I should've given you a chance to explain, though. I just—"

She gripped the bottle harder.

"I just got scared. A big public scene like that, it—it reminded me of all the reasons I don't like to mix my work life and my personal life."

I squeezed her shoulders.

"I understand." I chuckled bitterly. "Believe me, I do. I know what it's like to have your work life and your private life bleed into one another. It can get less than comfortable."

"You worked with Heather?"

"No, thank Christ! She did show up at my office, though, and she was not the first. I could tell you some 'funny stories.' Better yet, ask Alana. She tells them better."

Erin took my hand.

"That sounds awful," she said sympathetically.

"It was. But—"

I paused. I was getting into territory I'd never spoken about with anyone, but it felt safe to keep talking.

"The thing that bothered me the most was the way my co-workers would stop reacting after a while. When something crazy happened, they'd just shrug and say, 'Classic Nolan.' I became 'that guy,' and I never wanted to be 'that guy.'"

"You're not," she insisted, pressing my hand earnestly.

"Aren't I? Sometimes I look at my dad and I think—this is it. This is where you're headed."

She shook her head.

"Why would you think that?"

I hunched over as I spoke, like the truth was a monster I had to hide from.

"I've always looked like him," I muttered. "People used to comment on it all the time. They'd say, 'Isn't he just the image of his father?' or 'Nolan, sometimes I look at you and I could swear I'm looking at your father when he was your age.' As I got older, I looked more and more like him. I think that got hard for my mom when their marriage got rocky. Sometimes when she'd had a few, the line between me and him would get sort of... blurred. Anytime I'd screw up or do anything wrong, it would be, 'There you go, just like your father.' You get told something enough times, it gets in your head. I started to think—maybe I am just like him. That's why I always end up with women like Heather. I figure, I'm on a fast-track to hell—why drag anyone with me who isn't already halfway there?"

Erin ran her thumb over the back of my hand, causing a pleasant shiver to go through me.

"I think they call that a self-fulfilling prophecy," she said gently.

"That's what Alana says."

"Perhaps she's right."

"Perhaps," I agreed. "I'm trying to change things, though. In fact, I'm taking my own advice, at least as far as Heather is concerned. I got a restraining order. Or I'm getting one, anyway, so—"

I heard the note of hope entering my voice and hated myself for it.

"So you wouldn't have to worry about her popping out of the woodwork if you wanted to maybe hang out sometime."

Erin turned to face me, eyes shining.

"I do," she choked. "I do want to. I just got so confused. You were an egg in the work basket and I wanted to transfer you to the non-work basket, but the last time I did that, the egg burst like a piñata. Then all these gremlins popped out and they squashed all my work eggs. Then I was worried you were full of gremlins too and—"

By this point, the tears were pouring down her face and her

breath was coming out in huge, choking sobs. I wanted to console her but I wasn't sure what to do. In the end, I gathered her into my arms and held her to me. I rocked her gently until her sobs died down to occasional shuddering gasps.

She had buried her face in my shoulder while she cried, but I felt her shift slightly, turning to look up at me. Her eyes were red, and her face was blotchy, but somehow, she still looked beautiful. She was staring at me intently and it suddenly felt as though all the air had gone out of the room, but that didn't matter because my heart had stopped too. Tentative fingers reached up and stroked at the scruff along my jawline. I leaned into the caress, rubbing my face against her hand. Her other hand reached up, curling around the back of my head, and pulling my mouth towards her.

When she'd had her crying fit, I'd promised myself I wouldn't take advantage of her while she was drunk and vulnerable. The tiny voice in my head that questioned whether this was right was effectively silenced when she clutched at a fistful of my hair. Our lips crashed together, hungry and demanding. I could taste champagne and strawberries, mingling with the salt of her tears, and I felt like I was drunk all over again. Her teeth were sharp against my lip as she nipped at the sensitive flesh. It was an eloquent plea for more and I readily complied. I pulled her against me and swiped my tongue along her lip, prompting a delicious, needy little whine. Her sweet mouth opened for me and allowed my tongue to explore. I hissed as her nails dug into my back and she moaned into my mouth.

Rational Nolan was dimly aware that we were in public, but there had been a mutiny aboard my brain ship. Nolan Junior was firmly seated in the captain's chair. I put my hands on Erin's hips, urging her into a kneeling position. My mouth moved in a feverish frenzy as I planted kisses along her jaw and down her neck. She threw her head back and arched into me with a keening wail, her fingers digging into my shoulders hard enough to bruise. I brought my hand up and cupped her breast. My thumb circled the wet fabric of her bra until I found her nipple. It hardened instantly at my touch, and I groaned.

"Am I interrupting something?"

Erin shrieked as we sprang apart. I didn't need to turn around to see who had walked in on us. I recognized my father's malicious drawl.

Caught red-handed! Or should that be breast-handed?

Erin groped frantically for a moment before I handed her a towel. She wrapped it tightly around herself.

"Terribly sorry to bust in on you like this, but I was under the impression this was a public spa."

I reddened, unable to look at him. Partly because I was embarrassed and partly because I couldn't afford the therapy it would cost me to process his purple banana hammock. I stood up, placing myself between him and Erin as she covered herself.

"We got a little carried away," I grunted. "We were just leaving."

We had to pass him as we headed towards the changing rooms, and Erin almost ran to get out of his reach. I don't think I'd ever hated him more than I did at that moment. I'd almost reached the door to the changing rooms when I heard his voice behind me.

"Nicely done, son. Get her a little tipsy and then suggest the hot tub. Very clever."

"It wasn't like that," I snarled. "I just wanted her to relax."

"I bet you did," he leered. "That used to be my signature move. The combination of alcohol and the heat gets them all light-headed and suggestible. You really are a chip off the old block."

"You're disgusting," I spat, stepping into the changing room and slamming the door.

All the same, I felt as though my stomach had been

flooded with something icy. Those things he was saying—that thought hadn't even crossed my mind, had it?

I waited for Erin outside the changing rooms for a while, but she didn't show. Eventually, I concluded that she had escaped to bed.

Chip off the old block.

My father's words followed me up the stairs and into my room, playing on a loop in my head until I eventually sank into a restless sleep.

CHAPTER TWENTY-FIVE

Erin

I was awoken at 5.15 am by the shrill chirping of my phone. When I groped for the handset, I was seized by a wave of nausea. I clutched at the top of my head and groaned. How much champagne had I drunk last night?

My fumbling fingers grasped for my shrieking phone, but I only succeeded in knocking it off the nightstand. I managed to reach it by hanging off the edge of the bed.

Big mistake!

Fighting the urge to throw up, I peered blearily at the screen. The caller ID filled me with dread. If I were to make a list of the people I would least like to speak to whilst nursing a hangover, my landlady would be near the top.

Sticky Treats occupied the bottom floor of a five-story building owned by Mrs. Pasternak. A 67-year-old woman who smoked like an industrial chimney, Mrs. Pasternak was the punchline of every joke about "broads from Brooklyn." Most people have never encountered anything so terrifying wearing a housecoat that pink.

I accepted the call with mounting trepidation. Had there been an issue with my rent?

"Erin!"

I winced and held the phone away from my ear. Mrs. Pasternak's voice struck my aching head like a buzz-saw.

"Mrs. Pasternak, hi. Is there—?"

"I know, I know," she interrupted. "You're wondering why I'm calling at this ungodly hour. That's exactly what I said to the man from the security company when they called me at *4 a.m*. I said, 'Do you have any idea what time it is?'"

Did I mention she liked to talk?

"He said, 'It's company policy to notify the proprietor immediately in the event of a break-in.' So, I said, 'I don't give a rat's *tuchus* about your company policy. I'm an old woman and I don't—'" Interrupting Mrs. Pasternak when she was in full flow was difficult, but the word "break-in" had pierced the swirling fog in my brain.

"Did you say a break-in?" I ventured, raising my voice a little.

I heard a muffled click on the other end of the line as she lit a cigarette.

"Apparently so," she said, mumbling around the filter. "The alarm went off at the bakery at some god-forsaken hour of the morning. Word is someone broke in and trashed the place."

No.

It was that moment before an accident when everything slows down. I was acutely aware of everything—the wrinkles in my bedsheets pressing into my stomach, the cool plastic of my phone against my face, the vile taste in my mouth. I couldn't process it. Everything I'd worked for, my livelihood, destroyed. I sat mutely as Mrs. Pasternak prattled on. She loved a good crisis and this one promised to keep her going for days, if not weeks.

"The police are down there now," she informed me. "You'll need a copy of their report for your insurance company. Of course, *I'll* have to claim for the windows."

I clutched a hand to my forehead. It was too early for this.

"Was there much—?" I began.

"Of course, they're the real criminals if you ask me."

I frowned in confusion.

"Who?"

"The insurance companies; who else? I remember trying to claim for the funeral when my Al passed away. I said, 'You can't expect me to fill out a 20-page form. I'm a grieving widow. You should be ashamed of yourselves.' I tell you; it was like getting blood from a—"

"Do you have any idea who did it?" I interjected.

"I don't know," she grumbled. "I can't be sticking my nose into this city's underbelly. I'm a frail old woman. Sometimes I think my Al, may he rest in peace, left me a curse when he willed me this place. Just watch; I'll be pushing up the daisies before Thanksgiving."

Mrs. Pasternak regularly predicted her own death, but I had a strong suspicion she would outlive us all, a horrifying dinosaur in hair rollers.

"Do the police have any idea who did it?" I asked, trying to stop my voice from rising to an anxious scream.

"Degenerates probably," she snorted. "Degenerates on *drugs*. I warned you when you opened that bakery; there are certain parts of the human anatomy that have no place on a cake. 'You'll attract the wrong element,' I said. Like flies to manure; pardon my French."

People are already going to look at what you do and get the wrong idea. You don't need to add fuel to the fire.

Nausea hit me again as Stirling's words came back to me. I swallowed hard, trying to gather my racing thoughts. For all my landlady's theories about degenerates on drugs, I had a horrible feeling I knew who was behind this. Logically I had no reason to suspect him, but I had a nasty feeling in my gut.

I pinched the bridge of my nose, dimly aware that Mrs. Pasternak was still talking. Getting any useful information out of her was looking increasingly unlikely. I needed to get off the phone.

"— If you ask me, hanging's too good for them!"

"Right!" I agreed. "Anyway, I've got to check out of the hotel and get on the road so I can see to this mess. I'd better be—"

"Oh right! The wedding! How did it—?"

I knew it was rude to terminate the call while she was still talking, but desperate times called for desperate measures. I'd promised Granny V I'd stay for the wedding breakfast, but that was no longer an option. I had to get home *now*. I ordered a pot of coffee from room service and dragged my suitcase from under the bed. Mercifully, the panic and the chaos had scared my hangover away a little.

I was flying around the room like a whirlwind, hurling clothes into my suitcase, when I heard a soft knock at the door.

"It's open," I called, assuming it was my coffee.

"Erin?"

It was not my coffee.

Nolan stepped across the threshold of my room, looking pale and sheepish. He was wearing jeans and one of his comfy flannel shirts. It looked impossibly soft, and I wanted to bury my face in it. His green eyes swiveled around the room, taking in the random clothes exploding from my suitcase and the open drawers and closet doors.

"You're not staying for breakfast?" he asked.

"I can't."

I turned away, unable to look at the injured expression on his face. He took a half step forward, reaching for me and then pulling his hand back.

"Look," he said. "What happened last night. It doesn't mean that you need to leave. I know I shouldn't have done what I did, but we were both really drunk and—"

My head pounded. I was exhausted. I could feel an inevitable explosion of tears aching in my throat. I couldn't do this. This wasn't fair. Why was he making this difficult for me?

"I happen to have a crisis on my hands here," I shouted. "Not everything is about you."

I didn't know why I was yelling. It wasn't as though any of this was Nolan's fault. However, once I'd started, I couldn't stop. All the anxiety and tension I'd been containing over the weekend exploded, pouring out of me in a stream of semi-coherent vitriol.

"I told you," I shrieked, pointing at him like a vengeful spirit. "I warned you. Every time I let my guard down, something awful happens. But you were all," my voice dropped an octave as I mimicked his tone. "'Relax, Erin; you deserve it. What could happen?' Well, how about everything? How about my bakery getting broken into whilst I was drunk off my ass at your little hot tub party?"

"Erin—"

He stepped towards me, holding out his hands in a gesture of placation.

"I'm being punished."

My voice cracked and tears welled up in my eyes until Nolan was nothing but a blurred shape. In an instant, I'd transformed from furious harpy to helpless child.

The shape grew as he moved closer.

"No," he said firmly. "You're not."

"I mixed up the eggs and the gremlins came out."

A second later, I was surrounded by warm, downy flannel as he wrapped his arms around me. I burrowed my face into his chest and sobbed.

"No," he soothed. "No gremlins here. Just some rowdy Mogwai."

"I was supposed to be here working," I mumbled. "But all could think about was how much I—"

Shit.

It was too late to bite the words back. He placed his fingers under my chin and tilted my face to look at him. My eyes were burning, and my nose was running. I didn't even want to think about how hideous I must look. Nolan tenderly brushed a few strands of hair from my face, looking into my eyes with quiet intensity.

"How much you what?" he murmured.

"I—"

I quivered in his arms. My gaze travelled from his piercing eyes to his slightly parted lips. Our faces tilted imperceptibly, and I felt that same magnetic pull I'd experienced in the hot tub last night.

"Room service, Ma'am."

The smart rap at the door jolted both of us back to reality.

"I ordered coffee," I muttered, pulling away and hurrying for the door.

I couldn't decide if I was relieved or sorry that we'd been interrupted. Everything in my mind was so confused that I wasn't sure how I felt about anything, least of all Nolan.

Fortunately, the bellboy didn't seem to notice my appearance. I reflected that, at this time of the morning, he was probably used to being confronted with disheveled, bloodshot zombies. When I came back into the room, Nolan took the tray from me and took over the preparation of the coffee. I sank down on the bed and watched him. After my crying fit, I was experiencing that weird tranquility that came from being slightly out of sync with reality. When I was presented with a steaming cup of coffee, I accepted it numbly. He perched on the bed next to me and put a hand on my knee.

"Whatever's happened, we can fix it," he said gently. "Everything always looks worse before your first cup of coffee. True facts."

He gave me a half-smile. I could only summon a feeble grimace in response.

"Now, drink up, and tell me what happened, slowly."

I closed my eyes and took a deep breath. The familiar smell of the roasted beans acted on me like a tonic. I relayed everything that had happened since my phone woke me up. It was amazing how brief the saga became once I'd viciously edited Mrs. Pasternak.

"I just know it's Stirling; I can feel it." I sighed, staring into the dregs of my coffee.

"Hmm." I could see the gears in Nolan's head turning. He'd shifted into lawyer mode.

"You might be right, but it's pointless to speculate until we've been to the bakery and spoken to the police," he stated.

We?

He stood up and poured me another cup of coffee.

"We'll get some breakfast and get checked out. We can be on the road by 7.30 at the latest."

I voiced my confusion out loud this time.

"We?"

He stared at me in unfeigned puzzlement.

"Yes," he said slowly. "You don't think I'm letting you deal with this on your own, do you?"

"But—" I protested, my mouth searching for objections my brain didn't want to look for.

He took the cup from me and pressed both of my hands in his.

"Please, Erin," he entreated. "This is what I do for a living. Let me help you."

"What about your family?"

He flicked his hand, waving my words away.

"They won't mind. Liv's more than capable of driving the car back. And," he smiled slyly, "I'm willing to bet that Granny V won't mind me missing her wedding breakfast if she knows I'm with you."

I opened my mouth again, but he raised a hand before I could speak.

"I'm not taking no for an answer."

I couldn't talk him out of it.

Not that you killed yourself trying.

I squashed the snarky voice in my head and forced myself

to eat toast and marmalade while Nolan took care of checking us out. He left a message for his family at the front desk, and we were crawling down the country club driveway before the sun had fully risen. As we emerged from the gate, I glanced at my passenger. He was resting his chin on his hand and staring sleepily out of the window. Despite everything, I felt a warm flutter in my stomach. This could have been one of the worst mornings of my life, but I had never felt safer or more taken care of.

CHAPTER TWENTY-SIX

Nolan

"I spy with my little eye something beginning with 't'."

"Aren't we a little old for car games?"

Erin was gripping the steering wheel so tightly that her knuckles had turned white. She kept raising her thumbnail to her mouth, then yanking it away when she realized what she was doing.

"I'm here to support you," I reasoned. "Whatever's going on, we can't do anything about it for the next few hours. Figure the best thing I can do is distract you."

She snorted.

"And I spy was the best you could come up with?"

"Hey!" I protested. "I'd normally have had my morning latte by now. Besides, I'm at a disadvantage here."

"You are?"

"Yeah," I admitted, flushing a little. "All my best stories involve you."

Now it was her turn to blush. It looked a lot better on her than on me. She shifted in her seat and a reluctant smile tugged at the corners of her mouth.

"Alright," she relented. "Something beginning with 't'. Give me a clue."

"Hmm," I pondered. "I guess you could say it's a weight. It's a weight you're carrying right here."

I splayed my palms and slapped my chest. Erin glanced downwards and her eyes widened.

"Nolan!" she shrieked.

Realizing my mistake, I stumbled to clarify.

"No! God, no! I meant tension. You're very tense. You're carrying it in your neck and your shoulders and your... and the area below your shoulders. Oh, Jesus."

I slid down in my seat and put my hands over my face. I would have been tempted to hide forever if she hadn't burst into her infectious giggle. I parted my fingers and chanced a glance at her. Her shoulders had relaxed, and she was smiling properly now.

"At least I got you laughing." I sighed.

She shook her head.

"I'm starting to see why Granny V thinks she needs to set you up with girls."

"Not true," I protested. "When you're not around, I'm suave as fuck."

"Oh yeah? Why'd I get the short straw?"

I shrugged and stared out of the window. Even onion fields could look beautiful just after sunrise.

"I guess you're special."

I gnawed at my lip. Once again, I had revealed more than I had intended. This woman had a knack for stripping me of my defenses and leaving my raw feelings exposed. Every time I opened my mouth there was a deluge of sentimental mush. This couldn't go on.

There was something Freudian about my choice of "tension" for I spy. Erin might have been feeling pent up, but she wasn't the only one. From the moment we'd met there had been tension of another kind between us, and it was getting harder and harder to ignore.

I couldn't give in, though. After my father's little "pep talk" last night, I was already doubting my own motivations. Plus, Erin had enough to deal with; she didn't need me spewing feelings all over her. As the seconds ticked by, it felt like my words were hanging in the air like a buzzing neon sign. I scrabbled for something to fill the silence.

"Speaking of set-ups," I ventured. "You get the feeling there was a joke we weren't in on this weekend?"

"Huh?"

"Well," I said. "Let me put it this way. The first thing my grandmother did when I arrived was send me to help unload the cake. And she conveniently forgot to warn me about the change of arrangements."

"Ah."

Erin pursed her lips and nodded slowly.

"Well, I have to admit," she conceded. "I wasn't entirely convinced by Jayden's stomach flu, graphic commentary notwithstanding."

"You think they cooked up this little scheme together?" I asked, trying to imagine Jayden and Granny V as partners in crime.

"Oh," Erin chuckled, "you didn't see them at the bakery. They were always giggling and plotting together. I should have known I was in trouble when they hit it off so well."

"I think the *world* might be in trouble," I groaned. "The only question is, who's the bad influence?"

"It's definitely a chicken and egg situation," Erin agreed. "What I'd like to know is how they got Maddie on board."

"Your best friend?"

"Yep. She was a little too ready with that stylist appointment. Still," she shrugged, "at least I didn't have to show up looking like a hot mess."

"You'd have looked beautiful however you showed up."

Oh God. I can't stop. It's like my filter is broken.

Erin's eyes remained fixed on the road, but there were

spots of heightened color on her cheeks and her face had softened into that half-smile I'd come to adore.

"I can't be too mad at them, all things considered," she said softly. "I really appreciate what you're doing, Nolan. If it wasn't for you, I'd probably still be panicking in my hotel room right now."

"No," I argued. "I just sped things along. You're a tough lady, Erin."

She didn't reply. She just gave me a skeptical look.

"I mean it," I insisted. "Not only did you build a successful business on your own, but you came back from what that bastard did to you."

My fists clenched in my lap. Talking about her creep of an ex-boyfriend reminded me of how much I wanted to rip his head off.

"Trust me," I vowed. "If he had anything to do with the break-in, we'll nail him to the fucking wall."

We made good time on our way back. I did force Erin to pull over for coffee when she started looking exhausted, but we still made it back in under five hours.

I'd been hoping that the landlady had been exaggerating. Those hopes vanished as soon as we pulled up in front of the bakery. The police were long gone, but the exterior of the building was still covered with yellow crime scene tape. Broken glass crunched under my feet as I stepped out of the van. Every window and both panels in the doors had been smashed. Red paint had been thrown everywhere, giving the impression of a brutal slaughter.

"Oh."

It was somewhere between a tiny gasp and a sob. I stopped focusing on the carnage in front of me and turned my attention to the woman standing next to me. Erin was staring numbly at the shattered remains of her livelihood. She was chalk white and her face had slackened. I stepped in front of her as if hoping to shield her from the devastation. She barely reacted when I put my hands on her shoulders.

"It might not be as bad as it looks," I said, not entirely believing my own words. "You don't have to go inside. You can sit in the van while I go in and get a lay of the land."

She stared through me as if I hadn't spoken.

"Erin!" I raised my voice a little and gave her shoulders a gentle shake. She blinked.

"What were you saying?" she mumbled.

"I was saying you don't have to go inside. Get back in the van and let me handle it."

"No." She shook her head. "No, I can handle it. I need to see."

The inside was worse. No single piece of furniture or equipment had been left untouched and the floor was a technicolor mulch of squashed candy and chocolate shards. That wasn't even the worst of it. The word 'whore' had been daubed over the walls in every flavor of frosting you could think of. It was as if some giant toddler with Tourette's had been on a sugar-fueled rampage. Erin stared at the walls, arms hanging limply at her sides. Her face had taken on that glazed look again. Cursing, I picked my way across the sticky floor and put my arm around her. She started at the touch, but relaxed when she realized it was me.

"I guess my premiums are going up next quarter," she mumbled.

"Bastard really went to town, didn't he?" I spat.

There was no longer any doubt in my mind as to who was responsible. The writing was literally on the wall.

"The only question is, why now? Do you guys have some sort of anniversary coming up? It seems strange that after all this time he'd suddenly..."

I trailed off. She was biting her thumb and looking away.

"What's going on, Erin?" I asked. "Has he contacted you?"

She closed her eyes and took a deep breath.

"The messages started again that night we went out," she admitted. "He got angry when he thought I was seeing someone. Called you my new boy toy."

Her cheeks pinked when she said boy toy. It was adorable, but I was too worried and angry to enjoy it.

"Jesus Christ, Erin!" I groaned. "Have you even been to the police? Why didn't you say anything?!"

"Because I wasn't supposed to ever see you again," she cried, wrenching away and turning her back.

"I—I... Don't."

My tongue was thick and clumsy in my dry mouth. The pain of being suddenly pushed away felt like a punch in the chest.

Her voice was tight and choked.

"I did go to the police, as it happens. Maddie took me after —after he left something in my car."

"Left what exactly?"

She sniffed and swiped at her eyes, continuing to stare in the opposite direction.

"Some flowers and a note. It's not important. The police certainly didn't think so, anyway. They didn't take me very seriously."

"B—but, that's exactly why you should have called me," I blustered. "I could've—"

She shook her head.

"I couldn't."

Her voice had dropped to a hoarse whisper.

"I understand that you might not have wanted to see me," I reasoned. "Still, you should—"

"But I did want to," she sobbed, spinning around to face me again. She was breathing heavily, and tears were flowing freely down her face. "And that was why I couldn't. I wanted to see you again so badly it hurt. I knew that if I called you, you'd come. You'd hold me and comfort me and make me feel safe, and that was..." She gestured helplessly. "It was fucking terrifying."

I cocked my head and frowned.

"So, you're telling me you didn't want to call me because you were afraid that I'd make you feel better? I think I must be having an obtuse guy moment here because you lost me."

Erin raised her eyes to the ceiling and set her jaw.

"It's because I know where it leads," she gritted. "It might be all stomach flutters and head tingles now, but sooner or later we—w—we end up here."

She flung out an arm, indicating the ugly words on the wall.

"I'd never do anything like this," I protested.

"I know," she conceded. "But something else would go wrong. It always does."

Bending down, she righted a fallen stool and perched on it, resting an elbow on the counter.

"The more I look at all this, the more I realize that some people just aren't meant to be happy," she said bleakly.

I raised my arm and let it fall to my side. I wanted to gather her into my arms and kiss away all her doubts. I longed to tell her that she should trust the butterflies in her stomach, that she should give in to her feelings and give us a chance. But something held me back. Maybe it was the fact that I'd been having a similar argument with myself last night. I couldn't shake the conviction that she deserved better than me. Trying to break down her resolve when she was already vulnerable felt like the lowest move imaginable. It was something my father would have done.

I folded my arms and pushed my feelings down. It was painful, but not impossible. I was used to donning masks, and this situation called for professional Nolan.

"We need to talk to the police again," I said. "They'll have to take you seriously now."

She sat up and rubbed her hands over her face. She was no longer weeping, but she looked pale and blotchy.

"You're right," she said wearily. "I can handle it, though. You should go home; you've already gone above and beyond."

"No way," I said quietly.

She blinked.

"What do you mean, no way?"

"Exactly that," I stated. "I'm a lawyer and I'd like to believe I'm a friend. Looking at all this, I'd say you need both right now."

She opened her mouth to argue and then appeared to deflate.

"You're right," she admitted, sliding from the stool and gazing around glumly.

"Come on," I coaxed. "We can't do any more good here."

Moving gingerly, we picked our way towards the door. I reached out a hand to help her avoid a particularly large and gooey patch of marshmallow fluff. When her feet had reached solid ground, she didn't let go. She held on to my hand and squeezed.

"Thanks, Nolan," she murmured.

I shrugged.

"I didn't want you to get your shoes sticky."

"No, I mean, thanks for all this. You really are a good friend."

I tried to smile. I should have been happy that she considered me a friend, but somehow the word sent a pang of loss and regret straight through me.

"Anytime," I croaked.

Stepping outside had an immediate positive effect on Erin. She took a deep breath and shivered slightly, almost as though she was shaking off the oppressive atmosphere of her ruined bakery.

"Right," she announced, sounding more alive than she had

in hours. “We’ll go to the police station, then I can drop you off at home afterward.”

I shook my head firmly.

“Bad idea. I don’t think you should be home alone right now.”

“It’s ok. I don’t live above the bakery.”

“No,” I agreed. “But it’s obvious this guy’s not playing around, and I’m willing to bet he knows where you live.”

She sighed.

“There’s always Madison, I guess. But she just got back from her honeymoon. I don’t want to intrude.”

“I have a spare room.”

The words tumbled from my lips before I had a chance to think them through. She eyed me doubtfully.

“I know it sounds weird,” I said hurriedly. “But it’s really not safe for you to be on your own. I’d make this offer to any of my friends.”

It was a risky proposition. I was going to have to exercise some serious self-control.

“Just for tonight, at least,” I urged. “If you don’t feel comfortable, we can see about arranging something better tomorrow.”

“Ok,” she said cautiously. “I guess one night can’t hurt.”

Oh. Believe me. It’s going to hurt.

CHAPTER TWENTY-SEVEN

Erin

"I don't want to do this."

We were standing within a stone's throw of the police precinct and my legs had gone on strike. I stared at the double doors, my body refusing to carry me over the threshold.

"What's wrong?" Nolan asked, his expression creased with concern.

I shoved my hands into my jacket pockets and hunched my shoulders.

"The last time they completely dismissed me, and it was really embarrassing. I left with the feeling that *I'd* done something wrong."

Nolan put his arm around me.

"It'll be different this time," he promised.

"How?"

He released my shoulders and stood in front of me like he was preparing to deliver a lecture.

"Firstly," he said, counting the points on his fingers. "We have physical evidence. It's hard to argue with that much property damage. Hopefully, he'll have been dumb enough to smear his DNA on every available surface."

I wrinkled my nose.

"Eww."

"I'm talking about hair and fingerprints! Although," there was a thoughtful pause. "If he did leave anything else behind—"

I held up a hand, my stomach roiling.

"Let's not go there," I pleaded.

He nodded.

"Probably wise. But, physical evidence—that's the first point. The second point is that this time," he placed his hands on his chest, "you're going in with expert legal counsel."

I looked him up and down, taking in the rumpled jeans and plaid shirt.

"You don't look very lawyer-ish right now," I said, biting the tip of my thumb. "I feel like we should have brought you a briefcase or something."

He let loose with that resonant chuckle that made my stomach flip.

"I don't need a briefcase," he said, tapping his temple with his forefinger. "Everything I need to know is in here. And trust me, I can be just as intimidating in flannel as I can in Armani."

I did trust him, completely. But that was a terrifying train of thought that I refused to board.

"You have nothing to worry about," he continued. "There's no way on earth they won't take this seriously."

"I don't understand how you're not taking this seriously!"

I winced as Nolan banged his hand on the table.

Things had started so well. Nolan managed to coax me through the precinct doors, and I breathed a sigh of relief when I saw that it wasn't that same desk sergeant. Everything appeared to go smoothly. The incident report relating to the break-in had been logged in their computer system, so all we had to do was wait until an officer was available to speak to us.

Nolan's presence was even more reassuring than I'd expected. It was strangely compelling, watching him slip smoothly into his professional persona; compelling and more than a little sexy. A shiver went through me every time he said "my client."

Unfortunately, things soon went downhill. We were ushered into an interview room by a uniformed officer. He was a round-faced pleasant-looking guy in his late 20s. I noticed that he'd missed a spot under his ear while shaving and my eye kept drifting back to it as he talked.

It quickly became apparent that the main concern of the police was to hand over a copy of their incident report so I could square things with my insurance company. The young officer explained that nobody saw what happened and it hadn't been possible to identify the intruder from the security footage. When Nolan pressed for more details, the police officer spread his hands and shook his head.

"It was a masked intruder dressed in black," he explained. "Going purely on height and build, it was probably a male, but there's no way to know for sure."

"What about prints?" Nolan demanded. "Hair, clothing fibers. He must have left something behind."

The police officer scratched the tiny patch of stubble under his ear and shook his head.

"We didn't find anything," he insisted. "It's all in the incident report; you can read it for yourself."

He turned to me.

"I'm sorry, Ms. Donovan, but in the absence of forensic evidence or material witnesses, our chances of finding the perpetrator are slim to none."

"I find that hard to accept," Nolan said coldly. "My client has been subjected to a sustained campaign of harassment. She lodged a complaint at this very precinct less than a month ago. Given the vindictive and personal nature of the vandalism, it would seem unlikely that these two circumstances are unconnected."

The officer flipped through a file on the desk. His lips moved silently as he ran a stubby finger down one page.

"Our records indicate you made a complaint against a Mr. Stirling Bateman?"

I nodded.

"He threatened her," Nolan snapped. "And he's been following her. You need to get off your asses and do your damn jobs."

The officer reddened.

"Mr. Reid," he bristled. "We're doing everything we can within the purview of the law. Your client's complaint is on record, but we have nothing but circumstantial evidence to connect Mr. Bateman to this incident."

"What about his history?" Nolan challenged. "I know for a fact that if you plug his name into your system, you won't come up empty."

I looked at Nolan in surprise. This was the first I'd heard about any of this. Had Nolan already looked him up? A feeling of uneasiness crept over me, and I shifted in my seat.

"None of those claims were ever substantiated," the officer argued. "The charges were dropped in every single case."

"Yeah, because that never happens if the guy's guilty," Nolan snorted.

"I understand your concern, Mr. Reid, but our hands are tied. We can't act based on hearsay. Look, how about this?" He leaned forward and addressed both of us. "Given the complicated history of this case, I'd say we have decent grounds to ask Mr. Bateman some questions. We can have a little talk with him and perhaps give him a friendly warning, off the record. How does that sound?"

He presented this with the indulgent air of Santa Claus, about to pull an extra-large present from his sack. I opened and closed my mouth, but no sound came out. I'd been overtaken by a numb feeling of helplessness. Nolan, on the other hand, had no problem locating his tongue. He stood up and placed his hands on the desk, looming menacingly over the seated officer.

"Have your friendly word, by all means," he gritted. "But if any harm comes to my client as a result of the shocking negligence of this precinct, I will bury you in so much litigation that you'll never see daylight again."

The officer stood up, white with fury.

"I don't think I like your tone, sir," he stated. "I'd advise you to remember where you are."

Nolan's jaw clenched. I decided we should leave before my lawyer needed a lawyer of his own.

"Nolan." I put my hand on his chest and spoke soothingly in his ear. "Please. This won't do any good."

Out of the corner of my eye, I saw the police officer looking between us curiously. I cringed. We probably didn't look much like attorney and client right now.

I apologized to the officer and ushered Nolan out of the room. When we got back to the waiting area, he slumped on a chair looking dazed.

"I don't know what came over me," he declared. "I've never lost it in an interview like that. I'm supposed to be a professional, for fuck's sake."

He ran a hand through his hair and gave me a remorseful look.

"I'm so sorry, Erin."

I reached out and took his hand.

"That's ok," I reassured him. "It's hardly surprising; you're as exhausted as I am."

He flapped a dismissive hand at me.

"I'm fine."

I looked him over, taking in his gray complexion and the livid circles under his eyes.

"No you're not," I said gently.

Nolan shrugged and stared miserably at his knees.

"You put your trust in me and I let you down."

I squeezed his hand fiercely.

"Are you kidding?" I exclaimed. "You can't honestly think that after everything you've done for me. You were my hero today."

He swallowed hard, holding my gaze with suspiciously bright eyes. For a moment, I thought he was going to cry. Unsure of what to do but wanting to comfort him, I put my arm around his shoulders and rested my cheek on his head.

"Erin!"

I gritted my teeth and my eyes drifted closed.

Really? Now?

In the bleak brightness of the police station, Mrs. Pasternak's pink velour tracksuit and purple cat's eye spectacles were jarring. Unwinding from Nolan, I stood up to greet her, allowing her to plant an enthusiastic kiss on each of my cheeks. As usual, the heady cloud of floral perfume didn't conceal the rancid buttery smell of stale cigarettes.

"Hi, Mrs. Pasternak," I said, my voice bright and brittle. "What brings you here?"

"*Oy*, don't ask," she groaned, pushing her glasses up her nose. "I gotta collect a rainforest-worth of paperwork for that *farkakte* insurance company. It's enough to give me an aneurysm."

Her eyes slid over my shoulder taking in Nolan, who had stood up behind me. Her grimace evaporated and was replaced by a knowing smirk.

"But more importantly," she purred. "How long have you been keeping this tasty snack under wraps?"

Heat rushed to my cheeks. I needn't have bothered groping for an answer. Mrs. Pasternak steamrollered over me like a fuzzy pink tank and addressed Nolan directly.

"I'm Gayle Pasternak. It's lovely to meet you."

One hand flew up to fuss at her hair, while the other

reached out for a handshake. Her nails had been painted bright purple to match her glasses.

"I'm so glad that Erin finally found a nice boy."

She kept a death grip on Nolan's hand and leaned in confidentially.

"She's a lovely girl, but she's been on the shelf too long," she murmured. "I warned her. 'You're not getting any younger,' I said. Old age creeps up on you. One day you're young and carefree, the next thing you know, your tits have taken a nosedive and your legs look like a map of the New York subway."

Mortified, I stole a glance at Nolan. He was looking at my landlady with earnest attention, but his lips were twitching. I suspected he was trying to suppress a laugh.

"Mrs. Pasternak, Nolan and I are just friends," I said firmly.

Nolan cleared his throat and put on his most official voice.

"Yes," he stated. "Actually, I'm acting as her lawyer right now."

Mrs. Pasternak looked Nolan up and down and raised a harshly plucked eyebrow. I saw her taking in his crumpled jeans and faded shirt.

Damn! I knew we should have gotten him a briefcase.

"Hmmm, if you say so," she drawled. "But I don't remember no rules about lawyers bein' celibate. You snap her up, young man. You snooze, you lose. In fact..." She smacked her lips. "Between you, me, and the gatepost, you might just have some competition."

I frowned.

"What are you talking about?"

"Well," she began, positively swelling with anticipation. "You'll *never* guess who I saw earlier."

"Probably not," I said dryly.

Sarcasm had no effect on Mrs. Pasternak. It bounced right off her carapace.

"It was that other fella of yours. What was his name? Sherman!"

"You mean Stirling?" I asked.

My throat clamped down around the words and they came out sounding tight and strange.

"That's the one," she agreed. "Snappy dresser, good with computers."

"Where did you see him?" I demanded. "Did he come to your house?"

I tried to keep my voice calm. Nolan placed a soothing hand on my shoulder.

"Of course not," Mrs. Pasternak breezed, oblivious to my distress. "It was at the bakery this afternoon. I'd gone there to inspect the damage for myself. Wanted to make sure I took some pictures of my own. You can't be too careful with insurance companies. Anyway, I was snapping my photos, and Sheldon shows up out of the blue."

"Did *Stirling* say anything?" I asked.

My heart was racing. Nolan stepped forward and addressed Mrs. Pasternak with gentle urgency.

"This is very important, Mrs. Pasternak. We need you to tell us everything you can remember."

Taken aback by his serious tone, my landlady blinked owlishly behind her glasses.

"Well," she mused. "The first thing I noticed was the flowers."

"Flowers?"

I shuddered, remembering the roses in my car.

"Yes!" she confirmed. "He walked up with a bouquet almost as big as him. Looked like he'd bought up half the florist. Honestly, the way some of these young men carry on, you'd think they printed money. Mind you," she shrugged ruefully, "my Al was tighter than a gnat's hiney, so you can't win either way."

"Did Stirling leave a message?" I asked, desperate to keep her on track.

"He did," she said eagerly. "He said he was terribly sorry to hear about what happened and he was worried about you. Something about how vulnerable young women are when they live alone."

My legs swayed under me, and Nolan's hand tightened on my shoulder.

"He said that?" he growled.

Mrs. Pasternak's eyes widened.

"Well, he's not wrong, dear," she asserted. "I've always said it's not safe for a young lady to live on her own in this rotten world. You can wax as progressive as you like, but those are just the times we live in. You need a man about the house. If I didn't have my sons to come in and check on me, I'd probably be six feet under by now."

This was a frequent refrain. I had always nodded and smiled, but I was prepared to give Mrs. Pasternak good odds against anyone foolish enough to break into her house.

"I don't know what happened between you and this fella," she continued. "But if you ask me, he wants to get his feet back under the table."

The sudden beep of Mrs. Pasternak's cell phone was the most persuasive evidence I'd ever encountered that divine intervention existed. I don't know how we would have gotten rid of her otherwise.

After we left the police station, we drove to my apartment so I could throw some clean clothes into a bag. I didn't even bother suggesting to Nolan that he should wait in the van. He seemed unwilling to let me out of his sight and I wasn't inclined to argue.

When we pulled up to my building, a suffocating weight pressed down on my chest. The realization that I was afraid to enter my own home hit me with the force of a truck. Nolan took my hand when we entered the building, and I didn't pull away. If anything, I gripped back harder. I felt like I was a character in a horror movie, creeping around in the dark and waiting for the inevitable jump scare. Anyone watching me open my mailbox would have thought I expected to find a cobra inside instead of three bills and a cookware catalog. My heart was hammering as we got into the elevator. Taking a deep, shuddering breath, I closed my eyes and leaned back against the wall, dreading what I would find when I got to the front door.

CHAPTER TWENTY-EIGHT

Erin

I breathed a sigh of relief when I found my apartment undisturbed. After seeing the devastated remains of my store, I'd been expecting anything from the door hanging off its hinges to sinister ticking packages left outside. Instead, I just found myself staring at an innocuous, untouched white door.

"So far, so good?"

I jumped when I heard Nolan's voice behind me. Now that my immediate fears about my apartment had been addressed, I found time to be self-conscious. Nolan was going to be inside my home for the first time. I cast my mind back, trying to remember what sort of condition I had left the place in. It wasn't as if I was super messy, but when you live on your own, you don't keep track of things like what particular sets of underwear might be hanging out to dry. What if I'd left the bathroom festooned with voluminous granny panties? What if he saw my Bert and Ernie slippers? Then there was the snack situation. Things can get seriously out of hand when there's nobody around to judge you for your banana Twinkie consumption.

Maybe I should get a cat. They always look judgmental.

"Um, is there some sort of ritual with your front door, or are we waiting for your monkey butler?"

I blushed hotly. I hadn't realized how long I'd been staring at the door. Shaking my head, I fumbled for my keys.

"Sorry," I mumbled. "Must have zoned out for a minute there."

"Too bad. I love monkeys."

I rolled my eyes.

"You're such a goober!"

All the same, the clenching hand in my chest relaxed slightly. I left Nolan in the sitting room while I flew around grabbing essentials. My mind was racing at a thousand miles per minute. How long should I pack for? I wanted to be prepared, but I didn't want to look presumptuous. A suitcase would definitely be too much, but could I get everything I needed in the duffel? I'd packed and unpacked three times when I heard the muffled exclamation from the living area. My eyes widened.

Oh God! What has he found?

"Hey!" I yelled, hurling myself into the sitting room, still clutching a hairdryer. "I'll have you know there was a special on those Twinkies and—"

"Huh?"

He was standing by the coffee table with a large, gold box in his hands.

"Did you say something about Twinkies?"

"Nothing important," I said hastily.

He held up the box with a rueful grin.

"I was just admiring your DVD collection. I didn't know there was a special edition *Downton Abbey* boxset. Should I put up my hands and come quietly?"

Suddenly aware that I was pointing the hairdryer like a weapon, I cleared my throat and lowered my arm.

"Maddie got it for me as a Christmas present," I explained, wrapping the dryer cord absently around my fingers. "I guess it's a guilty pleasure when I'm feeling blue. Didn't figure you for a fan."

He rubbed at the back of his neck, smiling bashfully.

"Alana gave me shit about it, but yeah, I enjoyed it. My whole family likes it. We watched it on PBS. Abby asked if she could be British when she grew up. I think she might be in for a disappointment if we ever take her to England."

Shoulders relaxing, I smiled and gestured at the box.

"You're going to demand I bring that with me now, aren't you?"

He grinned impishly.

"Maybe just the last season? I haven't seen it yet."

Damn it! If his other likes include The Golden Girls and Chunky Monkey ice cream, it'll be confirmation that the universe is not playing fair.

Everything about Nolan's apartment screamed bachelor pad. It wasn't that it was untidy, but it was very stark. The walls were painted in various shades of dark gray and frosty blue, and lots of the furnishings were glass and chrome. It felt like a place where someone slept. Somewhere they came to exist between work and recreation. It didn't feel like a home. The only personal touches were the photographs of his family, arranged on the cabinet underneath the enormous television. He looked very shy as he gave me a tour of the place.

"I'm sorry. I don't entertain much. To tell you the truth, I'm not usually here a lot."

"Why not?"

He shrugged.

"I work long hours and I visit my sister a lot. I've lived in several places since college and they've always just felt like... I don't know."

"A place to crash?" I suggested.

"Yes," he said eagerly. "That's exactly it. I think for a house to truly be a home, you need..."

He trailed off, looking around the room like he thought the missing X-factor might jump out at him.

"Need what?" I asked.

He looked at me for a long moment and then shook his head as though violently brushing something off.

"It doesn't matter."

I hugged myself and looked away. All at once, the air was heavy with everything we were both holding back. I had the urge to grab my bag and flee. The tense silence was only broken when my stomach gave a loud growl. I flushed, but Nolan placed a hand over his own stomach and laughed.

"I second that." He chuckled. "Neither of us has had anything since breakfast. Plus, everything I know about being a good host, I learned from my grandmother, so I should have been force-feeding you since you walked through the front door."

He crossed the open-plan living room to the kitchen and opened the refrigerator.

"Hm. I have light beer and half a taco that should probably be carbon-dated. How does takeout sound?"

"Takeout sounds great," I agreed.

He pulled his phone from his pocket and thumbed through various ordering apps.

"Are you in the mood for noodles? There's a pretty good ramen place I order from sometimes."

I pursed my lips. Ramen was a little too close to pho, and noodle soup felt cursed for us at this point.

"How about pizza?" I suggested.

"Sure. What toppings should we get?"

I decided not to open the pineapple debate. That was a can of worms that should remain sealed, with a clearly written warning label. I couldn't handle any further evidence of our compatibility. After a brief negotiation and a few finger swipes, a stuffed crust pepperoni was winging its way to the apartment.

Nolan went to get us drinks while I flipped through the apps on the smart TV. The adage used to be that you could tell a lot about a person from their bookshelves. This can now be updated to include looking through someone's Netflix profile. I wasn't sure whether it was him or Abby who was responsible for the cartoons. Either way, it was hard not to have a soft spot for a guy whose suggested viewing included *SpongeBob SquarePants* and *The Powerpuff Girls*. There were documentaries too: wildlife, food and—

"Does that say what I think it says?"

"What's that?"

By this point, Nolan had come back, bearing two bottles of beer.

"There's a penis museum?" I asked, gesturing at the thumbnail.

"Oh yeah!" he said brightly. "In Iceland."

"Really? This is an actual museum, full of—"

"Yep," he confirmed. "It was all started by this one guy. He had a collection of them."

Something wrong with baseball cards?

I raised an eyebrow.

"I'm inclined to be suspicious of someone who collects body parts," I drawled.

Nolan sniggered.

"Tough talk from someone who bakes them all day."

I punched him on the arm, and he stuck out his tongue.

"Anyway," he continued. "It's not like that. These are scientific specimens from all different animals. Bulls, whales, polar bears—it's like nature's *Who's Who* of wangs. I'm surprised you haven't been."

"You are?" I asked, not sure whether to be insulted or not.

He shrugged and took a swig of beer.

"I figured it would basically be a research trip for you. You could write it off as a business expense."

"I'm honestly more focused on human anatomy."

"An artist shouldn't limit themselves, Erin."

"Ok, you've got a deal. As soon as I get an order for a polar bear penis piñata, we'll take a field trip to the wiener museum."

"Now I'm tempted to order one. No, wait, I have a better idea."

He put his beer down and swiveled to face me.

"You should make sweets for the gift shop!"

I blinked.

"There's a gift shop?"

"All museums have gift shops. Seriously, though, this is a match made in heaven. I can picture it already." He spread his hands theatrically. "Little selection boxes with names like 'penises of the world' or 'dongs of the sea.' And giant whale penises for sharing. You could even fill them with—"

"Don't finish that sentence," I pleaded, screwing up my face in disgust.

"Don't tell me you're squeamish."

"If we're talking whales, then yes, I'm squeamish."

Nolan shot me an evil grin and pulled his phone from his pocket.

"I'm totally e-mailing this guy right now."

"No way." I giggled.

His eyes and mouth widened in an expression of mock surprise. Raising a hand, he allowed his finger to hover over the touch screen.

"Look at that," he breathed. "It's moving, it's typing. We're powerless to resist. You can't stop the finger of fate, Erin."

"Hey," I shrieked. "Gimme that."

We started a tug of war for the phone. I barely noticed that I had climbed into his lap.

"I—am—not—going to Iceland—to—sculpt chocolate—

polar bear dicks," I panted, trying to prise the phone from his fingers.

"But you'd be so good at it." He laughed. "Admittedly I can only vouch for the quality of your cakes, but—"

"Oh shit!"

I released Nolan's phone and clapped both hands over my mouth.

"What's the matter?" he asked, his tone instantly reverting to seriousness.

"Cakes," I mumbled, the word muffled by my hands. "I completely forgot. I have an order to get in by next week and there's no way my kitchen will be ready in time."

I suddenly registered I was sitting in Nolan's lap, and I slid off hurriedly. He placed a comforting hand on my arm.

"Cancel it," he urged gently. "I think, given the circumstances, your client should understand. Plus, you could do with a break; you've been through the wringer recently."

I rubbed a hand over my forehead.

"You don't understand," I said miserably. "I can't let Mrs. Perez down."

"Why not? She can't be that terrifying."

I shook my head.

"It's not that. I can't let her down because I know what this order means to her."

"How do you mean?"

"I'm making breast cupcakes to celebrate her reconstruction surgery." I sighed. "She beat breast cancer last year, but she had to have a double mastectomy."

"Ouch." Nolan sucked in air between his teeth. "I see what you mean."

"She's had to wait months for the surgery. I think she sees it as sort of a new lease on life."

I picked miserably at a hangnail on my thumb.

"Anyway, now it's finally happening. She's throwing a 'booby shower' and I'm supposed to be providing her with four dozen cupcakes."

"But you have no bakery to cook them in?" he finished.

"That's about the size of it," I gritted out, suddenly furious. "God! I thought Stirling was finished trying to ruin my life."

"That's not going to happen."

Nolan took both of my hands and moved his thumbs in soothing circles.

"We won't let him."

"Well, what can I do?" I choked. "I can't wave a magic wand and have my kitchen ready to cook in by tomorrow morning."

Nolan released my hands and rubbed his chin thoughtfully. Finally, he gave me a sidelong glance.

"You could always use my kitchen."

CHAPTER TWENTY-NINE

Nolan

You could always use my kitchen.

The words fell from my lips so naturally that I barely had time to think about them. Watching everything Erin had gone through in the past 24 hours had made me angry. It made me want to rise up like the Incredible Hulk and smash every obstacle in her path. I had been unaware of Mrs. Perez's existence until a few minutes ago, but I couldn't stand seeing Erin so upset. Suddenly, Mrs. Perez getting her cupcakes on time was incredibly important to *me,* and I would move heaven and earth to get it done.

I was reasonably confident that my oven was up to the challenge. The literature had included a picture of a smiling woman holding a tray of freshly baked muffins; that had to count for something. Admittedly, my entire store of baking knowledge came from making chocolate chip cookies with Granny V. All of that was far enough in the distant past that I'd needed to stand on a stool to reach the counter. I gave Erin what I hoped was a confident smile, but she just frowned.

"No," she said, shaking her head.

My face fell.

"You don't think we'll have enough room?" I asked, trying not to sound injured.

"I—It's not that." She made a helpless gesture. "I can't let you do that."

"Why not?"

"Because—"

She placed a hand over mine and my heart skipped a beat.

"Because it wouldn't be fair," she protested. "It's an incredibly sweet offer, but you've already opened your home to me. I can't just waltz in and take over your kitchen too."

"You're not taking over anywhere," I insisted. "My kitchen's nowhere near what you have at the bakery, but it's clean and it has a decent oven." I paused, grinning sheepishly. "So I've read, anyway. I can't honestly say I've used it much."

She put her head on one side and studied me incredulously.

"Are you seriously suggesting that I could make my cupcakes here?"

"Of course!" I said breezily. "It'll be no problem. We can probably salvage some of your equipment from the bakery. We could even summon Jayden... or I could help you... maybe?"

"Help" might have been overstating my abilities. I was forcefully reminded of the time I'd challenged one of my frat brothers to a drinking contest. Unfortunately, the guy in question was a varsity shot-putter who outweighed me by at least 100 lbs. I'd thought my days of writing checks my butt couldn't cover were over. At least this time I was unlikely to wake up in a pool of my own vomit, wearing nothing but a blond wig and a pair of novelty breasts. A small gulping sound broke me out of my reverie. I looked up. Erin was weeping quietly, both hands over her mouth.

"What's wrong?" I asked, alarmed.

"N—Nothing," she whimpered. "I'm just really... I don't know what I'd... Thank you, Nolan."

"You don't have to thank me," I said gently. And then,

smiling feebly, "Definitely don't thank me until you've seen my kitchen skills."

She made a sound somewhere between a sob and a laugh. I opened my mouth to say something else, but the doorbell buzzed.

Ah, finally! Pizza.

I returned with the warm cardboard box and placed it on the coffee table. By this point, Erin's sobs had calmed to the occasional quiet sniffle. I laid a hand on her knee and gave it a squeeze.

"Let's not worry about it tonight," I urged. "What you need now is food, and sleep, and maybe *Downton*."

She wiped her reddened eyes on her sleeve and smiled shakily.

"Ok, Doctor," she said. "That sounds like a pretty good prescription to me."

"Good girl."

My heart stuttered. I'd slipped into the endearment without thinking. She didn't appear to have noticed. We ate the pizza ravenously. Less than halfway through the first episode of *Downton Abbey,* Erin's eyelids started to droop. Exhaustion plus hot food tends to have that effect. I held my breath when her head lolled onto my shoulder. I didn't dare move. As we ate and watched TV, we had gradually shifted closer together, but this was as near as we had come to snuggling.

Sometimes bodies can be evil. When you just ignore them, they can be comfortable for hours. However, when you desperately need to stay still, they will do everything they can to draw your attention. Your nose begins to itch, your foot wants to jiggle, or (as was the case on this occasion) your ass goes numb. Eventually, I shifted involuntarily, and Erin's head got jostled. I tensed, expecting her to come to her senses and jerk her head away as if she'd woken up with her cheek in something nasty.

But she didn't.

She made a sleepy noise of protest and cuddled farther into me, moving her head to a more comfortable position on my shoulder. I blinked in disbelief. Cautiously, I slipped an arm around her, holding her to me. She let out a contented sigh. After a few minutes, her breathing had settled into a steady rhythm, and I knew she had fallen asleep on me.

We stayed like that for hours. I told myself that I wasn't moving because I didn't want to wake her, but I was kidding myself. The truth was, I didn't want to let her go. Holding her like this felt right. It felt good. I experienced a sense of peace I'd never had before. I'd never had a woman fall asleep on me like this. I couldn't remember many times *I'd* fallen asleep with a woman. In my previous relationships, I wasn't much for sleepovers. It only happened when we both passed out drunk. Breakfast and Sunday trips to the farmer's market had never been a big feature of my hook-ups.

Erin and I weren't dating, and we'd certainly never hooked up, but this felt more intimate than all my previous encounters combined. I brushed some of the hair from her face. Asleep, she looked so artless and vulnerable. The fact that she'd allow me to see her like this made it feel like I'd been favored with an enormous amount of trust. Perhaps that was why I'd never liked staying over with a woman. Having someone around when you were sleeping made you vulnerable. I'd always sucked when it came to taking my armor off.

I fell asleep at some point. I opened my eyes to find the pale light of dawn seeping through the window. Erin was still fast asleep on my shoulder. I gave an inner chuckle when I felt the tiny damp patch on my shirt where she'd drooled on me. Gingerly, I eased my body from underneath her, all my muscles screaming in protest. Erin mumbled in her sleep and tried to burrow farther into the sofa. I smiled. She was possibly the cutest thing I had ever seen. Bending down, I scooped her up and carried her to the guest room.

I decided to lay her on top of the covers. Undressing her felt like a bad idea, but I did take her shoes off. It was extremely tempting to fall in with her. I was so tired, it felt like my eyelids were lined with sandpaper. Wrenching myself away, I stumbled back into the living room. I wasn't the greatest sleeper at the best of times, and it didn't take much to completely throw my schedule off. Besides, I wanted to make sure I could actually offer Erin some breakfast when she woke up.

A quick shower kicked my brain out of power save mode and into the realm of semi-functional. After a few minutes of sleepy fumbling, I located my phone and my keys and headed to the market for supplies. Somewhere between the apartment door and my car I realized I'd been ignoring my messages since last night. Opening my inbox had gotten slightly less scary since I'd initiated legal proceedings against Heather, but I still felt some trepidation.

There were two messages from Olivia. One letting me know she had gotten home safely and another that was just an adorable picture of Abby, sound asleep in bed. Granny V and Russ had posted an airport selfie. They'd be well on their way to Singapore by now—the starting point for their Far Eastern cruise. There was also a lengthy rant from my father about what an inconsiderate asshole I was for running out on my own grandmother's wedding. I gave it as much of my time and consideration as it deserved. Alana had somehow managed to email me my weekly schedule already. I promptly canceled everything for the next few days. Things were quiet at work; they could manage without me.

Erin was still asleep when I got back, so I put on a pot of coffee and started combing through the police report for anything useful. I also made a list of the things that needed to be done to get the bakery up and running again. I wanted to take on as much of the tedious admin as I could. Erin had enough to deal with without wrangling with insurance companies and contractors. I might not have known much about baking, but I had enough common sense to realize that my apartment was not optimized for producing culinary works of art. I put my chin on my hand and gazed across at my kitchen.

I should probably dig out the instruction manual for the oven.

CHAPTER THIRTY

Erin

The first thing I noticed when I awoke was the irresistible smell of fresh coffee. This was followed by the disorientation that always occurs when waking up in a strange bed. I knuckled at my eyes and took in my surroundings. The room was clean and tidy, but bare; all stark white walls and light pine furniture. I got the impression that Nolan's guest room didn't see a lot of use.

Looking down at myself, I registered that I was still dressed, but I wasn't wearing my shoes. I had no memory of going to bed last night, or even of falling asleep. The realization that Nolan must have carried me here immediately sent heat rushing to my cheeks. I hoped I hadn't snored or drooled all over his shirt.

I tiptoed into the living area, straining my ears for any sounds. I wasn't sure why I felt so bashful; it wasn't as though anything had happened between us last night. Still, waking up in his bed—even his spare bed—felt like we'd crossed an invisible barrier into unknown territory.

I found Nolan standing in the kitchen. He was wearing brown corduroy slacks and a green wool sweater. The first time we'd met, he'd been wearing an expensive tailored suit, but I preferred his casual clothes. His sweaters and flannel shirts made him look so soft and huggable. When he caught sight of me, he flashed me a sparkling smile and my expression shifted in sympathy. It was infectious.

"Morning, sleepyhead."

I glanced at the clock on the oven.

"Not for much longer."

"You were dead to the world; I didn't like to wake you. Plus, it gave me the chance to do some grocery shopping."

"So I see!"

He had laid out a full-on breakfast buffet. There were bagels, pastries, fruit, yogurt, cream cheese, marmalade, several kinds of cereal, and a large box of donuts. Nolan looked at the spread and rubbed his palms together slowly.

"There's um, there's hot rolls in the oven and I also have eggs. I didn't know what you'd like to eat so I—"

"Bought everything?" I suggested, fighting the urge to laugh.

"I may have panicked."

He ran a hand through his hair and looked at me shyly from under his lashes.

"I'm not very good at this."

I had a mental image of him at the market. Anxiously flitting from aisle to aisle, piling more and more items into his cart. Maybe putting some back and then grabbing them again. It was an endearing picture and it made me want to hug him.

"Thank you." I beamed. "I can't believe you did all this for me. I feel very spoiled."

"You deserve it," he said quietly.

I swallowed, becoming very interested in investigating the donut box. He took a stool on the opposite side of the counter and passed me a cup of coffee. I fell on it eagerly. I was no use without my morning visit from the caffeine fairy.

"I went over the police report while you were sleeping," he ventured. "There's a lot of damage, but your insurance company should cover it. You'll need to give them a call today and maybe see about booking a contractor. I've written down all the numbers you'll need to call. I also scanned the police report so you can e-mail it to the insurance company as soon as you're ready."

I had just bitten into a donut and a glob of purple jelly oozed over my fingers. I stared at him mutely, while sticky goop dripped steadily from my hand.

"Y—You did all that this morning?" I stuttered.

"Yes!" He reached across and handed me a napkin. "I figured you had a lot on your plate, and I wanted to help with some of the tedious red tape. I hope I didn't overstep my bounds."

"No. You're fantastic. I mean, it's fantastic."

I was so choked with gratitude that I could barely form words. If it came down to it, I could have dealt with these things myself. Normally it would have been a point of pride to deal with them myself, but not now. These last few weeks, I'd been balancing so many plates that there were times I thought my head would explode. It meant so much to have someone quietly step in and take one of the plates away.

Blushing, he waved my thanks away.

"It's nothing. My sister never tires of pointing out that my entire job is basically creating tedious paperwork for other people. Consider this my cosmic penance."

I chuckled, raising my hand to block the escaping spray of crumbs.

"Refill?"

Without waiting for an answer, he leaned across the counter and refilled my coffee cup. I couldn't remember the last time I had been pampered like this. I felt like a princess.

"Now," he continued. "You finish breakfast and freshen up, then we'll go on a retrieval mission."

I wiped my mouth with a napkin and gave him a puzzled look.

"Retrieval mission?"

"To the bakery," he explained. I've got the basics here, but I don't have mixers, or anything fancy, like," he waved a hand vaguely, "a melon baller."

I raised an eyebrow and he shrugged.

"It was the only fancy thing I could think of."

"Sounds good," I said, amused. "And on the way back we should obviously stop and get you a melon baller. I don't know how you've survived this long without one."

After breakfast, I telephoned Jayden and gave him the week off. He was beside himself when I told him what had happened, but I assured him there was nothing to worry about. I knew if I'd called him in, he would have done anything he could to help, but I wasn't ready to see him. I liked Jayden a lot, but he was an employee. I hated the idea of him seeing me when I was this fragile.

Going back to the bakery was hard. I thought I'd feel better about seeing it now that all the crime scene tape was gone, but that just made it worse. A crime scene implied that an investigation was happening. It meant someone gave a damn about finding out what happened. Seeing the building with the last shreds of yellow tape fluttering in the wind made me feel abandoned. If it hadn't been for the reassuring warmth of Nolan's one-armed hug, I'm not sure I'd have made it through the door.

It turned out that the damage in the kitchen wasn't as bad as the damage in the shop. There were lots of pans and utensils strewn across the floor, but the machines still seemed to be in working order. It takes some serious commitment to significantly damage industrial cookware. I had prepared a list of essential equipment, so we set to work packing things in boxes and loading them into the van.

When we were done, Nolan suggested I'd feel better if we cleaned up the worst of the mess. Part of me wanted to be done and gone as soon as possible, but I knew he was right. I didn't want to come back and discover the sticky mess on the shop floor had attracted wildlife. While Nolan made a quick run for cleaning supplies, I leaned on the counter and pored over my list. I wanted to be sure we had everything.

When I heard the door open, I looked up in surprise.

"That didn't take very—"

My throat constricted, cutting me off mid-sentence. The man standing in the doorway wasn't Nolan, it was Stirling.

I hadn't seen him for a long time. He'd been a malevolent, disembodied presence in my life for so long that it was almost a shock to see him looking so normal. No horns, no fangs. Just cold blue eyes and a calculating smirk. He was a tall, slender man with dark hair and high cheekbones. The gray turtleneck and black slacks were perfectly cut to emphasize his lithe, athletic frame. Most people would have called him handsome, but I found the sight of him repulsive.

"I wondered when you'd show your face here," he drawled.

He leaned against the doorframe regarding me coolly. Fear condensed in my chest like a clutching fist. I gripped the counter, grateful for its solid weight between him and me.

"Stirling," I gasped. "What are you doing here?"

He shook his head and smiled indulgently.

"I was worried about you, of course. I know what this place means to you."

He reached up and caressed the doorframe.

"I was there, remember? I was right there at the birth of your dream. In fact, I helped make it a reality."

My palms were so sweaty that my grip almost slipped on the counter.

"Stirling," I said, trying to keep the tremor out of my voice. "I was grateful for your help, but that's all in the past now. We both need to move on."

I wanted to sound firm, but I heard the hint of a plea enter my voice. He stepped into the shop and the windowless doorframe closed behind him. He continued talking as though I hadn't spoken.

"When I heard about what happened, I said to myself, 'Erin's business is the most important thing in the world to her. She'd never abandon it.' But then again—" He paused and inspected his nails. "That seems to be the person you are nowadays. Always ready to walk out on the things that matter."

His eyes snapped back to my face, piercing me with a frosty glare. The eerie calm in his voice was somehow more terrifying than rage. He moved towards the counter, and I stepped back instinctively, backing up until I collided with solid wall.

"I don't know how you can ignore me after everything we've been through."

His voice was still soft, but I could see the muscles working in his jaw. Despite my fear, I experienced a flash of anger. After everything he'd put me through, he had no right to show up and intimidate me like this.

"I think you do know," I ground out bitterly.

He raised his eyebrows.

"Are you still pissed about that internet thing?"

You can bet your ass I am.

"I admit that got out of hand," he conceded. "I lost my temper. But who drove me there, hm?"

I recognized his I'm-being-magnanimous tone and it made me bristle.

"You nearly destroyed me," I choked. "Everything I'd built. Everything you helped me build."

"And now I'm here to help you put things back together," he coaxed, stepping forward with his arms outstretched. "Look around you. Isn't all this enough to show you that you need me?"

"I've got all the help I need, thanks."

As soon as I said it, I cursed myself. I knew what his reaction would be. Sure enough, his features hardened instantly.

"What do you mean by that?" he demanded.

"Nothing," I said hastily.

"There's someone else, isn't there?"

Hearing the hard edge in his voice, my panic rose. My mouth had gone dry, and I could feel my pulse pounding in my ears.

"It's not like that," I insisted, trying desperately to shrink back farther.

"Who is it? That asshole I saw you with at the restaurant? I thought I made it quite clear how I felt about you seeing him. Is he here now?"

Stirling paused and looked about him. While he was distracted, I took my chance. I dashed from behind the counter, making a break for the door.

"Oh no you don't!"

Quick as lightning, Stirling lunged, seizing me by the upper arm. I struggled wildly, but he was too strong. His fingers dug into my bicep with a bruising grip.

"I've had it up to here with you ignoring me," he growled. "I came here to talk. That means you're going to shut your mouth like a good girl and listen."

CHAPTER THIRTY-ONE

Nolan

When I got back to the bakery, there was a strange car parked outside. The sight of it made me uneasy. Hurrying to the front door, I heard raised voices. It sounded like Erin was arguing with someone—a man. Hairs rose on the back of my neck, and I stormed through the door.

A slim, dark-haired man in a turtleneck had seized Erin by the arm. She was struggling in his grip, and he was shaking her viciously, like a terrier with a rat.

"Hey!" I shouted.

Startled, the man released his grip and spun around. Red-faced and panting, Erin scooted away from him, massaging her bicep.

The intruder recovered quickly. He stared at me coolly, the corners of his mouth curling in a disdainful sneer.

"Oh look," he drawled. "It's the new boy toy, heroically riding to the rescue. How heart-warming."

"I don't think I need to ask who you are," I snarled.

I was trembling with rage. I wanted to punch him so hard he saw stars. All the same, I held myself in check. I was smart enough to know I'd have no legal leg to stand on if he pressed charges, and I'd be no use to Erin if I was arrested.

"Has Erin been spinning her little stories?" he asked, glancing in her direction. "Did she blink those big doe eyes and play the damsel in distress? Don't feel bad, friend. That stuff usually works on gullible idiots."

"Erin doesn't need to tell me anything. I've been a lawyer for ten years. I know human trash when I smell it."

He tucked his thumbs into his belt and spread his feet a little wider.

"Am I supposed to be intimidated?"

"If you're smart, you'll crawl back under your rock where you belong."

Smiling sardonically, he boosted himself up to sit on the counter.

"Stirling," Erin pleaded wearily. "Please go. This isn't going to accomplish anything."

"But I want to hear more fascinating legal insights," he protested, folding his arms and looking at me expectantly. "Seriously, I love this shit. I'm a big *Judge Judy* fan."

How about I let my foot get some insight into your ass?

"Ok," I said, pausing to casually inspect my nails. "I can give you one interesting fact I've learned about criminals over the years. They always return to—" I slapped my hand on the bakery counter and looked around pointedly. "—the scene of the crime. I mean to see that you get your fix of courtroom drama. You'll get it when we haul you in front of a judge for harassment and breaking and entering."

He arched an eyebrow.

"Those are some serious accusations," he purred. "Isn't it lucky for me that you don't have a shred of evidence to back them up?"

My hand clenched into a fist. He might have slipped through the net for now, but there had to be some way to nail this bastard. I was going to find it.

"And yes," he continued, throwing Erin a sickly smile. "The police did come to see me. We had a cup of tea and a lovely chat. I'm sorry you both missed it, actually; I served my famous maple scones. Anyway, we had a talk and they told me all about Erin's little misapprehension."

I looked over at Erin. She was glaring at Stirling through a film of angry tears.

"That's partly why I'm here. I knew if Erin and I talked through this mess like rational adults, I could make her see sense."

He smiled at me maliciously, white teeth flashing.

"You don't know her like I do. She needs someone who'll tell her when she's being irrational—don't you, baby?"

Erin seemed to diminish in size before my eyes. She blushed and looked at the floor. By this point, my anger was threatening to boil over. I could barely keep my voice steady.

"That's how you've always gotten away with it, isn't it?" I demanded.

Stirling blinked, looking politely nonplussed.

"I don't think I follow you," he said smoothly.

"I wondered how you always managed to wriggle off the hook, but now I see," I growled, advancing on him slowly. "You lie through your teeth to the police and then you strong-arm the women into dropping the charges."

I was in his face now, practically nose to nose. He didn't move, but he did lean back slightly.

"I see someone's been doing some research," he hissed. "Did you enjoy digging around in my affairs?"

"I found it very illuminating," I shot back, crossing my arms in front of my chest.

"Ignoring for a moment the inexcusable breach of my privacy, if you'd read those files, you'd know that no evidence of any wrongdoing was ever found. Of course," he spread his palms wide, "I'm no legal expert, but I believe that leaves you up a creek without a vital implement."

I stared him down, fighting the urge to pound his smug, smirking face until it crumpled.

"Things will be different this time," I promised.

"Oh?" he said, looking amused. "And why would that be?"

"Because you're dealing with me."

Stirling tutted and shook his head.

"So fierce! I only came here to speak to Erin. I didn't expect to cross swords with her bodyguard."

"I think Erin has made it quite clear that she doesn't want to talk to you. So why don't you get out before I throw you out?"

"Careful, Sir Galahad," he warned. "Lay a hand on me and you'll be facing some charges of your own."

My teeth ground together as I forced myself to take a step back. Stirling leaped from the counter and dusted himself off. He sauntered casually towards the door, seemingly making to leave, but he turned around at the last moment.

"We'll talk soon, Erin," he said silkily. "Your boyfriend's skirts aren't wide enough to hide you forever."

She shrank farther against the wall as if hoping she could teleport through it.

"Is that a threat?"

He raised his hands in mock surrender.

"Wouldn't dream of it. I would watch *your* back, though. You're on my radar now."

"What's that supposed to mean?"

"It means you're not the only one who can use an internet search engine. Just you wait, Erin. I can turn up things about your shiny new boyfriend that would make your pretty hair curl."

He lifted a hand and curled his fingers in a wave.

"*Ciao*, for now."

As soon as he was gone, Erin's legs gave way. I rushed to steady her, almost over-balancing when my foot slipped in a patch of jelly. Gathering her in my arms, I hugged her fiercely. She quivered against me, and I heard a tiny sniffle.

"It's alright," I soothed. "He's gone. I've got you."

"I'm so glad you came back," she sobbed, the words muffled by my coat.

"I wish I'd gotten back sooner."

My jaw clenched at the memory of his hand on her arm.

"Did he hurt you?"

"No," she said, raising her head from my chest and wiping her eyes on her sleeve. "He just shook me up a little. But..." She looked up at me, eyes swimming with tears. "Those things he said before he left. He threatened—"

"And that's all it was," I said firmly. "A threat. He's blowing smoke because he knows he's lost."

I was reasonably confident that I was right. Erin had met Heather and my father. They were, by far, the worst skeletons in my closet. I was also sure I'd never done anything stupid that had ended up online. There might be the occasional social media rant from an ex, but nothing more sinister than that. Stirling Bateman didn't scare me.

"I don't know what to do," Erin whispered.

"Yes you do," I stated, taking her face in my hands and brushing away her tears with my thumbs. "We're going to clean up here, just like we planned. Then we're going back to my place and you're going to bake your damn socks off. We're not going to let him spoil anything."

Without thinking, I leaned forward and planted a kiss on her forehead.

Nothing wrong with that, I thought, as I scrubbed a chocolate stain from the floor. It was a friendly kiss. A kiss given in the spirit of friendship to support a friend. I scrubbed harder, pouring all my energy into the task. Because that's what we were. Friends. And *nothing* more.

In a couple of short hours, we were done. It was amazing how much better the place looked without the smashed treats and broken glass. Erin's spirits had risen in tandem with the progress of the clean-up, and she was even able to join me in a weary high five once the floor was sparkling and the debris was gone. We were tired and sticky, but overall, the day seemed to be looking up.

The buoyant feeling of accomplishment dissipated slightly when we stepped back into my apartment. I was immediately struck by the intuition that something was wrong. I couldn't put my finger on it. Everything looked neat and undisturbed, but there was a strange smell. It was new and jarring, yet somehow familiar. I left Erin in the kitchen unboxing the takeout we had brought for lunch, while I prowled from room to room, inhaling deeply. It wasn't exactly an unpleasant smell. It was heady and floral. Perfume perhaps? It was definitely nothing I wore, and I hadn't smelled it on Erin. I wracked my brains, trying to remember what days the cleaning lady came. Scratching at the back of my head, I frowned and headed back to the kitchen.

Erin had finished unpacking the Chinese food and the mystery smell was overpowered by garlic and five-spice.

"What's the matter?" Erin asked, handing me a carton of kung pao chicken.

"Nothing," I muttered. "I hope not, anyway. Might sound like a weird question, but did you notice a smell when we came in?"

She shook her head as she poured soy sauce onto her fried rice.

"Don't think so. After this morning, I think it will be a while before I can smell anything but sugar and Lysol."

Maybe that was all it was. Some weird olfactory hallucination brought on by over-exposure to the delightful aroma of candy and cleaning products. I shrugged it off. Whatever it was, it wasn't important right now. We had boobs to bake!

CHAPTER THIRTY-TWO

Erin

It was scary how much I was beginning to rely on Nolan. I was addicted to his smile, to the feeling of his arms around me. Over the last couple of days, he'd been a rock; he'd been there to pick me up every time I'd fallen down. Each time this happened, the little voice in my head that warned me that I was in too deep got fainter and fainter.

Thanks to Nolan, I had a clean shop and a place to bake. He'd also seriously cut down the amount of work I needed to do with the insurance company. He even insisted I take a nap after lunch while he unloaded the van. When I woke up an hour later and stumbled into the living area, I found all my equipment unpacked and laid out in the kitchen. Nolan stood behind the kitchen counter, beaming proudly. He'd even dug out an apron from somewhere. All he needed to complete the picture was a big, white chef's hat.

Fuck, he looks so cute!

"So," he said, rubbing his hands eagerly. "What do we do first?"

"Cool your jets, cowboy." I giggled. "Love the enthusiasm, but cupcakes need ingredients. Eggs, flour, butter, sugar, plus a little milk. I'm willing to bet you don't have those things in the quantities we'll need."

He deflated like a balloon. If he had been wearing a tall chef's hat, it would have flopped with a sad trombone noise.

"It's my fault," I assured him. "I should've thought of it on the way back from the bakery. Jayden and I were due to make a run to the wholesaler's this morning. I'll get my tablet; we'll go over my design and then make a list."

My tablet contained my original design and a photograph of a mock-up I'd made. Nolan leaned over my shoulder and whistled appreciatively.

"Wow! It looks so real."

I usually didn't know what to do with praise, but compliments from Nolan created a warm glow inside me.

"It's actually not that hard," I said modestly. "Cupcakes lend themselves pretty well to your basic boob shape."

Nolan snorted with laughter.

"What?!" I cried. "They do!"

"I'm sorry," he choked, trying to get himself under control. "But you sound like a pornographic Martha Stewart."

He adjusted his voice to a serene and soothing cadence.

"A simple cupcake can easily be transformed into a boob. It's a good thing."

"Watch it," I said, trying to sound stern but biting back a giggle of my own. "Or I'll put you on dishwashing duty."

"I am seriously impressed, though." He took another look at the screen. "How did you get that texture? It almost looks like real skin."

I shrugged.

"It's easier than you'd think. I just used a crusting buttercream."

He wrinkled his nose.

"That does not sound appetizing."

"I know what you mean," I admitted. "It might paint a better picture if we said 'crystallizing buttercream.' All it means is that you smooth it on, and it sets firmly. It's like armor for cakes. It protects the sponge underneath and it's easy to build on. Lots of people use fondant but it looks so flat and smooth. Besides, who really wants to eat a ton of fondant?"

Nolan grinned.

"Six-year-old Nolan would. Best part of the birthday cake, hands down."

"Yuck! I should go back in time and introduce you to Swiss meringue buttercream. It would have blown your tiny mind."

"Well, if you've got a time machine stashed away, I have a huge list of things little Nolan needs a heads-up about," he joked. "Speaking of lists, though." He pointed at my tablet screen. "Shouldn't we be making one?"

Taking Nolan to the wholesaler's was like taking an excited kid to a toy store. The look on his face when I told him we weren't going to be buying a five-gallon tub of gummi bears was priceless. It was weird to be shopping with him this way. I had the sensation of two worlds colliding. Even though I'd met Nolan through work, I'd met him as a customer. He got introduced to "front of house Erin." Going to the wholesaler's was "behind the scenes Erin." Watching him forlornly replace the gummi bears on the shelf, I thought about how much had changed since that night at the bachelor party. I'd only known Nolan for a couple of months, but he'd already had more glimpses of "behind the scenes Erin" than I usually revealed to anyone. I must have been staring vacantly, because he touched me on the shoulder, frowning.

"Everything alright?"

"Everything's fine," I lied. "I was just trying to remember if there was anything else we needed."

"Ok," he said doubtfully.

I wasn't surprised he didn't believe me. He had this uncanny knack for seeing straight through my bullshit.

Nolan was just as much of a kid in the kitchen as he was in the store. He was so eager to help that he was practically bouncing. I didn't have the heart to tell him that there probably wouldn't be a great deal that he could do.

The first thing on the agenda was to unpack the equipment. I'm usually fairly neat and organized, but I must have been distracted when I packed at the bakery because the boxes were a jumbled mess. When Nolan got back from a trip to the bathroom, he found me frantically rummaging in a crate and turning the air blue.

"What's wrong?"

"I can't find my nipple mold," I fumed.

Out of the corner of my eye, I saw numerous expressions chase one another across his face.

"Your what?" he asked eventually.

"My nipple mold," I repeated. "I need it for the tempered chocolate nipples."

He shook his head slowly.

"Ok, so I did hear you right." He cupped his chin pensively. "I definitely don't have one of those. Hey!" He brightened. "You know what you could use instead—"

I turned on him, brandishing a balloon whisk.

"If I hear any combination of the words 'kisses' and 'Hershey's' coming out of your mouth, I won't be held responsible for my actions."

Nolan held out his hands and took a step back.

"My bad. I had no idea this process would be so intricate. Where do you even buy a nipple mold?"

"I didn't buy it," I murmured, once again absorbed in rummaging. "I made it."

"Really?"

He sounded impressed.

"Yeah." I groaned, straightening up and massaging my lower back.

Despite the fact that I was busy and stressed, I found myself getting drawn into this conversation. I loved talking about my work, and it was flattering to find someone so interested in the crafting process.

"I started with an alginate impression, which I used as the basis for a hard cast. Then I had a sheet of molds made from food-safe silicone. They'd only just come in when I left for the wedding. Aha!" I held up the floppy sheet triumphantly. "Here they are. I'd forgotten how well they turned out. You can see—so much detail. Look!"

I thrust the molds at Nolan, and he blushed furiously.

"What's the matter?"

I watched his eyes flicker rapidly between the silicone sheet and my chest. My own cheeks burned.

"They're not *my* nipples!" I shrieked, holding a protective arm in front of my chest.

"T—they're not?" he stuttered.

"No," I huffed, trying to sound dignified. "You happen to be looking at a perfect silicone rendering of Mrs. Perez's new left nipple."

"Wow," he exclaimed.

He reached out a hand to touch the mold, then changed his mind and yanked it back.

"You really go in-depth with these projects."

I gave a one-shouldered shrug.

"I have to. You can't just use a generic nipple mold and have done with it. Have you ever seen two sets of nipples that looked the same?"

He rubbed the back of his neck and looked away, smiling shyly.

"You tell me," he teased. "Weirdly, you've probably seen a bigger sample than I have."

"True. I always destroy any material a client's given me

when I finish a project... unless they're happy to contribute to the database, that is."

He coughed.

"You have a database?"

"Yes," I said, clinging doggedly to my professional dignity. "If I'm making something less personalized, it's useful to have certain shapes already on file."

My mind drifted back to Nolan's striptease, and I bit my lip.

Don't ask him for a cast of his nipples! Don't ask him for a cast of his nipples!

"Is this why you mentioned wanting to cast my nipples when we were in that hot tub?"

Damn his elephant's memory!

I swear my face was on fire. I raised my hands to my cheeks and my skin felt hot to the touch.

"Well," I mumbled, the words muffled by my hands. "Drunk Erin might have been a little forward, but she did have a point. When you stripped at that bachelor party, I couldn't help but admire them—professionally, of course. If I'd bought any alginate with me, you might have been in danger."

I'm definitely in danger.

His smile was bashful, but he took a theatrical bow.

"Erin," he said solemnly. "I'd be honored to add my nipples to your database."

I laughed shakily and cleared my throat.

"Well, what girl could refuse an offer like that?"

He stepped forward and took hold of my hands, smiling softly.

"I'm here for you," he promised. "Anything you need. Paperwork, nipples, anything at all."

Acting on pure instinct, I hugged him around the waist and laid my head on his chest.

"Thank you," I whispered. "You have no idea how much that means."

Had I finally found a man who kept his promises?

Eventually, I managed to persuade Nolan that he wasn't needed in the kitchen, and he retreated to sort through my insurance paperwork. After a couple of grueling hours of baking, I was already exhausted and sweating. I'd forgotten how hot a small kitchen could get when the oven was constantly blasting. Unable to stand it any longer, I stretched and pulled off my sweater. When I emerged from my clothes, I discovered that a glass of wine had "somehow" materialized on the counter. I glanced around. Nolan was sat at the dining table with the paperwork, smiling innocently. I smiled back, feeling all gooey inside. He was so sweet and thoughtful.

Also, a mother-frickin' ninja. I didn't even hear him approach.

I wouldn't normally drink while working but this felt like a valid moment to make an exception. It had been a truly terrible week. Another hour went by, and I had done everything I could do that day. The cakes needed to cool before I could frost them, and I didn't have access to a blast chiller. I was tired and sore, but I felt a lot calmer than I had that morning. Mrs. Perez receiving her cupcakes before the heat death of the universe no longer felt like a pipe dream.

"All done?"

Nolan sauntered into the kitchen with two more glasses of wine. He was so easy to be around. Having people around while I was working usually made me edgy, but with Nolan, I was completely relaxed. Every now and then I'd looked up and caught him sniffing the air appreciatively. Baking always makes a home smell amazing. The air in the kitchen was heavy with the scent of chocolate, strawberries, and caramelized sugar. It was rich, complex, almost sensual.

I accepted the wine with a wry smile.

"If I didn't know better, I'd think you were trying to get me drunk," I teased.

In truth, I wasn't drunk. I wasn't even buzzed. I just felt

good. I couldn't remember the last time I'd felt so comfortable.

"I'm not," he protested. "I just want to help you unwind. Think of this as a reward for a job well done."

"And the first one?"

"Medicinal," he said promptly.

"Mm, you give the best prescriptions." I groaned, stretching out my shoulders with an audible crackle.

Nolan winced.

"As it happens, I've also got the prescription for that," he declared.

He put down his glass and walked over to stand behind me. I stiffened automatically when his hands went to my shoulders, but I quickly relaxed as he gently worked the tense muscles. He found knots I hadn't even known were there, his fingers smoothing and squeezing with the perfect amount of pressure. Soon I was boneless in his grip, purring like a contented cat. The warm, solid bulk of his body behind me felt so good that I leaned back against him. In no time at all, his skillful massage robbed me of my inhibitions and my groans of appreciation grew louder. After a particularly resonant and throaty moan, I felt something shift against my backside. I froze.

"Jeez! I'm sorry."

Nolan took his hands away and moved to step back. Instantly, my hands shot back and grabbed his hips, stopping his retreat. I don't know why I did it. All I knew was that I didn't want him to go away. I wanted to feel his warm body pressed against me. I wanted... more.

"Erin?"

It was no more than a hoarse whisper. We were both trembling. Moving gingerly, I shifted round to face him, our bodies still flush. Nolan stared at me in mute wonder, almost as though he had never seen me before. His eyes were dark, and his throat bobbed as he swallowed convulsively. Reaching out a hand, he tenderly stroked the side of my face. Sighing, I leaned into the caress and pressed a soft kiss to his palm. The rational part of my brain had completely switched off. I wasn't thinking, I was just reacting.

His skin was surprisingly soft, and I could detect the slight tang of salt. I kissed him again, brushing my lips over his hand, pausing to gently suck and nip at the flesh. At that moment, something between us broke. Hissing sharply, he brought his other hand to my face and claimed my mouth with his.

CHAPTER THIRTY-THREE

Nolan

It was like hurtling toward the edge of a cliff. We were racing to the point of no return and, this time, there was no one to stop us. I didn't care. I didn't want to stop. This woman was a drug, and I was addicted.

I pressed my lips to hers, tasting red wine and the rich bitterness of chocolate. My tongue tickled the seam of her lips and she shivered, opening her mouth eagerly. There was nothing chaste and patient about this kiss. It was hard and hungry. Every forbidden desire and unspoken urge that had been simmering since our first meeting poured into our frantic embrace.

We had kissed in the hot tub, but this was different. Kissing Erin for the second time was even more intense. It was like taking a second bite of a delicious and complex dish. When you're no longer overwhelmed by the heady rush of the new, you're free to enjoy all the subtleties and hidden depths of the whole.

As I kissed her, I caressed the side of her throat, stroking the tender skin behind her ear. She moaned appreciatively. Without breaking the kiss, I lifted her onto the kitchen counter, placing us eye to eye. She wound her arms around my neck and wrapped her legs around my hips, pulling me closer. I was already rock hard. My lips moved from her mouth to pepper kisses across her cheek and jawbone. When I took her earlobe between my teeth and nipped, she mewled needily and threw her head back. I kissed my way down her neck, pausing to suck gently at the hollow of her throat. She gasped and I could feel her pulse jumping. Running my tongue along the ridge of her collarbone, I tasted salt, caramel, and a hint of vanilla. I wanted to devour her.

Her hands flew to the back of my head, pushing me gently but insistently downwards. I nuzzled at her breast, grinning smugly when I felt the diamond-hard point of her nipple stretching the fabric. My hand went to her other breast and my thumb swiftly found the second stiff peak.

She pushed me backward and yanked her top over her head, throwing it aside. Her bra swiftly followed, and I gazed at her hungrily. My eyes traveled from her toned stomach to her firm breasts. Her nipples had crinkled into tight, aching points and her chest was heaving. She stared at me, eyes shining, lips slightly parted. Her cheeks were flushed, and she was breathing heavily. I had never seen anything more beautiful.

I reached for her tentatively, as if reaching for a mirage. I felt suddenly bashful and clumsy. Never breaking eye contact, Erin grabbed my outstretched hand and pressed it to her breast. When I felt the pebbled flesh of her nipple brush against my palm, my cock twitched. I groaned and leaned in for another kiss. Cupping her breasts, I softly pinched her nipples and she moaned into my mouth.

The next moment my eyes flew open as I felt her hand brush my crotch. She raked her nails lightly over the straining bulge in my pants, teasing me mercilessly. I growled and nipped her lip, drawing an adorable squeak.

"Lovely though this is," I murmured, placing light fluttering kisses over her eyelids and forehead. "I won't last long if you keep doing that."

There was a little whine of disappointment as I caught her wrist and moved her hand from my cock.

"Not yet." I chuckled.

I trailed my free hand over her belly to the waistband of her jeans and popped the top button open. I looked at her with a raised eyebrow, silently asking permission. She leaned back, giving me easier access. I opened the rest of the buttons, gradually exposing the lilac satin of her panties. When I began easing her pants down her legs, she lifted her hips, helping the movement. My mouth went dry when I saw a darkened patch of purple. I caressed her through the slippery fabric of her panties, tracing the outline of her swollen folds. I stroked her until she was gasping and whimpering. Her hips bucked into my hands, searching for more pressure.

"Please, Nolan," she gasped.

By this time, my cock was straining painfully against my boxers. The naked want in her unrestrained plea only made it twitch harder and I felt a tiny amount of pre dribble from the head.

Slowly, torturously, I hooked my fingers into the waistband of Erin's panties and slid them down her legs. I bit my lip and swallowed a groan. The blushing petals of her pussy were puffy and glistening. I ran two fingers through her slick folds and then brought them up to lightly circle her clit. I cupped her face with my free hand and gazed down at her.

"You're so beautiful," I whispered reverently.

"I—I," she panted. "Oh God. Nolan. Please don't stop. That feels so… oh."

Her entire bottom lip disappeared into her mouth as I sped up my circles. I shifted my hand so that my thumb was rubbing back and forth across the hardened nub of her clit, allowing me to carefully slide two fingers inside her. She shuddered and moaned as my fingers curled upwards, pressing against her front wall. I flexed my fingers back and forth and her hips lifted eagerly to meet my thrusts. My thumb sped up as I felt her walls clamp down around my hand, and her eyes rolled back in her head. I fucked her gently, drawing out her shivering climax. When she was spent, I straightened up and took her in my arms, cradling her against my chest.

"That was—" she panted. "That was just... wow."

"Yeah," I agreed, "it was."

I meant it too. I had almost blown my load when she came. She was breathtaking.

We stayed like that for a minute or two. Her still perched on the kitchen counter and me standing with her cuddled against my chest. It was strange. Even though I was still rock hard, I was also experiencing bone-melting levels of contentment. However, Erin clearly wasn't done with me. Gradually, her hands inched their way down my back until she was gripping my buttocks. I made a throaty, purring sound as she kneaded the flesh.

"Take your pants off," she whispered. "I want to feel you inside me."

Yes, Ma'am.

In no time at all, I had unbuttoned my jeans and allowed them to fall to the ground. I shivered as Erin's soft, cool hands brushed my stomach. Without preamble, she grabbed the waistband of my boxers away and pushed them over my hips. I sighed with relief as my cock sprang free. It was so erect it was quivering, and I felt it jump and pulse with each beat of my heart. Erin's eyes were riveted on my crotch, and I fought the impulse to blush.

Bad idea, Nolan. That blood is needed elsewhere right now.

She took my length in her hand and stroked my shaft. With every pass she swiped her thumb over the tip, catching the drops of pre that welled from the slit. Soon, my erection was slick and glistening and my breath was coming in short pants. I closed my eyes and bit fiercely at the inside of my cheek. I knew I couldn't hold back much longer.

Erin must have known it too. She stopped jacking me and

slid her ass towards the edge of the counter. I watched in rapt fascination as she braced her weight on her elbows and pulled her knees back to her chest. The movement exposed her pussy. It was pink, swollen, and practically dripping. Standing on the balls of my feet, I lined myself up, passing the head of my cock through her folds and allowing it to bump over her clit. Her breath caught and she thrust greedily, but I had to be certain.

I slid my arm around her back, supporting some of her weight, and looked at her earnestly.

"Are you sure this is ok?"

"Yes," she breathed.

Loose strands of hair were sticking to her sweating forehead and her cheeks were flushed. Her eyes were darkened pools of lust.

"Fuck me, Nolan. Please."

I thrust into her in one smooth movement, groaning as she surrounded me with her molten embrace. I tried to pull out, but she wrapped her legs around my waist, holding me to her. Her arms flew around my neck, and she pulled herself upwards, trying to take me deeper. Grunting, I put my other arm around her waist and stood up. She clung to me fiercely, her legs around my waist and her arms around my neck. Locking eyes with me, she lifted herself almost completely off. For a second, she stayed there, straining and quivering with effort, before allowing herself to sink back down. We cried out in unison as she impaled herself on my cock.

Bracing my ass against the kitchen counter, I supported as much of her weight as I could and allowed her to control the rhythm. By this point, we were both covered in a sheen of sweat and our skin slapped audibly together every time she fucked herself on my length. I could feel my climax boiling low in my belly, but I fought to hold it back. Erin's whimpering gasps had reached a new pitch and her chest was flushed. I knew she was close, and I wanted to us to fall over the edge together. Finally, she cried out and I felt her clench and flutter around me. The rhythmic squeezing of her walls triggered my orgasm, and it was truly volcanic. My vision blurred at the edges and I'm fairly sure I saw stars.

Panting, we both crumpled to the floor. Erin was shivering so I gathered her in my arms. I was sitting bare assed on cold tiles, but I swear, I could have fallen asleep. I felt peaceful and happy. For the first time, all my fears and nagging doubts were silent. How could it be wrong to feel this good? Erin's breathing had settled into the soft, steady rhythm that told me she was asleep. I placed a soft kiss on the top of her head and picked her up, bridal style. Stopping at the guest room door, I briefly considered putting her to bed in there and then dismissed the idea. Taking her to my bed felt like the right thing to do and, for once, I didn't second guess myself. I put her under the covers and climbed in next to her, spooning her. Without waking, she made a sleepy noise of contentment and pulled my arm tighter around her. She was so adorable that it caused a weird ache in my chest. An ache I hadn't felt in a long time.

I love her!

It came to me in a bolt of clarity, and I was struck to the core by its absolute truth. At any other time, this revelation might have terrified me, but in the euphoric afterglow of our lovemaking, it just felt right.

I fell asleep, feeling the steady thump of her heart and breathing in the light, floral fragrance of her hair.

CHAPTER THIRTY-FOUR

Erin

I woke up sprawled over Nolan's chest. His skin was warm against my cheek and my head moved gently up and down to the rhythm of his breathing. I was in no hurry to move. I'd had the best night's sleep I'd had in months, and I felt warm and comfortable.

It had finally happened. The thing I had been fighting against ever since we left the wedding.

Who are you kidding? You've been fighting it since you saw him do that striptease.

I chuckled softly at the memory. It made my body vibrate a little. Nolan made a sleepy grumbling noise and wrapped his arm tighter around me. Looking up at his sleeping face, it occurred to me that losing the fight with my feelings didn't feel so much like losing after all. What had I been so afraid of? I lifted my head and planted a light kiss on his cheek.

The eye closest to me flickered open and he smiled at me blearily.

"Morning," he mumbled.

I smiled back shyly.

"Morning indeed. That was quite a night."

"Yeah."

He rolled on his side to face me and brushed hair out of my face.

"How are you feeling?"

He looked apprehensive. He was asking something specific. I smiled warmly and pecked him on the lips.

"Never better," I declared.

His face immediately relaxed, and he leaned in for another kiss. Our mouths moved softly together, and he sucked lightly on my lower lip. I opened my mouth with a small, contented sigh. It was sweet, languid, and unhurried.

"Mm," Nolan crooned. "Definitely a drug."

I frowned.

"What's a drug?"

"You are," he stated, tapping me playfully on the nose. "And I don't think I can quit. I tried but—"

He shrugged helplessly. I caught one of his hands in both of mine and toyed with it.

"I tried too," I admitted, staring intently at his fingers.

"So," he murmured, brushing his thumb over the back of my hand. "What do you want to do now?"

"I..."

There were a million ways to answer that question. "Go to the bathroom?" "Have breakfast?" "Hold you and never let go?" I wanted to do all those things, but could I trust what I wanted? Taking the plunge with Nolan seemed a whole lot scarier now we were both awake and talking about it than it had a few minutes ago. Sensing my hesitation, he rubbed his hand up my arm.

"It's ok," he soothed. "I don't want to push you into any big decisions when you still have so much shit going on."

"I—It's not that I don't—"

My throat closed down around the words.

"I know how I feel about you," I choked. "I know in here." My hand came up to lie over my chest. "In lots of ways you're the best thing that's ever happened to me. I'm just—"

"Scared? Overwhelmed? Exhausted? All of the above?"

I nodded, still staring at our joined hands.

"Everything's so up in the air. There's Stirling and the bakery, and—"

He cut me off with a finger on my lips.

"Let's just take things one step at a time, ok? Starting with breakfast."

I snuggled into his side and laid my head back on his chest.

"I could make us something," I suggested.

"Absolutely not!"

"What?" I protested. "I can do regular cooking, you know. It's not all stripper cakes and chocolate nipples."

"I'm sure you can." He laughed. "But you're going to stay where you are and relax. I'll bring us breakfast in bed."

I ran my hand gently over his stomach and he shivered.

"If you keep pampering me like this, I'm going to get horribly spoiled," I purred.

He grinned.

"Good. That's been my cunning plan this whole time."

"But the kitchen," I argued. "It's a mess. I didn't have a chance to clean up last night." I glanced at him slyly. "I may have been a little distracted."

"Well," he pulled me closer and kissed the top of my head, "I'm sure I'm at least partly to blame for that."

"You and your massages," I teased, poking him in the belly. "Also, you should know by now, there are consequences when you give me alcohol."

The arms around me stiffened. Frowning, I looked up. Nolan was staring into the middle distance, his face clouded with concern.

"What's up?" I asked anxiously.

He took a deep breath and looked down at me.

"I—I really wasn't trying to get you drunk. I mean, I wanted you to relax and have a good time, but I had no ulterior motive."

I was stunned. For a moment I just gaped at him.

"That never even entered my mind," I said emphatically. "That's not the kind of guy you are, Nolan."

He gave me a feeble smile and kissed me on the forehead.

"I'd best make a start on that breakfast," he declared.

As I watched him go, I had the nagging feeling that something was wrong, but I dismissed it. For once, I was determined to stay out of my head and stop overthinking everything. Instead, I grabbed my phone and my stylus. I then proceeded to make valuable use of my time like a real adult. Translation: I did a quick check of my messages and then played *Cat Quest*.

Jayden had sent me a selfie at 3 a.m. It showed him half-naked in a crowded, darkened room, surrounded by foam. Clearly, he was managing to enjoy his impromptu vacation. Maddie had asked how I was and suggested several creative ways of getting back at Stirling. I couldn't help shuddering. The words "acid" and "enema" should never appear in the same sentence. Sometimes that girl worried me. The final message was from Mrs. Pasternak. She wanted to know how things were going with the bakery and whether "Stanley" had dropped by. The message was in all-caps, but I didn't read too much into this. Mrs. Pasternak had never gotten the hang of her touch screen.

After breakfast, Nolan told me he had taken the week off work, so we could spend the whole day together. It was as if we were in our own cozy bubble, oblivious to the world whirling around us. By evening, Mrs. Perez's cupcakes were beautifully decorated and waiting to be boxed and shipped.

Nolan and I cuddled on the couch with the spare cakes and binged *Downton Abbey*. As my head fell sleepily on his chest and his arm closed around me, I felt blissfully contented. It had been an absolutely perfect day. Feeling the weight of Nolan's cheek on my head, I smiled to myself.

The first of many, I hope.

CHAPTER THIRTY-FIVE

Erin

The next few months passed in a blissful blur. It took a while to fix up the bakery properly, but I was able to fill simple orders from home. In any case, the enforced lightening of my workload was well-timed. It gave me a chance to get my head straight.

I was amazed by the outpouring of support online. My Facebook and Instagram were flooded with condolences and well-wishers. After my shaky history with social media, it was extremely refreshing. I even felt confident enough to spice up my business page with some photo updates from my personal life. Me and Nolan at the park, me and Nolan at the beach, me and Nolan having bubble tea... There was definitely a theme to these pictures.

I moved back into my own apartment. Nolan made puppy dog eyes, but I held firm. Things between us were going so well. I didn't want to ruin it by rushing into anything. Plus, there had been nothing from Stirling since that day at the bakery, not a peep. It seemed he'd finally gotten the hint.

When the bakery was fixed up, we held a relaunch event and handed out free cupcakes. Within an hour, the cakes were gone, and our order diary was jam-packed. We were booked solid for the next six months.

About a week later, I was locking up for the evening when I heard a voice behind me.

"Erin? It's Erin, right?"

Blinking in surprise, I turned around and was confronted by a familiar face. I narrowed my eyes.

"What do you want?" I asked coldly.

I recognized Heather immediately. Big blue eyes, wavy blonde hair, and breasts for days. There was something different about her, though. The last time I'd seen her, she'd looked like the improbable love child of Marilyn Monroe and Jessica Rabbit. Smoky eyes, bright red dress, and lipstick to match. Now she was looking subdued, almost somber. She was wearing a gray sweater, black slacks, and very little makeup. She was acting differently too. Standing with shoulders hunched and eyes cast down, she looked sad and submissive.

"I'm probably the last person you want to see, huh?"

I kept silent. There was no reason to lie. If there was a definitive ranking of "people I least want to see," she couldn't claim the top spot, but she'd crack the top five.

"I don't blame you. Heck," she gave a shaky laugh, "there have been times over the last few months when I didn't really want to see me either."

Her face contorted for a moment, and she swallowed hard.

"That's the thing about hitting rock bottom," she choked. "You're confronted by all the shitty things you did on the way down. And you have lots of time to think about them too."

I bit my lip. I'd imagined confronting this woman several times. That night in the restaurant, she'd brought back some painful memories and ruined a top I was rather fond of. On the other hand, all my anger and devastating retorts had been aimed at the bottle-blonde bitch from hell. I didn't know what to do with this humble, contrite version of Heather. She was looking at me now. Her eyes were shining, and she was smiling tremulously.

"I know I behaved terribly towards you. But I'm trying to be a better person. I'm in a program and I've gotten in touch with my spiritual side. As part of my treatment, I'm supposed to apologize to all the people I've wronged."

I sighed. Everyone knows that it's hard to swallow your pride and apologize. What a lot of people don't realize is that graciously accepting an apology can be just as difficult. In Heather's case, it wasn't simply what she'd done to me. I'd seen how stressed-out Nolan had gotten over her vindictive hate campaign. As if reading my mind, Heather folded her hands together and looked down at them.

"I'd love to be able to apologize to Nolan too." She sighed. "But he felt he needed a restraining order, and I'm hardly in a position to question his decision."

"No," I agreed, my voice still hard.

I didn't know what to make of it. It was crazy but she seemed utterly sincere

"Look," she said. "I understand if you want to tell me to shove it. But I'd really like to talk if you're willing."

Could I really refuse her?

"Alright," I conceded. "One cup of coffee."

Occasionally, I'm struck by the feeling of being a passenger in my own life. As I sat, watching Heather draw lazy patterns in the foam of her decaf non-fat cappuccino, I had that feeling again. I had no idea what would happen next.

After an awkward pause, she put down her spoon, sat up straight, and placed her hands together like she was preparing to recite a poem.

"I'm so sorry for what I did to you," she said earnestly. "Throwing all that salsa over you—"

"Chili sauce."

She blinked.

"What?"

"It wasn't salsa. It was chili sauce."

Something flickered across her face. It had gone before I had time to analyze what it was, and her smile was back in place.

"Of course it was," she agreed. "But anyway, it was an awful thing to do. Covered in sauce like that with everyone staring." She leaned over and laid a hand on my arm. "You must have been so embarrassed."

Yes, I was. Thanks for bringing it up!

She drew back and placed both hands around her cup, staring into it meditatively.

"Seeing you with Nolan in that restaurant..." She paused, shaking her head. "I don't know what came over me. I wasn't like that before, you know."

I frowned.

"Before what?"

Her head snapped up and she looked at me intently. I fought the urge to look away. Her icy blue eyes were boring into me.

"Before him, of course," she said. "I never thought I'd be the kind of girl who'd lose my head over a guy. I was really into female emaciation."

I don't think that word means what you think it means.

I raised an eyebrow.

"You were?"

"Yes! I was a total feminist."

She sighed and stared wistfully out of the window with her chin on her hand.

"Anyway, that all changed when I met Nolan. I fell head over heels for him. I couldn't help it. He just seemed so perfect. You know what I mean, of course."

She caught my eye again, this time with a hint of a conspiratorial smile.

"I have no idea what you mean," I said stiffly.

I wasn't sure why, but I felt sick dread creeping from the pit of my stomach and into my chest.

"Oh, come on!" she cajoled. "You know how he is in the beginning. He treated me like I was the most important woman in the world—like a princess. I was swept away by it all. Without even realizing it, I'd become completely reliant on him."

My hands clenched around my mug. A memory had surfaced, crystal sharp in my mind. Getting the news about the bakery. Nolan flying to my rescue. The way I had clung to him. Straightening up, I gave my head a little shake.

That was different! We weren't even going out then.

"I guess when I think about it, I should have seen the warning signs," said Heather ruefully. "The fact is that, when it comes to women, our Nolan has a short attention span. In no time at all, I went from being the center of his world to simply an afterthought."

She paused for long enough to sigh dramatically.

"He always had an excuse, of course. Working late, family emergency. The usual suspects. I tried to hold on to him, but it was like trying to hold water. The more I clutched at him, the more he slipped through my fingers."

Her voice cracked and a single tear rolled down her cheek. She dabbed at her eye with a napkin and took a deep juddering breath.

"I was really mad at him for a long time," she confided. "But I've come to realize that's not healthy. His selfish, inconsiderate, borderline sociopathic behavior is obviously coming from a place of pain. My spiritual advisor always says that you can't spell badness without *sadness.*"

"Actually," I interjected. "I don't think that—"

"Deep down in the core of his unconscious selfhood, Nolan is a very unhappy man. I pity him."

This was said with a grotesque satisfaction that made me want to be sick. She placed her hand on my arm again and I fought the urge to jerk it away.

"But this isn't about Nolan. This is about *you.* I wronged you and now I'm here to balance the karmic scale."

"What are you talking about?"

I was filled with a sense of foreboding. I had a feeling I knew where this was going. I could feel Heather's eyes on me, and I tried to take a nonchalant sip of my drink.

"You can tell me it's none of my business. I wouldn't blame you. On the other hand, I won't be able to sleep at night unless I try to warn you."

"Warn me?"

My voice sounded like it was coming from the other end of a tunnel.

"Don't get too attached to Nolan," she advised. "He's a player. God knows what it takes to hold his interest." Her face twisted into a sympathetic grimace. "But it's probably not cake."

"There's more to me than just my job," I snapped.

I wasn't sure why I was justifying myself to this woman.

"Oh, sweetie," she cooed. "Of course there is. You're cute as a little button. Plus, that homespun, girl-next-door look is really in right now. But," she spread her hands helplessly, "for guys like Nolan..."

Trailing off, she shook her head.

"Don't offer him your whole heart, because I'm not sure he's capable of giving his in return."

My heart was pounding in my eyes. I wanted to take my coffee and fling it in Heather's smug, simpering face.

Rise above it, Erin. She's just trying to get in your head.

I sat up straighter and forced a complacent smile onto my face.

"I guess I'll just see how it goes," I breezed. "Nolan and I have only been going out for a couple of months. We're taking it slow."

Heather gave me a pained look.

"Are you, though? I saw your Instagram feed and it made me worried for you."

"What about my Instagram?" I said sharply.

"All those photos of the two of you."

This was uttered in the delicate tone you might use to tell another woman that her skirt is tucked into her panties.

"It seems like you're getting pretty invested. Now you've gone so public, it would be really embarrassing if anything were to go wrong."

I was way past done with this conversation. Everything in the coffee shop suddenly seemed too loud and too bright. I had to get away. Standing up hurriedly, I fumbled for my purse. Heather's eyes widened.

"Leaving so soon, sweetie?" she asked.

"Sorry, lots to do," I said shortly. "Thanks for your apology. I appreciate it."

"No." Standing up, Heather stepped around the table and clasped me by the shoulders. "*Thank you,* Erin. I feel very blessed that you opened your heart to me. I think this will be very healing for both of us. After all, we're both in the same boat. Maybe not right now, but..."

She broke off and pulled me into a hug. I gritted my teeth, trying not to breathe in too much of her heavy, floral perfume.

"Good luck, sweetie," she said, smiling sadly. "Call me anytime you need to talk."

"Thanks," I mumbled mechanically.

When she released me, I practically ran outside. The cool evening air woke up my brain and nearly sent me reeling. My phone buzzed in my pocket, and I experienced a flood of relief when I saw it was a message from Nolan.

Nolan: Hey, baby. Really sorry to do this, but I can't make our lunch date tomorrow. Emergency meeting. Talk later. N xxx

My relief soured in an instant and was replaced by a cold, sick dread. I stared at the message for a long time, people jostling past me in the crowded street. I didn't realize I'd started crying until one of my tears splashed onto the screen.

CHAPTER THIRTY-SIX

Nolan

"Look, this isn't easy for me to say, so I'm just going to come straight out with it. These last few months have been the best of my life. I know we haven't been seeing each other for very long, but I've never been so sure about anything. I honestly think we're ready to take the next step."

I slid a hand into my pocket and drew out a black velvet box.

"Sheesh! I know that chair offers good lumbar support, but don't rush into anything."

I jumped like a scalded cat and spun around. Alana was standing in my office doorway, smirking.

"How long have you been there?" I demanded.

"Just long enough to catch you making romantic declarations to the furniture. Maybe it's a good thing you didn't splurge on that reclining chair with the vibrating butt massagers."

"Very funny."

Blushing fiercely, I took the chair that had been standing in for Erin and tucked it under the desk.

"I had something I wanted to ask Erin. I'm a little nervous so I thought it might be a good idea to practice."

Alana perched on the desk and eyed me shrewdly.

"It sounded like you were gearing up to pop the question."

I took the box out again and turned it over in my hands.

"Not quite. Almost as scary, though." I held up the box. "This is a key to my apartment."

Alana raised her eyebrows.

"You're asking her to move in with you?"

I shrugged.

"Not exactly. She doesn't have to give up her apartment if she doesn't want to. I just want her to feel at home at my place. Come and go as she likes. Do you think it's too soon?"

Alana pursed her lips.

"No," she said finally. "I don't think it's too soon. But don't come on too strong, *jefe*. Weren't too long ago that you were both running scared from this."

"I know."

I was sitting down by this point, but I got up and started pacing restlessly.

"I'm just so excited. Things have been going so great between us. And it's been awesome to be with someone I can introduce to my family and friends. It's not even just that I can; I *want* to. I want to tell everyone I meet."

I expected Alana to complain that I was making her barf. Instead, she smiled indulgently, like I was a puppy who'd just learned to go to the bathroom outside.

"Love suits you," she remarked. "Besides, this is definitely the coolest person you've ever dated. Which is why," she stood up and adjusted my tie, "we're not going to let you fuck it up. When are you seein' her?"

"I'm taking her to dinner tonight. I felt bad that I had to blow off our lunch yesterday, so I booked us a table at that fancy new sushi restaurant."

Alana nodded her approval.

"Need anything before you go?" she asked.

"I don't think so. Unless..." I paused. "How much did you hear of my—?"

She smiled slyly.

"Your chair speech? I caught the highlights."

"How did it sound?"

"It was good. But you don't need to be all stiff. It's a romantic proposition, not a legal deposition."

I took a deep breath.

"Ok, loose. I can do loose."

"Speaking of depositions..." As she spoke, she started tidying the papers on my desk. "How are you both doing with your pet psychos?"

I rolled my eyes.

"If you mean Heather and Stirling, things have been pretty quiet on both fronts. Haven't heard a thing in weeks. I don't know whether to be pleased or worried. Neither of them has challenged the restraining orders, though, so those should be done and dusted soon. I want to take Erin on vacation when this is over. We both need it."

Alana nodded.

"Maybe you could propose then," she teased.

"Perhaps I will. I'm really getting a handle on this relationship stuff."

Despite my assurances to Alana, my stomach was fluttering by the time I pulled up to Erin's apartment building. When she let me in, she was still in her bathrobe, so I loitered in the living area while she went to finish dressing.

When she'd greeted me, her smile had been strained and there was something a little distant about her hug, but I dismissed it. She'd been working super hard recently. Business had been booming since the bakery re-opened. So much so that Maddie and I were trying to persuade her to hire another assistant. I was so proud of her. Smiling fondly, I leaned on the kitchen counter and helped myself to a banana Twinkie from the open box near the microwave.

I nearly gasped out loud when Erin emerged from the bedroom. Her bathrobe had been replaced by an off-the-shoulder, midnight blue cocktail dress. My mouth watered. The dress was tight in all the right places and the color suited her wonderfully. Sliding my arms around her waist, I kissed her tenderly on the mouth.

"You look beautiful," I declared.

"Wouldn't say that if you'd been here an hour ago. I swear, I found peanut butter cookie dough in my eyebrows."

"That doesn't matter to me. You could be covered head to toe in grape jelly and I'd still think you were gorgeous."

"Really?"

She was smiling, but there was a definite note of uncertainty in her voice.

"Of course!" I assured her, smoothing a hand over her hair. "What's brought this on?"

She made a face and shook her head.

"It's nothing. I'm just tired. We'd better go if you've booked this table for 7 p.m."

By now there was definitely tension in the air. It dogged us all the way down to the car. I could feel it like a third passenger in the elevator; an invisible barrier between us. I started to panic that I'd done something to upset her. A quick mental review of our interactions over the last few days didn't raise any obvious red flags. I glanced at her furtively as we buckled our seatbelts. The muscles in her jaw were clenched and her mouth was set in a tight line. I came to a decision. My body had started going through the motions of starting the car, but I stopped everything. Leaving the keys in the ignition, I took my hands off the steering wheel and leaned back in my seat.

"Erin," I said softly. "What's wrong?"

For a moment she didn't say anything, then her shoulders sagged, and she let out a shaky breath.

"I'm just feeling a little," she waved her hand, searching for the right word, "insecure, I guess. I mean, I've been thinking about all the women you dated before me. Lingerie models, backing dancers, tennis players. Heather's pretty damn stunning too, even if she is crazy. It's an intimidating act to follow."

That's all she's worried about?

The rush of relief was so powerful that I laughed out loud. It sounded unnaturally loud in the quiet car

"Baby!" I chuckled, squeezing her knee. "You don't have to worry about that. It's not as though I'm sitting here comparing; I wouldn't do that. Besides, I'm not dating you for your looks."

"I see."

It was two small words, but it dropped the temperature in the car palpably. The nervous lump rose back into my throat.

"I mean, there's so much more to us than that," I qualified hastily. "And there needs to be. Believe me, I learned that the hard way."

"What do you mean?"

This must be what it feels like to pick your way across a minefield in six-inch stilettos.

Her voice and expression were neutral, but I was still sweating. I started the car and chewed my lip as I groped for the right words.

"Things with Heather," I began. "They were always so shallow. Lots and lots of meaningless, animal sex."

"Lots?"

"Tons," I confirmed. "That was basically all we did."

"Sounds delightful."

The edge was back in her voice. I swallowed hard.

"It was fun at first," I admitted. "But after a while, it just wasn't very satisfying."

"Are you saying she got boring?"

My intuition told me there was a correct answer, but I had no idea what it was. I had the unpleasant feeling of blundering around in the dark. Up until now, everything with Erin had been so natural and relaxed. I drummed my fingers on the steering wheel as we crawled through the evening traffic. Assuming that I was right and there was no road map through this conversation, all I could do was be honest.

"I guess boring would be accurate," I said cautiously. "With you, it's different, though. Our connection runs deeper than that. I'd enjoy being with you even if we weren't having sex."

When she gave no reply, I blundered on. I could practically hear the crunch of the shovel as I dug myself deeper.

"I'm glad we are having sex, of course. The sex is awesome. I mean, I'm a red-faced male and I have needs."

Making sense was no longer a priority. I had to keep talking until I'd fixed whatever I'd somehow broken.

"Not that I'm some caveman and you're just here to fulfill my needs. I'm perfectly capable of seeing to them myself."

Her head whipped around to face me, and she raised an eyebrow. Belatedly registering the implications of my words, I nearly plowed into the car in front of us.

"Not that I'd go out looking for other outlets," I babbled.

I pulled into the restaurant parking lot. I'd been looking forward to this meal, but now I felt like I wanted to throw up.

"I'd never let anyone else near me. I mean," I took off my seatbelt and gestured at my crotch with both hands, "this dick has your name on it."

"Valet parking, sir?"

Erin's eyes widened. With a sinking heart, I followed her gaze over my shoulder. A young man in a red waistcoat was hovering by the driver's side window, smirking insolently. With some effort, I rearranged my face into a painful smile and wound the window down the rest of the way.

"Thanks," I gritted, thrusting my keys at him with more force than was necessary.

Feeling like I was walking through a nightmare, I stumbled from the car and groped in my wallet for a tip.

"Enjoy your meal, sir."

Nodding curtly, I took Erin's elbow and ushered her towards the entrance. From an early age, I'd learned that the only way to cope with humiliation was to keep moving. If you stopped to think about things, all was lost. Ultimately, the show must go on.

"You just gave him a hundred," Erin whispered.

Ah, nuts!

"I meant to," I said smoothly. "Valet parking is a valuable and underrated service."

The meal should have been wonderful. The surroundings were elegant, and the food was fantastic. We were presented with dish after dish of beautifully crafted sushi rolls and fresh, vibrant sashimi. Unfortunately, the atmosphere from the car never went away. I was so uncomfortable I barely noticed what I was putting in my mouth. At one point, I ate a large blob of wasabi that I'd mistaken for edamame.

I coughed into my napkin, eyes streaming. I could feel everyone in the restaurant staring at our table. Judging by Erin's blush as she handed me a glass of water, she could too. I contemplated leaving the little box in my pocket and saving my romantic declaration for another time. But what if I lost my nerve? It would either turn the evening around or it would blow up in my face and I could add it to the mounting list of public humiliations I had already endured that evening. I decided to roll the dice. As soon as the burning in my throat had dulled to a gnawing discomfort in my stomach, I drew the box out of my jacket pocket. Tentatively I placed it on the table and shoved it towards her. She gasped.

"Erin," I ventured. "There's something I want to ask you."

CHAPTER THIRTY-SEVEN

Erin

"Erin, there's something I want to ask you."

I gasped. Was he serious? I felt like I had vertigo. This whole date had been a crazy whirlwind of emotions. It was hard to imagine how the evening could have gone any worse.

The meeting with Heather had made me question everything I thought I knew about Nolan. And then every word out of his mouth since he picked me up seemed to confirm those suspicions. But now, he was presenting me with this.

The box was made of black velvet. It looked too wide and flat to be a ring box. I wasn't sure whether I was relieved or disappointed.

"Nolan," I breathed. "What is this?"

He gave a twitchy shrug and hunched his shoulders. It almost looked like he was trying to hide from me.

"It's a present," he muttered. "Well, maybe it's more of an offer. Or a question. Not *the* question, but it's still imp—"

He cut himself off with a rueful chuckle.

"It might be easier if you just open the box," he suggested.

I ran my hands along my thighs in a quick, discreet movement. My palms were slippery with sweat. Reaching out with trembling fingers, I picked up the box and opened the lid.

My eyes widened. I had been expecting jewelry of some sort, but Nolan obviously had a larger gesture in mind. The silver key was nestled innocuously on a bed of white cotton, its veneer burnished red in the dim light of the restaurant. A lump rose into my throat and tears prickled behind my eyelids.

"What do you think?"

Nolan was staring intently into his beer glass, but he kept peeking at me from under his lashes. I didn't know how to answer him. I was elated, terrified, and confused, all at once.

"I don't know what to say," I murmured.

"Did you say yes?" Maddie asked, fastidiously pouring syrup into each of the depressions on her waffle.

Madison had guessed something was wrong as soon as she picked me up for our monthly brunch date, and I'd finally cracked under her interrogation.

I reached into my purse and fished out the key. It was dangling from a sparkly cupcake keychain. My mom had put it in my Christmas stocking the year I opened Sticky Treats.

Maddie grinned.

"That's awesome, right?"

I tried to smile back.

"Yeah," I said tightly. "It's great."

"Ok, I know that look."

Maddie jabbed at me accusingly with a forkful of waffle. Golden droplets of syrup rained onto the tablecloth.

"Spill it," she commanded.

"I don't know." I poked morosely at my half-eaten stack of pancakes. "Don't you think it's too soon?"

Maddie snorted.

"Puh—lease! Claudie and I were already living together at this point."

"That's you, though," I pointed out. "You were happy to jump in with both feet."

She made a face at me.

"Is that your delicate and ladylike way of making a U-Haul joke?"

I chuckled.

"Of course not! I'm saying you're more spontaneous than I am. You've never been afraid to take risks."

"I don't see that you've taken any risk here," Maddie argued. "It's not like he's asked you to marry him or move across the country. You're not even giving up your apartment. These last few weeks you've been happier than I've seen you in years. Now, out of nowhere, you've got cold feet. What's going on?"

I set my jaw and took a deep breath. I should have remembered that my best friend was a human polygraph.

"I had a visitor a few days ago," I admitted.

Maddie's eyebrows drew together.

"Has Stirling been bothering you again?" she growled. "Because I swear, I'll rip his—"

"It wasn't Stirling," I interjected, cutting her off before she got too graphic. "It was Heather."

"The ex-girlfriend with the chili sauce?"

I nodded.

"The very same."

"What did she want?"

"To apologize."

Madison's eyebrows shot up.

"No way!" she exclaimed. "Did she find religion or something?"

I shrugged and sipped my coffee.

"Not quite. She said she was in a program of some kind, and she wanted to make up for all the shitty things she did."

Maddie whistled.

"That's a curveball and a half. What did you say?"

I held my hands wide.

"What could I say?"

"Oh, I don't know," Maddie mused, swabbing the last bite of waffle around her plate. "'That's very big of you. Here's the bill for my dry-cleaning?'"

I snorted.

"You're so charitable."

"I may be a little skeptical," she allowed. "What is this program, 'Skanky Hos Anonymous'?"

"I've no idea. She mentioned a spiritual advisor, but she didn't go into any more detail. Honestly, I didn't think to ask. The whole thing came out of nowhere. It threw me."

"Alright," Maddie reasoned. "Let's say Heather really is a reformed character. What does that have to do with you and Nolan?"

I bit my lip.

"She let some stuff slip."

Maddie frowned suspiciously.

"What kind of stuff?"

"Stuff about Nolan," I said miserably. "About what he was like when they were together. Apparently, she only did the things she did because he made her crazy. She said she wouldn't be able to sleep at night unless she warned me that—"

"Hah!"

Everything on the table jumped as Madison slapped her hand down triumphantly.

"I think that proves my point."

"It does?" I said uncertainly.

"Of course! This is 'shady bitch 101,' Erin. She was just trying to mess with your head. You didn't believe her, did you?"

"Well, some of it made sense," I protested. "Nolan flat out admitted that he dumped Heather because he got bored with her. A—and the other day, he sent me a message telling me he couldn't make our lunch date."

"Did he say why?"

"Yes," I mumbled. "He said he had an important meeting with a client that he couldn't get out of."

Maddie stared at me intently, pursing her lips.

"A corporate lawyer having to meet with a client? Sure, sounds fishy to me," she deadpanned. "He's having an affair. You should hire a PI immediately."

"Maddie!"

"Listen, Erin. It's real talk time."

Maddie pushed her plate aside and looked at me severely.

"When you and Stirling broke up, he left you with something."

"Emotional scars?" I suggested.

"No," she said gently. "He left a gigantic stick up your ass."

"I can't believe you just said—"

"Ah-ah. Not done. A gigantic stick that left you scared, insecure, and afraid to let go. I don't know what Nolan did, but he's been good for you. He's the only person who's even come close to wiggling that stick loose."

I narrowed my eyes.

"I'm not sure I like where this imagery is going. You think I'm overreacting, don't you?"

Madison's expression softened.

"Yes, I do," she said gently. "But that's only to be expected. You got seriously burned in your last relationship and you're still dealing with the fallout. It's only natural that something like this would rattle your cage."

"I—I guess," I stuttered, still unconvinced.

"You don't need to guess," she said firmly. "You know. If you truly think about it, you know. Does the guy Heather described sound anything like the guy you've been dating?"

"Not really, but—"

"Actions speak louder than words," Maddie insisted. "He just gave you the key to his apartment. Does that sound like a guy who's going to get bored and drop you? Because it sounds to me like a guy who's taking this very seriously. A guy who's in it for the long haul—and I think that terrifies you."

I stared at the table, twisting my napkin viciously in my hands. Madison's words were starting to have an uncomfortable ring of truth to them.

"Things are getting serious with Nolan, and you're scared," she continued. "You're all primed for something to go wrong."

"Maybe you're right," I conceded.

Maddie tossed her head and made a high-pitched noise of outrage.

"*Maybe* I'm right?"

"Ok!" I cried, holding up my hands in surrender. "You're definitely right. Forgive me for questioning your counsel, oh wise one."

"Hmm. I'll think about it. Seriously though." She reached out and took my hand. "If you let fear make your decisions for you, then Stirling's still calling the shots. He got away with it for too long while you were dating; there's no way he should get to live rent-free in your head now."

Her words hit me with the force of a gut punch. I'd never considered things that way before. Silently cursing myself as an obtuse moron, I squeezed my best friend's hand.

"Thanks, Maddie," I said hoarsely.

I felt emotionally drained, but somehow lighter. It felt good to know nothing was standing between me and Nolan except my own stupidity. I was grateful to have someone who knew me well enough to give me a good shaking before I fucked things up too badly. Perhaps everything would be ok after all.

"I don't know what I was thinking." I sighed. "I've been so caught up in—"

My sentence was cut off by the buzzing of my phone. I picked it up with a pleasant sense of anticipation bubbling in my chest. Maybe it was a message from Nolan. My excitement quickly evaporated.

"Oh no!" I groaned.

"What is it?" Maddie asked.

"It's an email from Heather."

To my surprise, Madison's face lit up in an evil grin.

"Open it," she urged.

"Now?"

"Yep. We'll compose a reply together. I've always wondered how many synonyms for 'bitch' I could come up with."

Shooting her a withering look, I tapped at my screen and opened the email. As soon as I saw the subject line, my stomach dropped. It simply read, "I thought you should see this."

CHAPTER THIRTY-EIGHT

Erin

The e-mail consisted of a wall of text and a video attachment. I couldn't process it. I had to read it three times before the words made any kind of sense.

> *Erin,*
> *I'm so sorry to have to do this to you. You seem like a totally nice person, so it kills me to be the one to break your heart. I didn't know whether I should show this to you at all. I thought maybe it would be better if you never knew. In the end, I asked my spiritual advisor and he said that you need to know so you can heal. Also, we have so much in common and we've been through so much together that we're almost like sisters. I think sisters should look out for each other, don't you?*
> *A well-meaning source, who wanted to remain anonymous, sent me a link to a certain website and I found the attached video. Honestly, I was like, in shock. Sure, Nolan is an asshole, but I never imagined that he'd stoop this low. He's always liked to record himself when he's doing you-know-what, so you probably know all about the cameras in the bedroom (the ones in the nightstand and on the picture rail above his bureau.) All the same, to upload the videos somewhere so public...*

Once again, I'm so sorry. I hate to see you humiliated like this. As someone whose business relies on good publicity, this is obviously devastating for you. Hopefully, you're not tempted to shoot the messenger, lol. I figure it's better that you know now, rather than allowing Nolan to make more of a fool of you than he already has. I appreciate that you'll need time to grieve, but I'm here for you if you need anything. Anything at all, I mean it.

Yours in sisterhood,

Heather xxx

A big part of me didn't want to click the link, but my fingers moved of their own volition. After a second of spooling, I was taken to a site that made me want to scrub my browser history with acid. It was plastered with triple X's and pop-ups advertising everything from flavored lube to crypto currency wallets.

When the video started playing, I was extremely glad my phone was muted. I recognized Nolan's bedroom immediately, and I had no difficulty identifying the writhing couple on the bed. I remembered that day. He'd surprised me with breakfast in bed. The tray was actually visible on screen. It was sitting innocently on the bedside table. We'd had croissants and then we'd...

"Erin!"

Maddie's voice sounded distant, as though she were calling from the other end of a tunnel.

"Erin, honey. What's going on? You're as white as a ghost."

The phone fell from my nerveless fingers and landed on the table with a clatter. Without saying a word, Maddie picked it up. Her eyes widened when she saw what was playing on the screen.

"Jesus!" she exclaimed, cheeks reddening.

If I'd been paying more attention, I might have reflected on how rare it was for Madison to blush.

"Erin, what the hell? This looks like some twisted revenge porn site."

"It's all in the e-mail," I muttered tonelessly.

I was feeling weirdly anesthetized. It was like being wrapped in a thick layer of foam padding. I watched indifferently as Maddie's eyes flew across the screen, the furrow between her eyebrows steadily deepening.

"I don't understand," she declared finally. "Is she claiming Nolan filmed the two of you having sex and then uploaded it to the internet?"

"Seems that way," I murmured dreamily.

There was an awkward pause.

"Did you know about the cameras?"

I shook my head.

"It's nothing to be embarrassed about if you did, Erin. A lot of people like to—"

"I didn't," I intoned. "He never said a word. Although," I snorted hysterically, "apparently I'm the only one who didn't know. Heather even knew exactly where they were."

"Ok," said Maddie, voice shaking slightly. "Ok. Let's just calm down."

"I am calm."

"No, you're not," she stated. "You're in shock. But I still say we shouldn't jump to conclusions. Something about this is seriously sus."

"Sus how?" I asked.

I still felt very distant from all this. I could have been asking Maddie to explain a complicated plot point on a TV show.

"It's a little too convenient," said Maddie darkly. "I find it difficult to believe that she just happened to stumble upon this. I wouldn't be surprised if this anonymous source doesn't even exist."

"Does that really make a difference? You saw the tape."

"You sure it's real?"

I swallowed convulsively and nodded.

"You can see our breakfast tray."

"Are you positive? From that angle, it could be—"

"Maddie!" I snapped. "Can you stop trying to make this better?"

"I'm not," she soothed. "I just don't want you to run off half-cocked, and I trust that bitch about as far as I could throw her."

I put my head in my hands and stared at the glass-topped table.

"I'm sorry," I mumbled contritely. "I just wish I knew what to do. I can't process this."

"Hm."

Maddie's eyebrows drew together, and her lips were pressed into a pensive line.

"Nolan at work right now?" she asked finally.

"I assume so."

I blinked stupidly at her as she began to gather her things.

"Wait. What're you—?"

Madison swung her bag onto her shoulder and huffed out a breath.

"We're going to put that apartment key to good use," she announced.

Nolan's apartment had undergone several subtle changes in the few weeks we'd been dating. The photos of his family had been joined by some framed photos of us—physical copies of the ones I'd posted on Instagram. There were also little traces of me everywhere: my sweater draped over the back of the couch, the banana Twinkies in the kitchen, my toothbrush on the sink. Each of these reminders created a pinprick of pain in my chest. I'd been stupid enough to let myself feel at home here.

The dreamlike state I'd experienced at the coffee shop had

faded as soon as we entered the apartment. Returning to the "scene of the crime" brought everything sharply into focus. I'd hated the numbness at the time but now I wanted it back. I stared at the bedroom door, unable to make myself go in.

"Eww! What the fuck?"

I jumped violently. I'd half-forgotten that Maddie was there.

"What's wrong?" I breathed.

I massaged my chest with one hand and tried to stop my heart from beating out of my ears. She bit her lip and glanced hesitantly between me and her phone.

"What?!" I demanded.

Was it possible that this could get any worse?

"There are more videos." Maddie grimaced. "I hate to say it, Erin, but it looks like your boy used this site a lot."

My legs threatened to give way, so I allowed myself to slump onto the couch.

"More videos of me?" I asked weakly.

She shook her head.

"No. Other girls. A lot of other girls, though. I guess he has some kind of weird—"

I held up a shaking hand. I didn't want to hear anymore. My eye fell upon the *Downton Abbey* boxset under the coffee table and tears welled up. I'd been such a fool. The couch moved as Madison sat down next to me and put her arm around my shoulders.

"I'm so sorry, honey," she said softly. "This was a bad idea; we should get out of here. Come and stay with me and Claudie until you feel better."

I closed my eyes and shook my head, trying to contain the sobs that were rising in my chest.

"I need to go in there," I said tightly.

"Need to go in where, sweetheart?"

I gestured with my head in the direction of the bedroom door.

"I have to know," I croaked.

Heather had told me where they were, but I needed to see them. I had to confront myself with it and make it real. The arm around my shoulders tightened into a squeeze.

"Want me to come in with you?" Maddie asked.

"No."

I stood up wearily.

"I have to do this myself. You go. I'll call you later."

The walk to the bedroom took a long time. It felt like I was walking, but the door wasn't getting any closer. It was like moving through invisible syrup. Finally, I reached for the doorknob, my sweaty palm sliding over the cool metal. With my stomach churning and my heart in my throat, I twisted the handle and pushed the door open.

CHAPTER THIRTY-NINE

Nolan

As soon as I opened the apartment door, I knew that Erin was there. Her perfume was never overpowering, but I was always conscious of it. It tickled pleasantly at the edges of my awareness. Whispering traces of roses and caramel suffused every room. I grinned. It was a nice smell to come home to. She was nice to come home to.

Before Erin, the idea that a woman could have let herself into my apartment without my knowledge would have been enough to bring me out in cold sweats. Now, it just made the place feel more like home. My smile widened when I spotted her coat slung over the back of the couch.

"Honey, I'm home!" I called jovially.

When I didn't get a reply or hear any sort of movement, I frowned.

"Erin?"

I threw my own coat and keys next to hers on the couch and moved towards the bedroom. When I saw the door slightly ajar, I got a warm, fluttering feeling in my stomach and my skin tingled with anticipation. I had been planning to surprise her by ordering takeout from her favorite sushi restaurant, but it looked like she had a different sort of evening in mind.

I pushed the door open and the butterflies in my stomach were doused in a torrent of ice water. Erin was sitting bolt upright on the edge of the bed with her eyes fixed on her lap. Her shoulders were stiff, and she was turning something over and over in her hands.

"Erin?" I ventured cautiously.

Her head snapped up as though attached to a wire. The uneasy feeling in my stomach increased tenfold. She'd been crying. Her eyes were red-rimmed, and she was pale and blotchy. She studied me incredulously as if she had no idea who I was or what I was doing there. This was starting to scare me.

"Erin, baby. What's wrong?"

"Are you actually going to pretend you don't know?"

Her voice was quiet, but it shook with anger.

"Er," I faltered. "I don't really need to pretend."

I put down my briefcase and moved to sit on the bed.

"Don't come near me!"

The pure loathing in her expression caused me to recoil. I stepped back and held up my hands.

"Ok," I began. "I can see you're very upset."

As soon as the words were out of my mouth, I cringed. I was using the exact tone Olivia used when Abby was having a tantrum. "Gentle parenting" probably wasn't recommended for use on girlfriends. On the other hand, I didn't know what else to do. None of this felt real. I wondered if I could step outside and come back in again. Maybe then, everything would be normal. Erin laughed harshly.

"Upset?" she scoffed. "Yeah, you could say I'm upset. What exactly were you expecting? That I'd be flattered? Turned on? Maybe you were just hoping I'd never find out."

"Erin—"

I closed my eyes and massaged my temples. My head was spinning.

"I'm truly lost here," I pleaded. "Can you just tell me what's going on?"

"Fine! You want it spelled out for you? How's this?"

She raised an arm and flung the object she'd been clutching at my feet. It was so small and light, it made no sound when it struck the bedroom carpet. More and more bewildered, I picked up the object and inspected it. It was a tiny black disc, no larger than a penny. When I squinted, I could just make out what looked like a lens in the middle.

"I found them," she spat.

"Er..."

"Don't play dumb, you deceitful bastard! You know exactly what that is."

"A camera?" I guessed. "I don't understand. Where did you—?"

"In the bureau and the bedside light, where you hid them. Don't bother denying it. I know about the videos too."

What the hell is happening?

"How could you? How could you do that after everything I shared with you? After everything that Stirling—"

Her voice cracked and she looked at me imploringly, eyes shining with tears. It broke my heart to see her like this, but I had no idea what she was talking about.

"What videos? You have to help me out, sweetheart. I still don't know what this is."

"Wow! I don't believe what I'm hearing," she breathed, outrage dripping from every syllable. "You're really committed to this, aren't you?"

"Committed to what?!" I exploded, my frustration finally boiling over. "Erin, you're not making any sense!"

"Here." She jabbed at her phone and then got up from the bed. I was dimly aware of my own phone vibrating in the pocket of my pants. "Enjoy! It's the last message you'll be getting from me."

She barged past me and out of the bedroom door. I hadn't been expecting her to move and she nearly bowled me over. As soon as I'd regained my balance I hurried after her. Catching up with her in the living area, I grabbed her by the arm.

"Erin, please," I begged. "Whatever this is, we can talk about it."

She froze in my grip.

"Take your hand off me."

She didn't sound emotional anymore, she sounded eerily calm.

"I mean it, Nolan. Don't ever touch me again."

I would have preferred it if she'd slapped me. In all the time I'd known her, she had never sounded so cold. It was as if all her feelings for me had simply been turned off. It scared me to death and created a horrible, gnawing ache in my chest. I dropped her arm and watched numbly as she put on her coat and threw her key on the coffee table.

I didn't move for a long time after the front door banged. I stood in the middle of the living area, staring at nothing, hoping this was a dream. Eventually, I stumbled into the kitchen, poured myself a generous measure of bourbon, and drank deeply. The alcohol scorched my throat and burned in my chest, but it did nothing for the knot in my stomach. The solution was clearly to drink more.

I still wasn't sure what had happened. I didn't know what to do, or what to think. I wanted to stop thinking altogether. After the third glass of bourbon, the sharp contours of my pain had begun to fuzz at the edges, and I remembered the message on my phone. Slumping into an armchair with a glass and the bottle, I stared blearily at the screen.

The message was a forwarded email with a video attachment. I nearly choked when I saw who the original sender was.

Sure, Nolan is an asshole, but I never dreamed that he'd stoop this low. He's always liked to record himself when he's doing you-know-what, so you probably know all about the cameras in the bedroom (the ones in the nightstand and on the picture rail above his bureau.) All the same, to upload the videos somewhere so public...

All the sordid pieces were falling into place. I had a horrible intuition about what I'd find when I clicked that link. I remembered the day I came back with Erin from the wholesaler's and noticed a strange smell in the apartment. I'd assumed the cleaning lady was trying out a new perfume. I couldn't recall ever giving Heather a key to my apartment, but what did that matter? There were a million different ways she could have gotten hold of one. She must have planted the cameras and then...

When I opened the video, my expectations were fulfilled down to the last sickening detail.

My fist closed convulsively around the phone as I fought the impulse to fling it across the room. I drained the bourbon glass and poured another measure. By this point, my hands were getting unsteady and some of the liquid sloshed over the side. I knew I shouldn't be drinking this much on an empty stomach, but I couldn't bring myself to care.

Just when I thought I'd finally shaken off my past, it had caught up to me and bitten me in the ass. Heather had popped up and sprayed poison over my newfound happiness like some spiteful crop-duster. What's more, Erin had believed her lies. I felt a surge of angry resentment and aimed a vicious kick at the coffee table. Dull pain shot up my leg and I took another large gulp of bourbon.

How could she think that of me?

Of course, I knew why. This kind of betrayal wasn't new to her. Stirling had humiliated her online and now I had too—well, my past had anyway, and that amounted to the same thing. She'd trusted me and I'd hurt her, just as I always knew I would. The thought of her on that disgusting website made me want to throw up. She'd shared something beautiful with me, and it had been stolen and turned into something sordid. Another casualty of the train wreck that was my life.

The room was swaying from side to side, and I was distantly aware that my cheeks were wet. When had I started crying? I hadn't cried since I was six.

I must have blacked out at some point. I woke up sprawled face down on the couch, with a foul taste in my mouth and a relentless pounding in my skull. I didn't want to open my eyes. Even though I was facing away from the window, I could sense daylight beating viciously at my eyelids. I shifted and winced as something hard dug into my chest.

Blinking groggily, I levered myself up onto my elbows. I had been lying on top of a framed photograph. It had been taken the day I surprised Erin at work and whisked her off for a picnic lunch. The memory of last night slowly trickled through the swirling brain fog and my stomach roiled. I ran my fingers over the surface of the photograph, wishing I could fall through it. I wanted to wind back time to the moment when Erin still smiled at me like that... and when I wasn't about to throw up.

After I'd finished heaving into the toilet bowl, I stood up to splash water on my face and realized that I was still clutching the photograph. Hugging it to my chest, I staggered across the living area and out onto the balcony. The cold morning air revived me a little, but I still felt like death.

No more than you deserve, you piece of shit!

I took my phone out and hovered over Erin's number. I thought about calling her. I could explain things, plead my case, beg for forgiveness. At the very least, I wanted to know whether she was ok.

Do you really think she wants to hear your voice?

You don't deserve forgiveness.

You're no good for her.

You destroy everything you touch. You can pretend all you like but, in the end, you turned out to be nothing more than your father's son.

I stood for a long time, staring between the photograph and my phone. All the while, the mocking voices in my head got louder and louder. Who was I kidding? I'd had my chance and I'd blown it. Despite all my efforts to protect her, my drama had swallowed her whole. She was better off without me, and she'd finally realized it. The only honorable thing I could do was let her go. My chest heaved and my face contorted but I refused to cry again. After several shuddering breaths, I put my phone back in my pocket and pitched the photograph off the balcony.

CHAPTER FORTY

Nolan

I winced as the insistent blaring of the horn sliced through my skull like a knife. Glancing up, I saw that the light had already turned green and the driver behind me was honking his impatience. Cursing, I gripped the steering wheel and stepped on the accelerator, squinting as the obnoxious glare of the sun pierced the windshield.

I hadn't planned on going to work that day. Initially, I was only persuaded to move from the couch when my body informed me in no uncertain terms that it was going to throw up. The idea of conquering my misery and my hangover to the extent where I could face the outside world seemed ludicrous. I was where I belonged. What better place for a piece of shit than wallowing at home, clinging desperately to the toilet bowl?

The thing that changed my mind was the bourbon bottle. Stumbling back from the bathroom with my stomach churning and my head pounding, I saw it on the kitchen counter. I'd drunk over half the bottle last night, but there was still enough in there to banish my hangover and bring me to a blissful state of numbness. I couldn't miss Erin when I was preoccupied with other things, like the room slowly revolving through 90 degrees, or the fact that I couldn't feel my face anymore. I was actually reaching for the bottle before I came to my senses and pulled my hand back.

Nuh-uh, Nolan. Slippery slope, my dude.

At that moment, as if fate was giving me a little extra poke, my phone buzzed. I'd been ignoring it all morning. The videos had somehow made their way onto all my social media feeds, and I'd been inundated with messages. There were even some official-looking ones from various platforms telling me that my content "violated their terms of service." Otherwise, reactions were split fairly evenly between disgust, laughter, and people asking whether I had been hacked.

I wondered what the senior partners would think. Would they finally decide they had to let me go? They'd tolerated my "antics" up until now, but this was a whole new level of scandal. I tried not to think about the fact that my grandmother and sister would probably have seen the videos by now. I'd always been reasonably confident that they would love me no matter what, but maybe this was a step too far. Liv might decide she didn't want me around Abby anymore. Why not? I'd already lost everything else that mattered.

These thoughts were sloshing queasily in my aching head when my phone went off again. Deciding I needed a distraction, I picked it up and glowered at the screen. I ignored the 87 Facebook notifications and my eye jumped straight to two messages from Alana, both sent within the last five minutes. The first just asked where I was and whether I was ok. The second was more colorful.

> *Alana*: If you don't get your lazy ass into work in the next hour, I'll call Granny V and tell her you're sick. Don't you fuckin' think I won't.

She was clearly worried. She had used her trump card. The idea of my grandmother hammering on my apartment door, armed with chicken soup, was too much. I messaged her back to tell her I was on my way—and that she could forget getting donuts with her coffee for the next month.

I regretted my life choices as soon as I stepped out of the door. The light was way too bright, and sounds were far too loud. Every time someone yelled or slammed a car door, I felt it through my teeth. I'm not sure how I made it to the office in one piece. I was so tired that my eyelids burned, and my mind kept drifting. Things with Erin had been amazing, and then Heather and her videos had appeared out of nowhere like some ghastly blip or glitch. I couldn't escape the idea that if I could somehow rewind time and start yesterday over, I could fix things.

Unfortunately, attempting to will yourself into the past can divert your attention from present problems. Problems like the delivery van you're about to rear-end at a busy intersection. I slammed on the breaks at the last minute and the impact threw me forwards with bone-jarring force. I slumped back in my seat, panting. My heart was hammering against my rib cage and the taste of vomit scorched the back of my throat. The car behind me didn't appreciate my sudden stop. I let my eyes drift closed as the screaming of a second angry horn pierced through the dense swirl of my mental fog. Adrenaline was coursing through my body and my temper was frayed, but I forced myself to take several deep breaths. I didn't need to add road rage or assault charges to my mounting heap of problems.

Things didn't improve once I had arrived at work. I'd just pressed the button for the elevator when I heard a shout behind me.

"Nolan! Buddy! Didn't expect to see you. You going up?"

Larry's exuberant yell hit me like the sound of a buzzsaw shearing through rusty metal. Somehow I managed a nod and a sickly grimace.

"Hey, Larry."

He gave me a sidelong glance as we entered the elevator, and heat rose under my collar.

He probably knows by now. Everybody knows. You've lost the woman of your dreams and now you're a laughing stock. It's the garnish on the shit sandwich.

I set my jaw and told myself I didn't care. My co-workers thought I was an asshole anyway. This probably hadn't even surprised them. Classic Nolan strikes again. I just had to put my blinkers on and get through it.

After a few seconds of awkward silence, Larry cleared his throat.

"You, uh. You look like hell."

"Thanks," I muttered wryly.

"You tie one on last night?"

"Something like that," I gritted.

Larry was irritating me more than usual. There was something in his manner I didn't like. His lips kept twitching with the suggestion of a smirk and his voice was bubbling with suppressed excitement. It was painfully obvious that he was dying to tell me something and I was sure I wouldn't like it.

"So, I hear things went south with that bakery woman."

I didn't respond. I just stared straight ahead. When he mentioned Erin, I had the overpowering urge to punch him in the face. It dawned on me that they had all seen her. Not just the strangers on that seedy website, but everyone I knew. My family, my co-workers, friends from high school. Every jackass I'd ever friended on Facebook or followed on Instagram had seen my Erin...

I wanted to be sick again.

What have I done?

"I'd actually been meaning to thank you."

"What?"

I started and blinked.

"I mean, I'm sorry it happened and all, but between you and me, I made out like a bandit."

"Larry..."

I pinched the bridge of my nose. He was making less sense by the second, and his conspiratorial leer was setting my teeth on edge.

"Larry. I'm not in the mood for guessing games. So, either tell me what you're talking about or shut the fuck up."

He stepped back, eyes widened in affronted surprise.

"Sheesh, man. Lighten up."

The elevator doors swished open, and I stormed out. Larry followed, yapping at my heels like a neglected terrier.

"I was gonna offer to cut you in, but if you bite my head off, I won't bother. Maybe I'll just pay bakery girl a visit now she's on the market. Looked like she was a demon in the—"

He never got to finish that sentence. It was cut off when I seized him by the front of his jacket and hurled him bodily against the coffee machine. The buzzing hum of office chatter ceased abruptly like someone had pressed a mute button. Larry's plump, wobbling face had gone white and he squirmed pathetically in my grip.

"C—c—calm down, Nolan," he stuttered. "It was just a joke, I swear."

"Ha-ha," I said flatly, not loosening my grip. "Now, listen up, dick-weasel. I'd advise you never to talk about Erin like that again. Unless you decide you don't particularly enjoy solid food."

By this point, sweat was beading on Larry's forehead and his voice had risen to a frantic squeak.

"Look, Nolan," he babbled. "I didn't mean anything. I swear it was just—"

"A joke," I interrupted. "Yeah, you said. Well, since you love jokes so much, why don't you tell me about this joke I'm apparently not in on?"

I glanced around. Several people had paused mid-task and were staring at me with files in their hands or coffee cups halfway to their mouths. One of the paralegals had been watering a spider plant on her desk. She'd drifted several inches wide of the mark and a steady stream of water was trickling onto a pile of deposition forms.

"There was a p—pool," Larry spluttered, still trying to twist out of my grip.

"What kind of pool?" I growled.

A flush crept over Larry's pale cheeks.

"People were placing bets on how long it would take for this thing with the cake woman to crash and burn. We didn't mean anything by it. We were just having fun."

Something ugly uncoiled in my chest. I wanted to squeeze Larry's throat until his eyes popped out of his stupid head, like one of those stress relievers.

"How many people were in on this little bit of fun?" I spat.

I looked around the room again. Somehow, everyone failed to meet my eye.

"Quite a few," Larry admitted. "Most people said you wouldn't last a week. I said you'd string it out for at least two months."

He gave me a beseeching smile. Was he hoping I'd be flattered? My grip on his jacket slackened and he sagged with relief. My anger evaporated and I felt cold and empty. Turned out I could be relied on for something. People were sure I'd screw up; they were prepared to stake money on it. At least I'd beaten the odds.

"How much did you win?" I asked tonelessly.

"Seven hundred dollars." He laughed weakly. "Guess the first round's on me this Friday."

"Congratulations," I mumbled.

Turning from Larry, I walked through the open-plan workspace as if in a dream. Multiple pairs of eyes burned into my back, but I was past caring. By the time I got to my office, I was seriously considering drafting my resignation letter on the spot.

CHAPTER FORTY-ONE

Nolan

Alana was at her desk, eyes glued to her laptop. She was wearing earbuds and didn't immediately register my entrance. I didn't bother to greet her. Dumping my coat and briefcase on the floor, I walked around my own desk and threw myself into the high-backed leather chair. From that vantage point, I could see Alana's screen. I froze.

There was a video playing. I couldn't hear the audio, but I didn't need to. The setting and the actors were horribly familiar. Well, one of the actors was. To my overwhelming shame, I didn't recognize the girl.

Watching myself writhing naked on Alana's screen was even more humiliating than the office pool. I saw myself through the cool, detached gaze of my PA. A weird specimen on a microscope slide, fascinating but repulsive. Above all, I felt betrayed. Alana had been one of the few people I could confide in without fear of judgment. Now she'd turned against me too.

I watched the video for a few more seconds, until my mortification twisted itself into a form I could cope with. Unfortunately, it chose rage.

Storming over, I plucked an earbud from Alana's ear and

slammed my hand on the desk. Uncharacteristically, my unflappable PA jumped.

"What the fuck?" She panted, massaging her ear.

"Me, apparently," I snapped. "Can't be sure, though. Not used to seeing myself from this angle. Having a good laugh, were you? I suppose you had a good chuckle over the pool too. I'd ask if you won anything, but I already know Larry scooped the grand prize."

I stomped across the room and kicked the Yucca plant over. It fell with a soft rustle, spilling a comet streak of dirt across the carpet.

"Or maybe you were appraising my technique," I shouted. "Replenishing your arsenal of devastatingly witty quips. I hired you as my PA, but you deliver the whole package, don't you? Filing, appointments, and acerbic director's commentary whenever my life takes a particularly shitty turn. It's nice to know that when I'm really feeling down, there's somebody here to kick me in the nuts."

I underscored my tirade by stamping viciously on the upturned plant pot, reducing it to tiny plastic shards. By the time I was done, I was sweating, dizzy and wheezing like an asthmatic bull.

Throughout my entire rant, Alana had stayed silent. Now that I'd run out of steam, she plucked the earbud from her other ear and stared at me with an infuriating air of calm.

"Are you done?"

"I—"

"I was about to explain what I was doing, but if you'd rather rant some more, I can wait."

Impotent rage is usually helpless in the face of self-possession. I gaped at her stupidly.

"Hate to deflate your ego, *jefe*, but there's a long list of things I'd rather do than watch my boss doin' the horizontal hula."

"Then why did you—?"

She held up a hand.

"As you pointed out a moment ago, I'm your PA. And despite what you just did to Audrey IV, I still consider myself your friend."

She scowled at the spectacle of her felled Yucca. I rubbed guiltily at the back of my neck. Audrey IV had joined the firm when Alana had. I once asked her what had happened to Audreys I through III. She had given me a withering look and pointed out that I and II were fictional. She eventually admitted that she forgot to water III.

"As your friend," she continued, "I thought I should start figurin' out who put these videos together. Not like I had anything else to do while I waited for you to quit feeling sorry for yourself and pull your head out of your ass."

"Y—You don't think I uploaded—?"

"Like to think I know you better than that," she said simply.

I felt a lot of emotions at once. Gratitude, remorse, relief. I tried to say thank you or at least apologize, but I'd lost the ability to make words happen. Alana gave me a small smile and I knew that I didn't need to.

"Besides," she turned back to her screen and snorted derisively, "I know a crappy deepfake when I see one."

"Deepfake?"

I grabbed the client's chair from the other side of my desk and pulled up next to her.

"You mean this isn't real?"

"You gonna tell me you ever met that woman in your life?"

I made a face.

"I don't recognize her," I admitted. "But I assumed I must have been really drunk."

Alana rolled her eyes and shook her head.

"Disturbing insights into your personal life aside, it's easy to spot if you know what you're looking for. The video of you and Erin, on the other hand—that looked genuine."

She shot me a sympathetic grimace and squeezed my knee. I put my head in my hands and groaned.

"This still feels unreal. I'm finding it hard to accept that someone shot a sex tape of me without me knowing and then uploaded it to the internet."

Alana gaped at me.

"Are you serious, *jefe*? What century are you living in? Give me two minutes on Google and I can Fed Ex an HD camera small enough to hide inside any household appliance you want. Then it's just a matter of breakin' into your apartment and hiding it. Come on. You're a lawyer; you should know this."

"Exactly," I grumbled. "I'm a lawyer, not James Bond."

"You don't have to be James Bond. More likely you're a twitchy suburban housewife who doesn't trust her nanny. Anyway, I'm guessing once they had the real footage, whoever did this just recut it a bunch of times with other women's heads on Erin's body. Didn't you wonder why the same breakfast tray kept appearing in shot?"

This was a lot to take in. I rubbed a hand over my forehead. I could feel a fresh headache gathering my temples.

"Honestly, I didn't watch them all," I sighed. "I was more than a little preoccupied with the first one I saw. I care a lot less about the others. Although honestly, I'm amazed she went to this much trouble."

"She?"

I gave her a meaningful look. Alana had always been quick on the uptake. It didn't take long before understanding dawned.

"Ah."

She blew out a breath.

"I usually applaud that level of determination and initiative but..."

She trailed off and shook her head.

"What have I done?"

I leaned back in the chair and put my hands over my face. I

heard Alana rustling in a drawer. Seconds later she handed me a packet of Tylenol.

"I assume Erin didn't take it very well," she said softly.

"Yeah, you could say that. She, uh. She never wants to see me again."

I started to stand up and move to the water cooler. Alana pushed me back down with a firm hand on my shoulder and went herself. I gratefully accepted the paper cup of blissfully cool water and tossed back two of the painkillers.

Alana sat back down and gave me a hard stare.

"Please tell me you at least tried to explain things to Erin."

"I tried to tell her it wasn't me," I said dejectedly. "But she didn't believe me. To be honest, I think she was too angry to even hear me."

I leaned back in my chair and began to shred the empty paper cup.

"It doesn't matter anyway."

Alana's mouth fell open.

"Excuse me? Did I hear that right? Your psycho ex breaks into your apartment, films you and your girlfriend without your consent, then posts the footage to a revenge porn site and all your social media—alongside some laughably sloppy deep fakes, I might add."

Alana had started pacing. She always got very animated when she was annoyed.

"As if that wasn't bad enough," she continued, "she frames you for it. She destroyed your relationship and humiliated you in front of all your friends and family. You're trying to tell me that doesn't *matter*?"

Her voice had steadily risen until it was almost a shriek. I winced, pressing two fingers to the side of my head.

"I'm saying," I said doggedly, "that Erin would have found out sooner or later that I'm no good for her. I've destroyed every relationship I've ever been in. Erin's better off out of my drama. I can't hurt her anymore now. I know what

Heather did was bad, but maybe it was karma. Maybe I had it coming."

The slap caught me off guard and nearly knocked me from my chair.

"Ow!"

I reached up and rubbed at the side of my face. My ears were ringing, and my cheek burned. Apparently "mean right hook" could also be added to Alana's formidable skillset.

"What the hell was that for?!"

"Someone needed to knock some sense into that thick head of yours."

Alana folded her arms and glared down at me, eyes blazing.

"No offense, *jefe,* but you are one self-centered, self-indulgent asshole sometimes."

"Me? I—"

"Exactly!" she said. "Me. I. You are thinking about no one but yourself."

I goggled at her, temporarily speechless with outrage. The accusation was so unfair. Letting all this go and not pursuing Erin felt about as far from selfish as I could get.

"If something in your rat's maze of a brain has decided you deserve this, that's fine," Alana snapped. "But what about Erin? Did she have it coming too?"

I didn't get much further than opening my mouth. Alana plowed on relentlessly.

"You weren't the only one on those videos, you know. You're not the only one Heather humiliated. Everything that you're going through right now—the heartbreak, the embarrassment, the betrayal. Erin's going through it too. If you're prepared to just sit there and let that go, then you're not the man I thought you were."

Fuck.

Alana's words floored me. She was right. I hadn't thought about it, not really. I hadn't allowed myself to.

Bet she's a demon in the sack.

Larry's comment floated through my mind. It echoed around my skull until one voice became a million. I imagined a million leering Larrys clicking onto that website and perving over Erin. I shuddered. For the first time, it dawned on me that she was probably imagining it too. I'd been so focused on my pain and what I deserved that I had barely given a thought to what she must be going through.

I had no business asking Erin to take me back, but I owed it to her to make Heather pay for what she'd done. Perhaps I could get the videos taken down, do some damage control before things got out of hand. If I hadn't spent so much time wallowing, I could have made a start on that before now. I wanted to kick myself

"Fuck," I groaned. "Jesus, Alana, I've been so stupid."

For the second time in 24 hours, hot tears prickled behind my eyelids. I squeezed my eyes shut, fighting to hold them back. I felt the firm pressure of Alana's arms around me and for a few moments, I clung to her fiercely.

"It's ok, *querida*," she soothed, rubbing gentle circles on my back.

It felt good to let go. For a few moments, I let myself be comforted. Once the burning behind my eyes had subsided and the raw ache in my throat had dissipated, I drew back and took a shaky breath. I still felt miserable, but I had a goal. It was enough to pull me together.

"Feel better?"

I looked up and gave Alana a feeble smile.

"A little," I croaked. "You were right, as usual. I was being a moron."

I took one of her hands in both of mine.

"I can always count on you to kick my ass when I need it."

"Eh," she breezed. "It's what I'm here for."

"Although," I touched my throbbing cheek experimentally, "I prefer it when it's a metaphorical ass-kicking. I didn't expect someone that tiny to hit so hard."

She drew herself up to her full height and narrowed her eyes menacingly.

"You're just lucky I didn't take a leaf out of my *abuelita's* book. You haven't known pain until you've experienced *la chancla*."

"The what?"

"Never mind. The important question is, what now?"

"Well," I mused. "I need to work out how she broke into the apartment. I can speak to building security. Get them to go over the tapes. As for all the computer stuff, I'm a little out of my depth there," I admitted.

Alana's mouth twitched into an enigmatic smile.

"I might know someone who can help with that. Just give me a minute to send a message. Which reminds me."

She paused in the act of tapping at her phone and gave me a significant look.

"Do you think you should contact Erin? Let her know what we're doing."

My stomach tightened. I wanted to speak to Erin very much. Even thinking about her created a yearning pang that hit me like physical pain. But, even if she was prepared to listen, I still had no idea what I'd say to her. I wouldn't know how to begin. More importantly, once I'd started talking to her, I'd probably forget my resolution. Just because I'd agreed to confront Heather, it didn't mean I should ask Erin to take me back. She deserved better than the shiftless son of Gabriel Reid. Nothing could persuade me otherwise.

Alana sensed my hesitation and sighed.

"How about I poke her on Facebook?" she offered. "There's no reason she won't talk to me, and I might be able to find out how she's doing."

"Ok," I said reluctantly. "Don't tell her anything yet. Just check in with her."

"Sure, but eventually you're going to have to— What the fuck?"

"What? What is it? Is she alright?"

I was at her side in an instant, leaning over her shoulder to look at her phone.

"There's a message on the Sticky Treats page. It says they're closed until further notice. You don't think she might—"

"No."

I straightened up and waved the thought away firmly.

"Erin's business means everything to her. She'd never let something like this affect things. No matter what happens, she'll never give up Sticky Treats."

CHAPTER FORTY-TWO

Erin

"You're selling Sticky Treats?"

"I don't know. I'm thinking about it."

I wrapped my hands around my coffee mug and stared listlessly out of the window. It was a bleak, gray morning and Maddie's front yard looked sad and water-logged. It had rained heavily throughout the night, reducing the breadcrumbs on the bird table to an unpleasant, anemic sludge.

I'd been staying with Maddie and Claudia since I stormed out of Nolan's apartment. They'd welcomed me with open arms and tried to take my mind off things. It hadn't worked. Maddie seemed confident that all I needed to bounce back from this was time. But now a week had gone by and, if anything, I felt worse. I was more depressed than I had ever been.

They tried to be tactful around me, but I wasn't blind. They were newlyweds in love. Their obvious happiness suffused them both with a revolting glow. I was happy for them, but I felt my loss all the more acutely whenever I caught them snatching a tender moment.

Rational Erin spent a lot of time telling me that Nolan was

clearly never the guy I thought he was, and it was silly to miss something I had never truly had.

Rational Erin could go jump in a lake. A lake infested with mutated sharks. Laser beams were optional.

I missed Nolan like crazy. The Nolan who had tucked me into bed and panic-bought every single breakfast item from the market. The Nolan who begged for gummi bears at the wholesaler's. Above all, I missed the Nolan who made me feel safe and secure and loved.

My usual response to emotional crises was to throw myself into work. Now, thanks to Nolan's little stunt with the videos, I didn't even have that option.

"You can't do that."

I started. I'd been so absorbed in my miserable reflections that I'd lost track of the conversation. I'd been doing that a lot lately. I dragged my gaze away from the front yard and focused on Maddie. She was sitting at the dining table, nursing her own mug of coffee, and wearing her best "you're being silly" expression.

"Why not?" I asked dully. "Have they changed the law in some way I don't know about?"

"You know exactly what I mean," said Maddie sternly. "Don't try to ward me off with pedantry. Do you remember me telling you about that guy I dated who tried to mansplain the difference between 'less' and 'fewer'?"

"Hm," I murmured. "I did wonder if they ever found his body."

"Ha-ha. My point is, giving up Sticky Treats makes no sense. This was your dream. It was going so well too."

"Yeah, really well," I snorted. "First it led me to Stirling and then to Nolan. Nolan, who managed to convince me that he was different. Face it, Mads, I'm a jerk magnet."

"You are not," Maddie intoned. "You've just had some bad luck with guys. That doesn't mean their shitty behavior reflects on you, and it certainly has nothing to do with Sticky Treats."

"Doesn't it?" I demanded fiercely.

I could feel the frustration gathering, tight and painful in my chest. Maddie didn't get it. She never had.

"Stirling was right," I declared bitterly. "People look at Sticky Treats, at what we sell, and they make assumptions about me. I was a naïve idiot to think it could ever be any different."

"*Stirling was right?*" Maddie squeaked. "Erin, did you hear yourself? I can't believe that, after all this time, you're still letting that conniving, sanctimonious hemorrhoid get in your head. It was bullshit he cooked up to control you and it's still working. This is the 21st century. You can't possibly believe that people still think like that."

"You think so? You think you know it all, but you don't know shit."

I slammed my mug down on the dining table a little harder than I'd intended and some of the coffee slopped over the side. Madison winced. I felt a stab of remorse and tried to blot at the small, dark puddle with my sleeve.

"I'm sorry." I sighed. "I know you're trying to help. It's just..."

I gestured helplessly, as though attempting to pluck the right words out of the air. Eventually, I blew out an exasperated breath and pulled my phone from my jeans pocket. I navigated to my e-mail inbox and slid the handset across the table.

"Here," I said softly. "Take a look at those. Feel free to open them. I've stopped bothering."

Blinking in confusion, Maddie picked up the phone. As she scrolled, I watched a myriad of expressions flit across her face. Her eyes narrowed, then widened. After a while, her whole face scrunched up with distaste.

"Eww!" she exclaimed, swiping vigorously at the screen. "Why do guys do that? Half of them haven't even bothered to get a good angle. And seriously, if you're going to send someone a picture of your... private garden, you could at least make sure you've trimmed the bushes. Ugh!"

She delicately placed my phone face down on the table.

"I think I need to get my eyeballs bleached."

"Lovely, isn't it?" I said dryly. "I'm just glad I thought to turn off comments on my website and Facebook page."

Maddie shuddered and sipped her coffee.

"There are so many of them. Is this all because of those videos?"

"The videos made it worse."

I squirmed and tried to ignore the flush that was creeping up my neck. I twisted in my chair so I wouldn't have to meet my best friend's eye.

"I always got one or two a week," I admitted. "It wasn't nice, but I could deal with it. This has just been too much, though. It hasn't been this bad since my website got vandalized."

"I had no idea."

Maddie's voice quavered a little. I wasn't used to her sounding so shocked.

"I wasn't trying to gross you out or make you feel bad," I continued. "But I—I wanted to show you that this wasn't all in my head."

Without saying a word, Maddie got up and moved behind me. Her arms went around my shoulders and her hair fell across my face in a ticklish, blonde curtain. My self-control crumbled as she held me. My eyes welled up and my throat constricted.

"I know it sounds dumb," I said tightly, trying to hold myself together. "I look at them all day, have done for years. It's different when it's work, though. There's—there's a barrier there, a boundary. Plus, I know who and what I'm looking at before I open the picture. I guess, in a way, I've... consented?

These pictures make me feel dirty. And these guys, the things they say..."

Even thinking about it made me sick to my stomach. My throat shut down completely, strangling any further words. Maddie felt the tell-tale quaking of my shoulders and hugged me harder.

"I—I can't do it anymore, Maddie," I choked. "I'm tired."

We stayed like that for a long while. Madison didn't say anything. She simply held me and let me cry myself out. When my shoulders had stopped heaving and my sobs had calmed down, she straightened up and went to fetch me a glass of water. I shivered when her weight left my back, like someone had yanked the covers off on a chilly morning.

"What will you do now?" she asked, handing me the glass.

I took a small sip and shrugged.

"Not sure yet," I confessed. "I think I'll go stay with my parents for a couple of weeks, and then, I don't know. I guess I could go back to textbook illustration."

Maddie pulled a face.

"I thought that always bored you."

"Kind of," I conceded. "But at least I always felt like I was doing something useful. I don't think anyone will ever save the world with chocolate penises."

"Maybe not," Maddie allowed. "You made a lot of people smile, though, and that's worth more than you think." Her expression became mischievous. "I don't think anyone will ever forget my wedding cake."

"Especially not your grandma Mabel," I replied, smiling despite myself.

Madison snorted.

"Sadly, I think everyone's most vivid memory of my wedding will be her loudly asking me how I expected my guests to be comfortable chowing down on an enormous, cream-filled hoo-ha."

"Actually," I countered, "I think the thing everyone remembers is the answer you gave her. I thought she was going to faint."

When we had recovered from our fit of giggling, Maddie wiped her eyes and reached for my hand.

"You've made up your mind, haven't you?"

It wasn't a question. When you know someone well enough, there are things you can just sense. I swallowed and nodded.

"This thing with Nolan was the last straw. I'm going to go away and clear my head for a couple of weeks, then I'm putting Sticky Treats on the market."

CHAPTER FORTY-THREE

Nolan

"You're gonna wear a hole in that carpet."

At the sound of Alana's voice, I stopped pacing and glanced nervously at my watch.

"I'm guessing it's five minutes later than it was the last time you looked."

"I'm sorry," I muttered. "I'm being annoying, aren't I?"

"Extremely," said Alana smoothly, eyes still fixed on her computer screen. "I don't get why you're so worked up about this."

"I think I've been worked up about a lot of things lately," I admitted, perching on the edge of my desk.

I tried to look casual and relaxed, but I couldn't work out what to do with my limbs. I experimented with crossing and uncrossing my legs, eventually settling on stretching them out and contemplating the toes of my shoes.

"Honestly, I'm—I'm not sure this is such a good idea."

I felt Alana rolling her eyes.

"Thought you were set on nailing Heather for this."

"I am."

"In which case," Alana reasoned, "you need all the evidence

you can get your hands on. You said yourself that the security tapes won't hold up in court."

She was right about that one. The building's security footage had revealed a strange woman entering my apartment. Unfortunately, large dark glasses and a headscarf made it impossible to get a positive ID. I'd be prepared to bet any amount of money that the intruder was Heather, but it made no difference. In my experience, judges and juries didn't care how sure you were if you had no proof.

"I do need evidence," I agreed. "I'm just not sure your girlfriend is the one to provide it. Not that Jess isn't great, of course."

I backpedaled hurriedly, noticing that Alana had gotten that dangerous look in her eye.

"She's one of the smartest people I've ever met. But she's also a high school guidance counselor. I don't see how that helps me. I'm not looking to sit down and rap about my problems."

"Guidance counselor is her day job, and it's not why I've asked her to come in. Jess has," she paused delicately, "other talents. Talents she's agreed to use to help us figure out what the deal is with those videos."

I coughed nervously.

"She's seen the videos?"

"Of course. She had to."

I ran a finger under my collar, blushing from the tips of my toes to the roots of my hair. If I'd been a cartoon character, there would have been steam coming out of my ears.

"Don't sweat it. She's seen worse."

"Thanks, I think. So, you're saying that by day Jess is a guidance counselor, and by night she's some kind of ninja techno-whiz?"

"I think if you asked her, she'd say she preferred to be called a hacker."

My eyes widened.

"Ok, now I know this is a bad idea."

"Relax," Alana soothed. "Hacking has a bad rep, but it's not all credit card fraud and corporate espionage. Jess is a white hat hacker."

"A what?"

"Have you even started that *Criminal Minds* boxset I loaned you? Never mind. Just trust me on this one. She uses her powers for good."

I got up restlessly and moved over to the window. Rolling my shoulders, I took a deep breath, but the knot in my stomach continued tightening. It wasn't that I didn't trust Alana, it was more that I'd just been through the week from hell. It was hard to trust anything anymore.

Those damned videos were following me everywhere like a curse. Half my friends and family weren't speaking to me, and I'd become a virtual pariah at work. The senior partners had called me into a meeting and informed me they had "certain expectations regarding the public conduct of their firm's representatives." Fortunately, my case history worked in my favor, but they made no bones about the fact that I was "on thin ice."

Six months ago, this would have been devastating. Now it barely registered. Losing Erin made everything else matter much less. A doctor once told me that bodies can only process so much pain at one time. If you tripped and broke your ankle, the headache you'd been nursing all day would probably magically disappear. It was the best analogy I could think of. With Erin gone, everything registered like a paper cut to someone with a major stab wound.

After a moment, Alana joined me at the window.

"Have you heard from her?" she asked, showing off her uncanny ability to read my mind.

"No, nothing."

I refrained from mentioning that I had been to her apartment building and driven by Sticky Treats several times in the last week. I'd been avoiding my own apartment as much as possible. I'd never really had my heart broken before. Now it had happened, I was discovering that homes gathered memories like sticky surfaces accumulated lint. Erin and I had only been dating for a couple of months, but she had left her mark on every corner of my apartment. The couch where we'd always watched TV. The kitchen where we'd baked those cupcakes. The bed where we'd...

Everywhere I looked, there was something to remind me I missed her. I took refuge in aimless drives around the city. Drives that always ended up with me "coincidentally" driving past Sticky Treats or parked outside Erin's apartment.

Of course, it didn't do me any good. The lights were always off in the apartment and the windows of Sticky Treats were firmly shuttered.

The only thing that had prevented me from losing it completely and turning into a pathetic stalker was the fact that Olivia and Granny V had stuck by me throughout this whole ordeal. They had even defended me to the rest of the family. My grandmother usually occupied the role of peaceful mediator, but all bets were off when my great aunt Norah called me a "perverted degenerate." Granny V had eviscerated her, not to mention "the horse she rode in on."

"Psst! I'm here. Are you ready for me?"

Alana and I turned from the window and did a mutual double-take. If Jess hadn't spoken, I might not have recognized her. On a normal day, she was exactly what I'd expect from Alana's girlfriend: hair a different color every time I met her and an intimidating array of piercings. In terms of clothing, she usually opted for torn jeans and t-shirts with provocative slogans. Today, she'd pulled off a jaw-dropping transformation. Her hair was mahogany brown and pulled into a sleek bun at the back of her head. Most of the piercings were gone and she wore a dark gray business suit, all sharp creases and hard angles. It was a severe look, but it suited her. The effect was only slightly ruined when she giggled at our dumb-struck faces.

"What do you think?" She grinned proudly. "I'm *incognito.*"

At least she isn't insisting on codenames. This would have been Alana's surprise birthday party all over again.

By way of a reply, Alana slunk towards her and closed the door with her foot. Whatever Jess had been about to say next was swallowed when Alana pushed her against the wall and kissed her hungrily. I coughed, suddenly becoming very absorbed in organizing the papers on my desk.

"If I'd known it was going to have this effect on you, I'd have shown it to you last night." Jess chuckled, slightly out of breath from the kiss.

"Maybe I should take an early day," Alana purred. "Then we could—"

I cleared my throat pointedly.

"Hate to interrupt, ladies, but I need you to focus. Jess is here for a reason."

Alana sighed dramatically, but she pulled back from her girlfriend and tugged her towards a chair.

"Ok, baby," she said. "What've you got for us?"

Jess made herself comfortable, which, for her, meant she had a device in her hands. In this case, it was a Nintendo Switch. One of Jess's many quirks was that she was more comfortable making eye contact with a screen than a person. The fact that she was glued to *Mario Kart* did not necessarily mean that she wasn't listening. I'd idly wondered how that worked with her job. By all accounts, the kids found her incredibly easy to talk to.

"First of all," she began, tilting her chair back, "I think I need some industrial browser bleach after poking around that website. It had more pop-ups than one of those Bible stories books they give you at Sunday school. Not to mention, back doors for days. Seriously shady stuff."

I shifted in my seat.

"Yeah, I got that impression," I said tightly.

Jess screwed up her pretty face and cursed under her breath.

"Stupid blue shell! Your videos have quite a lot of views, by the way. Which I guess isn't really a good thing, now that I think about it."

There was an awkward pause in which she shot me an apologetic smile.

"On the plus side, the production values are terrible. There aren't that many clear shots of you. Not of your face, anyway. Although, while we're on the topic, if you've never actually had that mole checked out, you should probably—"

Alana took pity on me.

"*Cielo*," she interjected gently, "I think what Nolan actually wants to know is whether you got anywhere with findin' out who uploaded the video."

"Ah. Right. That."

Jess stuck her tongue out of the corner of her mouth and leaned to one side as her kart navigated a hairpin bend.

"I've got good news and bad news."

My knees had begun to jiggle under the desk. Noticing for the first time, I planted my feet more firmly on the floor.

"The good news is, we can be fairly sure that you didn't upload the video. The bad news is, it's hard to say who did."

"How do you mean?" I asked, trying to school the disappointment from my face.

Jess took a deep breath and bit her lip.

"Hmm. How to explain," she mused. "Do you know what an IP address is?"

"Not entirely," I admitted. "I've heard the term before, but I'd have a tough time explaining what it was."

"Well," Jess said. "The simplest way of putting it is that an IP address is a string of numbers assigned to each device connected to a network. Your IP address is assigned to you for as long as your browsing session lasts. Think of it as an ID badge for your computer when it's on the net. In *very* simple terms, it's internet traffic control. It identifies the links in a network, allowing data to get where it needs to go. Anything you do on the internet, like sending an e-mail, or uploading a video, can potentially be tracked to your IP address."

I could feel my brain beginning to dribble from my ears. I wasn't what you'd call a Luddite, but computers had never been my thing.

"So, what you're saying is that if someone wanted to know if I'd uploaded a video, they'd see if it had been uploaded from my IP address. Is that what you did?"

Jess glanced up from her handheld and gave me a pitying look. To my horror, it was the same look Olivia gave Granny V when she mispronounced GIF or referred to "the Facebook."

"It's a little more complicated than that," she said. "You see, there are lots of occasions where people would rather their internet activity couldn't be traced back to them. It could be anything from wanting to see what was on British Netflix to watching skeevy porn, or even regular porn if you're the sort of person who gets embarrassed about that stuff. The point is video hosting websites usually take certain steps to protect the privacy of their users. In most cases, IP addresses are encrypted. That's where I come in."

She leaned farther back in her chair and favored us with a shit-eating grin.

"I was able to work my magic to punch through the encryption and peek behind the curtain."

I crossed my legs. I'd had enough of people peeking behind my curtain.

Probably best not to ask how illegal this is.

"This is where we get to the bad news," Jess went on. "Those videos bounced their way through multiple proxy servers before they reached their destination."

I stared at her blankly and she gave an exasperated sigh.

"It's a way of covering your tracks," she explained. "People use proxy servers when they want to conceal where data originated from."

"And in this case, it means you can't tell me where the video came from?"

"It's not all bad news, if you think about it," Alana put in. "We can't prove who did it, but we can prove that someone put a lot of effort into hiding it."

"Good point," I murmured, rubbing my hand over my chin. "Jess, this multiple server thing—it's advanced stuff, right?"

Jess gave a one-shouldered shrug.

"Relatively, I guess. You wouldn't need to be Oracle, but you'd need some idea of what you were doing. I'm fairly sure you couldn't do it. No offense."

"What are you thinking?" Alana asked.

She wrapped her arms around Jess's shoulders and rested her chin on her head, eyeing me curiously.

"I'm not sure," I muttered, standing up and thrusting my hands into my pockets. "I'm not saying Heather's dumb, but I don't remember her being particularly good with computers."

"You think she had help?"

"Yep," I said darkly. "And I think I know who from."

CHAPTER FORTY-FOUR

Erin

"Thanks for doing this, Mads. I'm not sure I could've faced it on my own."

Maddie shot me a smile as she glanced over her shoulder and maneuvered into a parking space.

"Don't mention it, sweetie. I've always got your back. You know that."

The wind whipped around us as we stepped from the car. It was only September, but there was already a hint of fall chill in the air. Locked up tight with the shutters down, Sticky Treats looked sad. As I faced it from across the street, I experienced a stab of guilt. I imagined that the building itself was looking at me reproachfully, asking why I had abandoned it. Pulling my coat tighter against the cold, I shook my head. I needed to get it together.

Maddie's arm linked itself through mine and squeezed gently.

"Are you really sure about this, Erin?"

Setting my mouth in a firm line, I gave a jerky nod.

"I am," I declared. "I'm not saying I won't miss it. Sticky Treats has been my life for more than three years. But it's time to move on. I have to do what's right for me."

It was time to face facts. I wasn't cut out to work in this industry. The world of adult confectionery was too hot for me. When I started it had been fun. I honestly never saw my creations as daring or risqué. As far as I was concerned, I was simply translating my artistic skills into something lighthearted and joyful. It was different now. Between them, Stirling and Nolan had contaminated it. They had made it dirty. Ever since the videos had gone online, I could hardly bear to leave the house anymore. It felt like everyone was looking at me. I didn't want to live like that. It was over. I'd given Mrs. Pasternak notice on my lease, and today we were clearing out my personal belongings. The packing and selling of equipment could be dealt with later.

I felt movement next to me as Maddie sighed.

"I remember how excited you were when you opened this place," she reflected. "It feels like such a waste."

"We made cupcakes with boobs on them." I snorted. "Doubt it will leave much of a void in the world. Shutting down Sticky Treats isn't going to affect anyone."

"Have you told Joker Junior yet?" Maddie asked pointedly.

Damn it! How does she do that?

The guilt came surging back. This time it had reinforcements and siege weaponry.

"Not exactly," I mumbled, shoving my hands in my pockets and contemplating a scuff on the toe of my boot.

"Meaning?"

"I told him I hadn't decided what I was planning to do yet."

Maddie puffed out an exasperated breath.

"Erin," she scolded. "You have to tell him. This isn't fair."

"I'm still paying his salary," I protested. "That makes it a little better... right? Plus," I added hastily, seeing Maddie open her mouth to argue, "I'm going to give him an awesome recommendation. Really glowing. Radioactive even. He'll find another job in no time. A couple of weeks won't make a difference. Come on. Let's get this over with."

I tugged at her hand, and we crossed the busy city street at a nearby crosswalk.

"It sounds to me," Maddie observed, eyeing me shrewdly as I fumbled in my coat for my keys, "like you're clutching at any excuse to put this conversation off."

"What's that supposed to mean?" I demanded. "Damn it! I'm sure I put them in here."

A search of my pockets had produced cough drops, a Chapstick, a bent bobby pin, and a hair scrunchie, but no keys. I began rifling furiously through my purse.

"I think telling Jayden would make all this too real. You're hoping if you stall long enough, something will turn up that will change your mind."

I rolled my eyes at her.

"Stop it," I warned. "Don't go all Dr. Phil on me."

I finally dug out my keys from the inside pocket of my purse and pushed the door open. The displays had been stripped bare, and everything was covered in a fine layer of dust. I felt an ache of longing in my chest. It didn't matter what I said to Maddie. I couldn't deny what this place meant to me. I closed my eyes and inhaled. There had been no baking here for more than two weeks, but I could still smell faint traces of chocolate and caramel. Opening my eyes, I looked around. Awards and reviews were displayed on the wall. Several of the frames showed me my own face, grinning brightly, glowing with pride.

It was easy to be rational and objective when I was sitting at Maddie's dining table. But now I was actually here, there was nowhere to hide. I was proud of what I had accomplished with Sticky Treats. What's more, I missed the place. I missed it like an old friend.

Rose-tinted spectacles! I scolded myself severely. I couldn't get sentimental at the last moment.

"Hey, Erin. Look at this."

Maddie emerged from a door behind the counter, carrying a large stack of brightly colored envelopes.

"I went to get your mail and I found all these."

"Probably thank you cards," I said casually. "Guess they built up over the last couple of weeks."

"You get these often?" she asked, thumbing through them.

"Fairly often. If you look under the counter, there's a box file where I keep them all."

She ducked down and pulled up the file.

"I can see what you mean," Maddie drawled, pulling out cards at random and examining them.

I winced. When I'd stored them, I'd been adhering to a strict filing system.

"It's obvious no one's going to miss this place at all. Nothing says 'not caring' like taking the trouble to send a business a thank you card."

I folded my arms and gave her a withering look. The sarcasm fairy was working overtime today.

"I *thought* you were talking out of your ass when you said that Sticky Treats never did anything important for anyone, but this has convinced me."

She plucked out another card and pursed her lips.

"I mean, how important is a wedding cake, really? This woman claims you 'made the happiest day of her life even happier,' but she's probably just some deranged weirdo."

She tossed the card dismissively over her shoulder and reached for another.

"I'm sure this charity fundraiser would have been just as successful without the $7000 worth of cake pops they sold. Very generous of you to only charge them for materials, by the way."

"Maddie!"

"Mrs. Regensburg claims you put the magic back in her marriage. Wouldn't imagine it meant much to her, though. I'm sure most people 'rekindle passions long-forgotten' at the drop of a hat."

"Are you done?" I demanded. "You're supposed to be helping me clear this place up, not making more mess."

"Do you see my point, though?" she pressed. "You made a real difference to people's lives, and they were so grateful that they took the time to mail you actual cards. That's huge. Most people can't even be bothered to leave a Yelp review these days."

"I—I'm not saying people didn't enjoy my stuff," I faltered. "I'm just—"

I was saved the trouble of scraping together a decent rebuttal when the doorbell jingled. My relief was short-lived when I saw who was standing in the doorway.

"I knew you'd show up here eventually. If I didn't know better, I could've sworn you were hiding from me."

Stirling loomed in the doorway, smiling coldly. He wasn't a big guy, but he seemed to occupy the whole frame at once. I opened my mouth to speak, but Madison got there first.

"What do you want, asshole?" she demanded, placing a hand on her hip.

Stirling shot her a venomous look. He and Maddie had hated each other from day one.

"Actually," he said frostily, "I came here to speak to *Erin.* If you wanted to do the classy thing, you'd step outside and let us talk privately."

"Unlikely," Maddie jeered. "You just want to get me out of the way so you can bully her."

"Not at all," Stirling shot back. "It's a fairly blustery day. I was hoping if you stood in the open for long enough, someone might drop a farmhouse on you."

My lips twitched traitorously. For a fraction of a second, I glimpsed the man I had fallen for. No one could deliver a zinger like Stirling. Of course, Maddie gave as good as she got.

She stepped from the other side of the counter and moved into his personal space.

"I understand that the idea of a powerful and confident woman might seem like witchcraft to you, Stirling. Yet more evidence that your brain is as microscopic as your dick."

Stirling's jaw tightened and his hand twitched at his side. Recognizing the danger signals, I stepped forward and took Maddie's arm, pulling her back.

"It's alright, Erin," Maddie said calmly, keeping her eyes fixed on Stirling. "I'm not afraid of him, and you don't need to be either."

"I'm not afraid," I lied.

It was difficult to rationalize the effect that Stirling had on me. Whenever I was in a room with him, he radiated this aura that made me want to fold in on myself. He made me smaller. In my darker moments, I'd wondered whether his power over me came from the fact that he represented a louder, more solid version of the fear and anxiety that had plagued every major decision I'd ever made.

I'd always been scared to take risks. Anytime I reached a crossroads, I was assaulted by a choir of inner voices telling me it wouldn't work out. That I wasn't brave enough or strong enough, or smart enough. Sticky Treats was the riskiest thing I had ever done, and it had terrified me. I was sure it wouldn't work. People would never accept it, it just wasn't me, it was too controversial. When Stirling had swooped into my life and given these fears a voice, the effect had been devastating.

As if reaching in and plucking the thoughts from my head, Stirling turned to me with a sympathetic smile.

"You should have called me when all this happened, Erin," he scolded. "I was worried about you."

Maddie snorted loudly. Stirling ignored her.

"Of course, I did try to warn you. None of this would've happened if you'd listened to me. Without me protecting you, it was only a matter of time before you were preyed on by some pervert. It's clear that this Nolan took you in completely."

I folded my arms and looked away, blinking back tears. Hearing him talk about Nolan was too much. The wounds were too raw. Even hearing his name felt like a knife through the chest. Stirling placed his fingers under my chin and tried to tilt my head, forcing me to look at him. His touch caused tendrils of revulsion to coil throughout my body. I longed to jerk my head away. My brain sent screaming commands to my muscles, but there was no response. As usual, my best friend came to my rescue. Quick as lightning, Madison reached out and slapped Stirling's hand away.

"Hands off, dirtbag," she snarled.

Stirling's icy blue eyes flashed.

"If Erin needed a guard dog, she could get one. I doubt she'd need to resort to a rabid bitch," he sneered. "Now, I'm asking you one more time to leave. You could save me the trouble of calling you a cab by telling me where you left your broomstick."

"Your mom's ass."

She really has a thing about butts lately.

I didn't recognize the gesture she made, but it was safe to bet it was obscene. I threw up my hands and retreated behind the counter. I always appreciated Maddie's help, but if the discussion had deteriorated to the point of trading "your mama" insults, I needed to tap out for a few minutes.

Desperate for something else to focus on, my attention wandered to the stack of mail Madison had brought in earlier. One of the envelopes was considerably thicker and heavier than the others. Frowning curiously, I picked it up and opened it. Nestling inside were a gift certificate, a card, and two carefully folded pages covered in small, neat handwriting. I'd received letters of thanks before, but never one this long. Blocking out the rising crescendo of Stirling and Maddie's voices, I unfolded the pages and read.

Dear Miss Donovan,

Thank you so much for the amazing cupcakes. It's hard to explain just how much they meant to me. Celebrating my breast reconstruction was the end of a very harrowing journey and the start of a new one.

The party was my way of ensuring that the next stage of my life started with a bang, and I could not have done that without you.

I'd never ordered from an erotic bakery before. I never even realized such things existed. I admit I was very nervous about the idea when I first contacted you, but you immediately laid my fears to rest. At every step, you were kind, approachable, and solicitous. I was surprised and gratified by the sensitivity and compassion you brought to this commission.

When the cakes arrived and I opened the box (my hubby will confirm this), I immediately dissolved into floods of tears. They were perfect in every way. You have been blessed with extraordinary talent.

I am extremely grateful to have survived my battle with breast cancer. At times it was awful, but I also feel it was an experience that altered me for the better. I'm braver, more decisive, and I'm determined never to be ruled by fear. Now I've had my reconstruction I'm ready to grab the gift of life with both hands. I hope you can derive satisfaction from the knowledge that your little cakes were a big part of that process.

I wish you nothing but success and happiness for the future. Please keep doing what you're doing. People need to celebrate their bodies for all sorts of reasons. Sometimes the people in question will be fragile, vulnerable, and wounded. These people need a gentle soul like you to take their hand and help them celebrate their beauty.

There will always be naysayers. Ignorant people will try to tell you that what you're doing is wrong. Before my diagnosis, I was the type of person who would allow people like that to get in my head. Now, hopefully, I can pass on some of the wisdom I have gathered on my journey in case you ever need to draw strength from it. Be bold. Never apologize and never be ashamed. You're doing exactly what you need to be doing.

I hope the gift certificate goes some way to repaying your kindness. Pamper yourself. You deserve it.

Kindest regards,

Lucia Perez

When I got to the end of the letter, my cheeks were wet with tears. I reached up and hastily brushed them away. There was a warm, euphoric feeling bubbling from my chest and spreading through my body like a healing balm. Thinking back to that crazy baking session in Nolan's kitchen, my face split into a smile. It was the first time in weeks that anything related to Nolan had made me smile. Now that I'd started, I couldn't stop.

In all the excitement over the last couple of months, the saga of Mrs. Perez's cupcakes had slipped my mind. What were the odds that she would pop up now and tell me exactly what I needed to hear? It felt like fate. Mrs. Perez had reached out and reminded me what really mattered. Everything that had happened in the last few weeks suddenly seemed unimportant. I was through being afraid and I was way past done with feeling ashamed.

Maddie and Stirling were still ripping shreds from one

another. It was a figurative bloodbath. If I didn't step in soon, it might stop being a metaphor. I drew in a deep breath and imagined my newfound resolve flowing into me.

Time for the best angry teacher voice ever.

"Shut up, both of you!"

I barely recognized the clear, confident voice that rang from my throat. It cut through Stirling and Maddie's yelling like a scythe.

"That's better," I said primly. "Now, Maddie, thank you for all your help and support, but I think I can take it from here. And Stirling—"

I turned to my ex-boyfriend, trying to project the entirety of my rage into one piercing gaze. I wish I could have seen the expression on my face. It must have been quite something, because he actually took a step back.

"Stirling, get the fuck out of my life."

For a moment, he simply goggled at me, mouth working soundlessly. He was in full-on goldfish mode.

"Erin," he eventually managed. "I don't think you know what you're saying."

"Oh, I know exactly what I'm saying. Get out. I never want to see you again. I never want to hear from you again."

My words turned him to stone. He stood, completely expressionless and silent, for almost a minute. In the end, it was the sound of Maddie's appreciative applause that snapped him back to reality. He glared at her, his lip curling.

"Stay out of this, bitch. You've done enough already. Erin." His gaze swiveled back, and he jabbed his finger in my direction. "I'd think carefully if I were you. You know what happens when you make me angry. I mean it. Remember what happened when we broke up? I can make that look like a picnic."

I'd been ready for that.

"Go ahead," I breezed, inspecting my nails nonchalantly.

Stirling's face had gone white, save for two livid spots of color rising in his cheeks. He was literally shaking with fury.

"Are you making fun of me?" he asked incredulously. "Because I'm not playing around here, Erin. I helped build your reputation and I can destroy it. You don't know what I can do. Those videos of you and your precious Nolan—I can make sure the whole world sees them."

"Is that supposed to worry me?" I asked innocently. "It just means that everyone will know that you're a worthless creep and that I have truly fantastic tits. You might have helped me set up a website, but *I* built this place. It was *my* talent and *my* work."

Maddie whistled piercingly.

"Wooh! You go, girl!"

"I'll be showing people what I knew from the start," Stirling hissed. "That you're a slut. A worthless, pathetic slut!"

I wrinkled my nose as he sprayed me with spit.

"You can't hurt me anymore," I stated defiantly. "Say what you like. Post all the filth you want online. You can never undo this."

I strode over to the box file, seized a handful of cards with zero regard for their proper filing, and threw them at Stirling. They smacked him in the chest and fluttered around his feet like confetti. It felt so good that I wanted to do it again. I grabbed a fistful of cards as though I were arming myself with their missives and I hurled them across the store.

"Nothing that you do can undo this, or this or *these!*"

I kept going until the box file was empty and Stirling was cringing from the colorful missiles. My fear of him had miraculously evaporated. How had I never noticed how weak and pathetic he was?

"I let you tear me down once," I breathed. "I won't let you do it again. I'm making people smile and I'm helping them celebrate their bodies. It's nothing to be ashamed of and it's too important to let someone like you ruin it for me."

"Erin," Maddie interjected, sounding uncharacteristically timid. "Does this mean what I think it means? You're not giving up Sticky Treats?"

I turned to my best friend, smiling broadly.

"Why would I do a silly thing like that?"

Maddie's face split into a matching grin.

"Is it too late to call Mrs. Pasternak and tell her you've changed your mind?"

"Probably not," I mused. "I'm not going to, though."

"But you just said—"

"I know I did, and I meant it," I assured her. "I'm not giving up Sticky Treats, but I do think I need a fresh start. I'll go to my parents' for a few weeks and then I'll start looking for a new space. A better one, in a bigger city. I might even branch out and open a Sticky Treats coffee shop. Who knows? The world is my proverbial oyster. We should get out of here and celebrate. Stirling can see himself out."

The astonished expression on Maddie's face was priceless. I linked my arm through hers and she allowed herself to be steered through the door as we swept past my equally dumbfounded ex-boyfriend. I couldn't help feeling that the scene needed a crescendo of triumphant music, but the rising tide of happy excitement was a more than acceptable substitute.

CHAPTER FORTY-FIVE

Nolan

I'd been right. The investigation revealed that Stirling had been behind everything. It hadn't been easy; we'd hit multiple dead ends before Jess came up with the idea of hacking into Heather's e-mail account. I'd wrestled with the ethics of this, until Jess assured me that she'd only look at the relevant e-mails. The memory of Erin's anguished face when she'd confronted me over the videos might also have swayed my views on the sanctity of Heather's inbox.

The information we found left no room for doubt. There was an incriminating trail of emails going back almost six weeks. I thanked my lucky stars that Heather had lacked the foresight to purge them. The correspondence gave me more than enough evidence to build a solid case against them both. It also simplified the process of approaching the website and getting the videos taken down.

From an official standpoint, I was well on my way to putting this horrible mess behind me. That just left the question of what to do about Erin. I'd toyed with simply not telling her. She'd been through so much already. The kindest thing might have been to just leave her to get on with her life. I could prove I hadn't posted the videos, but my fucked-up past had led to their creation. I could hardly absolve myself of responsibility. After a lot of soul-searching, I decided that whatever she thought of me, she'd at least feel better for knowing that the videos had been taken down and the perpetrators were being held responsible.

Phoning or emailing her seemed like a bad idea. She might just delete the messages without opening them. I decided to go old school. I reasoned that the novelty of receiving snail mail might be enough to keep her reading, even if she guessed where it came from. Sitting down with a pen and paper felt alien. It had been years since I'd handwritten anything longer than a grocery list. Perhaps that was the reason my mind went so blank.

Dear Erin,

I'm writing to inform you that...

No. Too formal.

Dear Erin,

This is just a short letter to explain that...

Lame.

Dear Erin,

How are you doing?

Lamer.

Dear Erin,

I miss you more than words can express. I'd crawl 50 miles over broken glass if I thought there was even a chance that I could get you back.

I was sitting with my third cup of coffee amidst a sea of crumpled paper when the door buzzed. My heart sank when I heard my grandmother's voice over the intercom. I flew frantically around the apartment, scooping up the empty takeout boxes and any other debris I'd been too depressed to clean up. The overall effect wasn't bad. Many adult children will confirm that a surprising amount of cleaning can occur in the time it takes an elderly relative to climb a set of stairs. As I headed to the front door, I caught a glimpse of myself in the hallway mirror and winced. I hadn't shaved in two days, and I was wearing my rattiest t-shirt and sweatpants combo. It was an outfit that positively encouraged probing questions about my mental well-being.

Forcing a sunny smile onto my face before I opened the door was painful, but it was better than the alternative.

"Granny!" I boomed jovially. "What brings you here?"

My grandmother gave me a critical once over and leaned in to kiss my bristly cheek.

"Since when do I need a reason to visit my grandson?" she demanded.

I shrugged.

"You don't, but you hardly ever come here."

"And you've hardly ever gone a clear five days without visiting us," she reminded me severely. "I wanted to check you were ok. And I wanted to reassure little Abby that her uncle hadn't vanished in a puff of smoke."

I experienced a harsh stab of guilt. Had it really been that long? The days had sort of run together. The investigation had been taking up a lot of my time, and I hadn't exactly been feeling all that sociable recently.

"I'm sorry. I've been a little busy," I mumbled.

My grandmother narrowed her eyes and pursed her lips.

"Not with work," she stated. "Alana told me you'd taken some unexpected leave."

Snitch!

"So, if you're sat around here on vacation, you can make some time for your old granny," she continued briskly. "Stop standing in the doorway like a lummox and go and make me a cup of tea."

To my immense relief, Granny V made no comment on the state of the apartment. Even after my hurried efforts, the place was far from pristine. Housekeeping was one of a long list of things I'd been neglecting recently. While I waited for the kettle to boil, I filled my grandmother in on the progress of my investigation. She didn't say much, but some of the faces she pulled were eloquence itself. I can confidently say that if it were possible to incinerate people with thoughts, Stirling and Heather would have been crispy and smoking by the time I'd told her everything.

I added a generous drizzle of honey to her tea and brought our mugs into the living area. My grandmother's unerring instincts had carried her to my desk, and she was busily sifting through the mess of wastepaper.

"What's all this, dear?" she asked.

I sighed. Lying seemed pointless at this stage.

"I'm writing Erin a letter. Thought I should let her know what I'm doing. Update her on the progress of the case."

"I see."

My grandmother picked up my latest draft and peered at it. Her eyes flew across the page as she scanned the lines. I fidgeted uncomfortably. The last thing I'd expected was for her to crumple the letter into a ball and throw it over her shoulder.

"Granny! What are you doing?"

"I'm doing what should be done with trash." She sniffed. "Which in your apartment is clearly to throw it on the floor."

I blushed and began gathering some of the discarded pages and stuffing them into the nearby wastepaper basket.

"You don't think I should be writing to her?" I inquired irritably.

"Correct," she said crisply. "I think you should take a shower, put on your nicest shirt and go tell her all of this yourself."

"I can't," I grunted, storming off to the kitchen and beginning to load coffee mugs into the dishwasher.

My grandmother wasn't prepared to let me escape that easily. She pursued me out of the room doggedly.

"Why not?" she asked." Nolan, you're innocent! I don't understand what Jessica did with her computer, but I do know that she proved you had nothing to do with those vile videos. Now, I don't know everything that happened between you and Erin, but it looks like you're letting the love of your life slip through your fingers because you're too proud or stubborn to go and talk to her."

"It's not that," I said quietly.

Turning my back on my grandmother, I took more time than was necessary making sure all of the mugs were perfectly stacked and aligned.

"Then what is it?"

I closed my eyes and leaned my head on the dishwasher door. I had a feeling this conversation would be easier if I could pretend that I was confiding in my kitchen appliances.

"I—I'm afraid that if we get back together, I'll hurt her again," I admitted.

My voice was barely above a whisper, but I knew my grandmother caught every word. I heard the soft tutting noise she always resorted to when she was exasperated.

"Why on earth would you think that?"

"Because I always do!" I blurted.

Maintaining the crouch was getting uncomfortable and I allowed myself to slump to the floor. I flinched as my butt struck the tiles a little more forcefully than I'd intended. Vaguely aware that I looked ridiculous, I kept my back to my grandmother and hugged my knees.

"All my relationships end up the same way, and they always will. Deep down, I know I'm just like—like Dad."

"Is that what you think?"

There was something in my grandmother's voice I'd never heard before. It was only when I'd shuffled round and seen the expression on her face that I realized what it was. She sounded heartbroken and suddenly frail. I knew she was 79, but she had never looked or sounded old to me before. I didn't like it.

"Is that really what you think?" she repeated.

I shrugged unhappily. Granny V looked at me for a long time before letting out a very heavy sigh.

"Nolan Aloysius Reid," she declared.

Uh-oh.

"If you were just a little smaller, I'd put you over my knee and spank you! Now, you listen to me. You are *nothing* like your father."

"What makes you so sure?" I asked gloomily.

"Because I know you. Gabriel is my son, and I love him to death, but I'm not blind. I know what sort of man he can be. And don't let your Aunt Norah fill your head with nonsense. She's always had a bad habit of talking out of her derriere."

I gaped up at her, lost for words. I'd always assumed Granny V was utterly oblivious to her son's faults. This was the first time I'd ever heard her say a word against him. She wasn't done either. She pressed on, warming to her theme.

"For example, when your sister was abandoned by that layabout, what did you do? You tracked him down and hauled him in front of a judge. It's thanks to you that Olivia got what was owing to her in child support. You didn't stop there either. You stepped in to fill the void he left behind. You've been there for Abby all her life. Does that seem like something your father would have done?"

"I guess not."

This had genuinely never occurred to me before.

"I don't have to guess," said Granny V grimly. "Gabriel's never been overly concerned with taking care of his own children, never mind anybody else's. But that's by the by. The main reason I know beyond a doubt that you are nothing like your father is that I raised both of you. Do you really think I'd be fool enough to make the same mistakes twice?"

I stared at my grandmother, unable to speak past the lump in my throat. I was feeling a lot of things at once. Things that were too big and important to reshape into words. I genuinely didn't know whether I felt happy or sad. I was bone tired, yet somehow euphoric. As usual, my grandmother knew just what to say.

"Come on." She folded her arms and made a quick, jerking motion with her head. "You going to get up off that floor and give your granny a hug or are you going to make me get down there?"

"Oh, Granny."

I hauled myself to my feet and pulled her into my arms. I'd been taller than her since I was nine. By the time I was 14, I was able to rest my chin on her head. She hugged me to her fiercely, then she stepped back and looked me over tenderly, like she was checking me for damage.

"You've made some bad choices, Nolan," she said, smoothing imaginary wrinkles from my t-shirt. "Everybody has. But that doesn't make you a bad person. You deserve to be happy and so does she."

For the first time in weeks, I dared to entertain a faint flicker of hope. Could she be right? Was there still a chance?

"What if I've left it too late?"

I looked at my grandmother helplessly, wordlessly pleading with her to make it better. I felt all of six years old.

"Only one way to find out," she reasoned. "Let's go and see her."

"Now?"

"No. Next Christmas. Of course now!"

All the customary energy and sharpness was back in my grandmother's tone. It was extremely comforting.

"You going to try telling me there's anywhere else in the world you need to be?"

It took a nanosecond to make up my mind. When I stopped overthinking it, it was the easiest decision I'd ever made.

"I'll go grab a shower," I said, giving my grandmother one last peck and hurrying towards the bathroom.

"Oh good," she enthused. "I'll send Alana a message. Tell her we'll be down in a few minutes."

"What?"

I skidded to a halt and spun around.

"What's Alana doing here?"

CHAPTER FORTY-SIX

Nolan

"Oh, Nolan! Do stop sulking," Granny V scolded.

"I'm not sulking."

I jerked irritably at the sun visor, trying to ward off the harsh glare beating through the windshield.

"I just don't see why the whole world has to weigh in on my business."

"Alana is not the whole world," Granny V retorted. "She came with me because we were both worried about you. We decided it would be best if she waited in the car, so you didn't feel like everybody was ganging up on you."

"But I was ready to tag in if she needed an extra pair of hands to yank your head from your ass."

I scowled through the rear-view mirror at the smirking figure in the backseat.

"Hope for your sake your resume's up to date," I growled.

Alana yawned and lazily flipped me the bird.

"Stop it, you two," Granny V chided.

She reached between the seats and handed Alana a travel mug of coffee. Apparently, she'd been busy in my kitchen while I took a shower."

"Where's mine?" I demanded petulantly.

"Don't be silly; you're driving."

My frown deepened and my jaw worked furiously.

"I appreciate that you both cared enough to hatch this little conspiracy. But I would like to remind you that I'm a grown man. I can take care of—"

"Of course you are, dear," Granny V soothed. "Now, stop pulling silly faces. If the wind changes, you'll get stuck like that."

There was a poorly suppressed snort of laughter from the backseat. I spent the rest of the journey plotting creative revenge on my smartass PA. I could bring her decaf. Or I could replace her ringtone with "Baby Shark." Maybe I'd yank Audrey IV from her fancy new pot and feed her into the shredder, leaf by leaf.

Of course, I'd never actually do any of those things, but thinking about them stopped me from feeling so nervous. My stomach was fluttering with a heady mix of excitement and terror. The thought that there might be a chance for me and Erin was exhilarating. On the other hand, I had resigned myself to losing her. What if, after all this time, I put myself out there and she rejected me? I swallowed hard and tightened my grip on the steering wheel.

When I finally pulled into a parking spot two blocks down from the bakery, I turned to my grandmother and my PA and eyed them sternly.

"Listen," I said. "This is how this is going to work. We're going to Sticky Treats to see if Erin is there. If she is, you two will wait outside. I mean it. I don't need an audience for this."

"It's ok, dear," Granny V assured me. "We're not going to cramp your style. Alana's taking me shopping for some specialist equipment."

"Specialist equipment?" I asked, momentarily derailed.

Granny V smiled coyly and began unnecessarily tidying her hair.

"Nothing fancy," she demurred. "Just some orthopedic...

marital aids. Trust me, when Shakira gets to my age, she'll mean something entirely different when she claims that her hips don't lie."

"Ok," I said, promptly exiting the car. "I think we're done with share time now."

Shaking my head vigorously, I tried to dislodge the truly disturbing images forming in my brain. I allowed my mind to drift to Erin instead. It had only been a few weeks, but it felt like an eternity.

Will she be pleased to see me?

Of course she won't. She still thinks you're an asshole.

I hadn't even begun thinking about what I'd say to her. Hopefully, she'd give me at least some time to explain myself before she threw me out of the shop or skewered me with a cake... sword?

In the rush of hope and excitement that followed my pep talk with Granny V, I had forgotten that Sticky Treats had been closed every time I'd driven past. When I saw the shutters down and the "to let" sign in the window my happy bubble burst. It stopped me as abruptly as a malicious foot stuck out across a track, tripping me up and sending me sprawling. Where was she? When did this happen? Was she even still in town? Questions multiplied in my head like crazy Jenga bricks. Looking at those blocky white letters on the harsh red background made me feel like I couldn't breathe. There was something so final about them. I didn't say anything. I stood mouth agape and heart in my shoes, not knowing what to do next. Granny V was the first to break the silence.

"Oh, dear!" she said quietly.

"Yeah," I croaked. "That pretty much sums it up."

"Maybe she's at her apartment."

"Calling now," said Alana, tapping at her phone and taking a couple of steps away.

"She won't be there," I murmured bleakly.

I don't know how I knew, but I did. I was too late. It was over.

"Giving up already?"

Startled out of my gloom, I whipped around.

"Liv?" I blurted. "What are you doing here?"

Somehow, my sister and Abby had snuck up on us. By itself, this seemed impossible. Abby usually responded to the sight of me or Granny V with hypersonic squeals that were incompatible with a stealthy approach. Yet there they were. It was a windy day and their hair was whipping around their faces in vivid red tendrils. Abby, docile and quiet for once, was holding my sister's hand and clutching Olaf to her chest.

I started to suspect that none of this was real. Perhaps I'd dozed off at my desk and fallen into one of those bizarre dreams where everyone you've ever known turns up completely out of context.

"Nice to see you too," she replied tartly. "I came here because I love my baby brother and I don't want him to screw his life up. Granny texted me and said that she'd finally talked some sense into you, so I came here to make sure you didn't do anything dumb."

"We like Erin," Abby added. "I want her to do the cakes for my next birthday, but this time I want them to be dinosaurs."

I closed my eyes and pinched the bridge of my nose.

"I love that everyone has so much faith in me," I gritted. "Does the concept of privacy mean anything to this family?"

"Nope," said Olivia cheerfully. "So, what's our next move?"

"Well, she's not at her apartment. I tried three times and got voicemail."

Alana didn't look remotely surprised to see Olivia. Apparently, my life was being run by a committee—a committee I hadn't been invited to join."

"Ooh!" Granny V exclaimed, clapping her hands together. "Jayden might know where she's gone. I'll give him a call."

"Oh right," I said wryly. "I'd forgotten you guys were BFFs."

Granny V raised the phone to her ear and held a finger up to shush me. Jayden picked up on the second ring.

"Hello, dear. It's Granny V. How are—? Where am *I?* I'm outside Sticky Treats. Why do—?"

We all took a step back as the shutters whirred into life, slowly rising to reveal a familiar green-haired figure standing at the window. Jayden's face lit up when he saw Granny V but darkened the instant he spotted me.

This should be interesting.

For a moment, I thought he might refuse to let me in, but however much he hated me, he couldn't resist Granny V. After a couple of seconds of awkward fumbling with the keys, he opened the door and hugged my grandmother warmly.

"Hey, Granny V. Haven't seen you in forever," he enthused. "How was the wedding? No, wait, don't tell me. I want to hear about the honeymoon."

He waggled his eyebrows suggestively and Granny V gave him a playful slap on the arm.

"Stop it, you naughty boy," she chided. "I'll give you all the juicy gossip on sundae Sunday. Right now, we need your help."

What the hell is sundae Sunday? And why wasn't I invited?

"Anything for you, Granny V, you know that."

"Do you know where Erin is? It's important."

Jayden shot me a venomous scowl over Granny V's shoulder.

"Huh," he grunted. "I wondered what ass-face was doing here."

"Ah-ah." Granny V poked him in the chest. "You mind your language, young man. That's my grandson you're talking about."

"Sorry, Granny V," said Jayden, still glaring at me. "I don't want to disrespect you or anything, but he broke Erin's heart. The whole reason she's leaving is because of him. Well... some of the reason. Probably. She said she just needs a fresh start, but we all know what that's code for. I know I'd want a fresh start if half the pervs on the internet had seen my bazongas."

"What are bazongas?"

"Not now, Abby."

"Fresh start?" I repeated, zeroing in on the pertinent part of his speech. "She's leaving?"

"What, you're surprised?" he scoffed. "She was totally devo'd."

"Jayden, you have to listen," Granny V insisted. "Nolan never uploaded that video. He didn't even know it existed."

Jayden narrowed his eyes.

"So he says."

"It's true," Alana put in. "Could show you proof if you want, but we might need my girlfriend and a laptop."

"Say what?"

"Well, you see, Jess is—"

"Look, it doesn't matter!" I exploded. "What matters is that I would never do that to Erin. I love her. I love her like I've never loved anyone. I thought I was no good for her. I thought I could never be any good for anyone, but I was wrong. I'm not perfect. I screw up sometimes. Actually, I screw up a lot of the time, but I've never been more certain about anything. I want to find Erin and devote the rest of my life to making her happy. If after all this, she still doesn't want me, that's fine; she probably deserves better anyway. But I need her to know how I feel, and right now I'm terrified that I've left it too late."

There was a ringing silence, only punctuated by the sound of Granny V blowing her nose. I blushed, keenly aware I'd just loudly professed my love in front of family, friends, and several curious passers-by. Jayden ran a hand through his hair and puffed out his cheeks.

"Wow, dude!" he said finally. "There's some intense feels

there. I guess—I guess if you really mean all that, I can tell you where she's gone."

"Thank you, Jayden," I gushed. "You've no idea how much this means to me. Where is she?"

"She's going to her parents for a few weeks to get her head on straight."

"Ok, I can work with that. When's she coming back?"

He grimaced.

"That's the thing," he said awkwardly. "She's not. You saw the sign. I'm here to pick up the last of my stuff. She's got her eye on a new business space in Columbus. Said there's an open position for me. Super tempting, but I'm going to have to give it some serious thought, I mean... Ohio?"

"Jayden," I said, grasping him by the shoulders. "This is very important. When is Erin leaving and where can I find her?"

Jayden bit his lip and looked away. Something that looked suspiciously like guilt flitted across his face.

"Ok," he began. "I want you to promise me you're not going to panic."

"How can I not panic after you've said that?!" I sputtered.

"It's possible that time might be a slight factor here," Jayden admitted nervously.

"How much of a factor?" I growled.

"She's leaving today. Her train leaves at..." He looked at his watch and paled. "Her train leaves Central Station in 40 minutes."

"Why the hell didn't you lead with that?" I bellowed.

Jayden flinched and Granny V laid a hand on my arm.

"Calm down, Nolan," she soothed. "There's still time."

"She's right," said Alana. "If we put our foot down and the traffic gods are with us, we'll make it."

Granny V did a quick headcount.

"We won't all fit in one car."

"It's ok," said Olivia. "We're parked at the soft play a couple of blocks down. I can meet you there."

"I don't think you all need to come."

I might as well not have spoken. Jayden's crestfallen face suddenly lit up with inspiration.

"I've still got the keys to the Sticky Treats van," he offered. "I can drive you."

"Why would you do that?" I asked.

"Honestly, man, it's no trouble."

"No, really," I insisted. "*Why* would you do that?"

"Are you kidding?" He grinned. "This is going to be dramatic as fuck; I don't want to miss it. Ooh, hang on."

He disappeared into the darkened depths of the store and returned in less than 30 seconds with a large cellophane bag of popcorn. Abby squealed with joy.

"We had some stock left over," he explained.

He actually brought popcorn. There's no way this isn't a dream.

"Fine," I snapped. "There's no time to argue. Let's go."

So, there we were. My grandmother, my sister, my niece, my PA, and a green-haired teenage heckler, racing across the city in a bakery van to win back my girlfriend. Jayden, Granny V, Olivia, and Abby were squashed into the front seat, while Alana and I sat in the back. I held my breath at every light and crosswalk, willing the vehicle to go faster.

"You know what," said Granny V suddenly. "This is just like that movie."

"What movie?" Olivia asked.

"Oh, you know, that movie, the famous one with the girl and that chap, whatshisname. One of them has a change of heart at the last minute and they have to race to the airport."

"Love Actually?"

"Sleepless in Seattle?"

"How to Lose a Guy in 10 Days?"

"Notting Hill?"

"Frozen!"

"No, there's no airport in *Notting Hill.* He has to get to a press conference."

"Same idea, though."

I leaped out of the van while Jayden found somewhere to park. I ran back a couple of seconds later, red-faced and sheepish. I'd suddenly realized I had no idea what train I was looking for. People turned to stare as we barreled across the atrium. I didn't blame them; we must have made quite a spectacle. After frantically consulting the departures board, we found the right platform and pelted for the stairs. We arrived at the ticket barrier panting and sweating. With rising dread, it dawned on me that I had slammed headlong into an impenetrable obstacle.

"Damn!" I shouted, slamming my fist into the silver metal.

"You could go back and buy a ticket," Olivia gasped.

Jayden consulted his watch and shook his head.

"Might not make it if we do that," he breathed.

I looked at the barrier. Imagining the train slowly rolling Erin out of my life, I made a snap decision. In one swift movement, I vaulted the barrier and sprinted for the platform.

"Sir! Sir, come back. You can't do that. Hey!"

I ran on, heedless. The last thing I heard was Alana's apologetic voice.

"It's ok, sir. We can explain. Have you ever seen *Love Actually?*"

CHAPTER FORTY-SEVEN

Erin

"This isn't what I expected from our last brunch."

Maddie deposited the paper cups of coffee on the table. The station coffee shop was noisy, and we had to hunch close to make ourselves heard.

"Are you saying you don't like over-priced coffee and greasy croissants?" I joked, trying to pull my stack of luggage farther into the booth.

"Of course not. They get a whole chapter in the journal of my girlish hopes and dreams. What I don't like is saying goodbye to you."

I reached across the table and squeezed her hand.

"It's not goodbye forever," I promised. "We can Zoom, and I'll come back and visit a ton. Once I'm settled, you and Claudie can come visit me in Ohio."

Maddie groaned and slumped forward. Her forehead hit the table with an audible thump.

"It's not that bad!" I protested. "I got offered a really good deal on the space for my coffee shop. I couldn't pass it up. Plus, I've been doing some research and there's actually a lot to do in Columbus. There's the Schwarzenegger statue, the Doo-Dah parade, and that area with all the corn sculptures."

My best friend raised her head and looked at me balefully.

"Wow," she deadpanned. "No way we could cram all that into one visit."

"Come on," I cajoled. "It wasn't all that long ago you were worried I'd run off to Peru. Ohio has to be an improvement on that."

"I guess." Maddie picked disconsolately at her pastry. "I just don't see why you have to leave town just because your ex-boyfriend is a jerk."

I shrugged.

"I'm trying to view this as a positive transition. It's like how *Buffy the Vampire Slayer* ended."

Maddie shook her sugar packet, concentrating all the grains at one end.

"An apocalyptic explosion and hordes of rampaging undead?"

"No! I mean yes, but that wasn't the important thing," I insisted. "The important thing was that Buffy knew when it was time to move on with her life. She'd let go of the past and she was taking the next step. There'd been some pain and struggles along the way and some really bad stuff had happened, but that wasn't what mattered. In the end, her struggles were what made her who she was—a strong mature woman with the world at her feet."

I sat up straighter in my seat and punctuated my speech with a self-affirming nod. Maddie leaned her chin on her hand and raised her eyebrows.

"Well, I guess when you put it like that," she drawled. "I should just be grateful you had your epiphany without needing to blow up the town first."

"True. That was a little inconsiderate of her."

"Or stick something pointy through Nolan's chest."

I flinched.

"I'm not angry with Nolan anymore," I said quietly.

I eased the top from my coffee and carefully blew on it.

Maddie looked at me skeptically.

"You're not?"

"No," I declared. "I mean, sure, he lied to me, humiliated me, and then completely broke my heart, but that's not how I want to remember our relationship. There were good times too, and that's what I want to focus on."

Maddie took an enormous bite of her croissant.

"That sounds very healthy," she mumbled, spraying me with crumbs.

"It is!" I agreed, deliberately ignoring the hidden barb. "I need to take my memories and put them through a sieve until all the sadness has been sifted out and all that's left are the happy times."

Madison put her head on one side, weighing my words as she chewed.

"Wouldn't that mean all the sadness would end up in the cake?" she asked.

"Oh... yeah. That metaphor actually works better the other way around. Maybe I should have said I was separating an egg."

I put my head in my hands.

"I don't know," I sighed. "I guess I'm better at baking than I am at relationships. There's no recipe for love." I paused thoughtfully. "Unless you believe those algorithms on dating sites."

Maddie edged around the booth and leaned her head on my shoulder.

"You're pretty good at friendship," she murmured. "That's a kind of relationship."

"I'll miss you too," I said, resting my cheek on her blonde waves.

She wanted to stay until it was time for my train to leave, but I wouldn't let her. I hated teary farewells and I needed some time to get my head straight. Sitting on the platform, I felt small and scared. A very little woman, surrounded by gigantic suitcases, about to voyage into the unknown. Well, the unknown, via a short layover at my parents' farmhouse in Wisconsin. I didn't feel like Buffy. Buffy had weapons, superpowers, and a cadre of sidekicks. All I had was a train ticket and the "power of positive thinking."

I was supposed to be taking the next step. This was meant to be exciting. I'd reached a whole new place where I was comfortable with my career and with myself. In many ways, the future looked bright and hopeful. So, why did striding confidently into the sunset feel so much like running away?

Because that's exactly what you're doing.

After staring at the same page on my Kindle for five minutes. I admitted defeat and put it in my bag. Sitting back on my cold bench, I stared listlessly into space. I wasn't running away from the videos, or from seeing him. I was running away from missing him. I couldn't stop thinking about him. Even if what we had was based on a lie, it was real for me at the time, and I couldn't just wish those feelings away.

My work, my home, my friendships. He'd left little traces and imprints on every aspect of my life and I couldn't handle the constant reminders. I wasn't Buffy. I was that heroine at the end of every romantic movie, about to leave to start a new life. She makes some philosophical speech about it all being for the best, while the audience yells at the screen. They know that however promising her new life looks, she'll be miserable and unfulfilled without Mr. Right. If this were one of those movies, it would be time for Nolan to appear with an impossible quantity of flowers, a boombox on his shoulder, and a compelling reason I should take him back.

The worst thing was, a traitorous part of me wanted it. I'd caught myself stalling as I packed, unconsciously leaving an extra few hours for a dramatic intervention of fate. I was doing it right now. The train had arrived. It was leaving in less than 15 minutes, but I was still sitting on the platform, stealing hopeful glances at the ticket barrier.

It would never happen. Nolan wasn't Mr. Right. He'd broken my heart and that was all there was to it. It would be too much to hope that he would suddenly—

"Erin!"

I blinked, convinced I must have been hallucinating. He was here. He didn't have flowers or a boombox, but he was here. Red-faced, sweaty, and disheveled but definitely... here.

"Erin!" he gasped, bending double and resting his hands on his knees.

He looked like he'd run a marathon.

"Erin, please don't get on that train. Or don't get on yet. I know I'm probably the last person you want to see, and you have every right to be angry, but I need you to hear me out because I think I might get arrested in a minute."

"Arrested? Wh—?"

"I didn't do it," he blurted.

"What do you mean? If you didn't do it, why are you getting—?"

"No, I mean the video thing. I didn't do it and I can prove I didn't do it, but that would take time we don't have. The important thing is that I had to tell you before you left, because even if you still think we don't have a shot, I had to know that you knew it wasn't me and that I'm trying to fix it."

He was still panting and his words were starting to run together. I wasn't doing much better. My brain had ground to a screeching halt.

"I really feel like you should have a boombox," I murmured, teetering precariously on the edge of hysteria.

My fantasy was coming to life, but no one had written either of our lines, and the improv was getting surreal. I had the crazy urge to poke him. It was the only thing I could think of to confirm he was truly here.

"I would've told you all this before," he continued. "But I'd convinced myself I wasn't good enough for you. I told myself that if I really loved you, I'd—"

"You love me?"

It came out as a strangled squeak. Tears blurred my vision.

"Of course," he said, sounding slightly confused at the question. "Of course I love you, but I told myself you'd never—"

I seized him around the neck and cut off his next words with a frantic, breath-stealing kiss. There are moments of clarity that happen only once or twice in a lifetime. Often, we're not aware of life-altering moments as they happen, we only recognize them for what they are later. However, I knew this was a moment I would remember for the rest of my life. There was a time to talk and a time to shut the hell up and just feel. I clung to Nolan like my life depended on it, pouring all my emotions into that kiss. It was searing, intense, and passionate, but it also felt like coming home. As we pulled apart, I was distantly aware of cheering coming from somewhere behind us. Nolan raised an eyebrow at me, and we turned as one.

Every movie moment needs its audience, and ours even had popcorn. Granny V, Jayden, Olivia, Alana, and Abby were standing in a little cluster. Nolan gulped when he saw they were accompanied by a man in a station uniform, but he needn't have worried. It was strange to see a 6ft 4-inch man with a large beard blowing his nose noisily and helping himself to Jayden's popcorn. Quite a few of the random people on the station platform were clapping and cheering too. I was surprised by how embarrassed I wasn't.

Nolan smiled down at me, caressing my cheek with the back of his hand. He was looking at me like I was the most precious thing in the world.

"Guess this means you'll be missing your train?" he said hopefully.

"Nope."

His face fell for a moment, until he saw the grin slowly spreading across my face. A plan was taking shape in my mind, and I was prepared to go with it, captivated by my own daring.

"It means you're getting on with me. I can't wait to see Mom's face. I haven't brought a boy home since college."

Nolan had a dazed, punch-drunk grin on his face as he loaded my bags on the train. He kept coming back and stealing kisses as I rapidly texted our plans to Alana. Once we were settled in the train car, I lifted the arm of the seat and nestled back against him.

"You know this is—"

"Crazy?" I offered. "Impulsive? Apparently, you have that effect on me."

He chuckled and kissed the top of my head.

"Don't worry," I assured him. "It won't last. I already feel a list coming on."

"What kind of list?"

I sighed.

"How about a list of bribes I could offer Mrs. Pasternak to take me back as a tenant?"

His arm tightened its hold around me.

"I don't want you to give up your dreams for me," he said softly. "We can work something out. It's not like they don't need lawyers in Ohio."

"I don't know," I pondered. "Honestly, Columbus is sounding less and less appealing."

I wriggled, snuggling closer to him.

"We can talk about it later. We have all the time in the world."

As the train pulled out, we waved out of the window at our cheer squad. Granny V looked almost as ecstatic as we were. Nolan gave me a sidelong glance.

"You know she's already mentally planning our wedding," he warned.

"Fine by me," I laughed, not pausing in my waving. "As long as someone else does the cake."

EPILOGUE

"What are these supposed to be again?"

Nolan slid his arms around Erin's waist and peered over her shoulder at the tray of cupcakes. Each intricately sculpted confection was molded to resemble a mottled eggshell with a dinosaur bursting from the top. Erin's tongue poked from the corner of her mouth as she carefully adjusted the angle of her airbrush.

"Someone's been slacking on their paleontology," she murmured. "It should be obvious that these are Micropachycephalosauruses."

"Of course!"

Nolan smacked himself on the forehead dramatically.

"How silly of me."

He put his head on one side.

"Was the Micropachycephalosaurus known for having a giant sparkly horn in the middle of its forehead?"

"Not traditionally," Erin admitted. "These are hybrids. They're dinosaurs, but they also happen to be unicorns."

"I don't even want to guess how that came about."

"Life finds a way, Nolan. It's not our place to tell a dinosaur who it should love. Besides, I take my client's brief very seriously. These were designed following an extended conference with the birthday girl."

"Best aunt ever." Nolan chuckled.

He leaned closer and kissed the sensitive skin behind her ear. Erin shivered as his caress sent a delicious wave of prickles across her skin.

"Careful," Erin scolded. "If you keep doing that, I'll mess up the veneer on these eggshells. I want them to be perfect. I owe the poor kid that much after what I brought to her last birthday."

Nolan rested his chin on her shoulder.

"The kitty cakes turned out awesome," he insisted. "Plus, you brought yourself to her last birthday and that's even better. Abby's crazy about you. And so am I."

He began to lightly kiss and nip at the side of her neck, and one of the hands around her waist slid upwards to cup her breast through her sweater.

"Nolan!" she squeaked. "I have to get these finished."

"As the attorney representing the interests of your fiancé, I'm obliged to insist you take a break. You're nearly done, and the party isn't until tomorrow."

Erin giggled.

"Do you think my fiancé will mind that his attorney is sucking on my earlobe?" she teased.

"Well, I suppose I could be persuaded to keep my mouth shut."

Erin put down the airbrush and wriggled around to face him. She ran her hands over his shirt-clad chest and stared up at him through her lashes.

"What's your price?" she asked mischievously.

"A kiss."

Erin wound her arms around his neck and raised herself onto her tiptoes.

"I think that can be arranged," she purred.

At first the kiss was tender, almost chaste. Erin cupped his jaw, enjoying the prick of his stubble as his mouth moved slowly over hers. When she felt the tickle of his tongue brushing her lower lip, she opened her mouth with a soft sigh. The wet, welcoming warmth of her mouth triggered a groan that reverberated pleasantly from Nolan's chest. The groan turned to a grunt of surprise when Erin slid her hand between them and gave his nipple a sly pinch through the fabric of his shirt.

"You're a wicked girl," he growled, gripping her ass and pulling her hard against him. "And you know what happens to wicked little girls."

"Ahem!"

Nolan and Erin sprang apart at the sound of someone loudly clearing their throat.

"Oh, don't stop on my account," said Olivia dryly. "Although I was hoping Abby's birthday cake was safe from your libido this year."

"Jesus, Liv!" Nolan hissed. "Wear a bell next time."

"This is *my* kitchen, Hugh Hefner."

"Sorry, Olivia," said Erin contritely. "I'm almost done, though. Come look."

Olivia's exasperated expression melted when she saw the cakes.

"These are incredible," she gasped, pulling Erin in for a one-armed hug. "I still don't know how you landed this woman, Nolan. Or how you tricked her into marrying you."

"Don't scare her off," he warned. "I haven't sealed the deal yet."

"Relax," Olivia scoffed. "If Granny didn't scare her, I don't stand much of a chance. Speaking of sealing deals, I believe congratulations are in order, Erin."

Erin flushed, eyes sparkling with excitement.

"Thanks! It still hasn't quite sunk in. They actually accepted our offer on the place."

"Well, we were able to offer them a good price," said

Nolan, kissing the top of her head. "It was worth it too. Prime location, lots of foot traffic. You can really start putting Sticky Treats on the map."

"Poetic justice," Olivia said vehemently. "I can't think of a better use for that ass-wipe's settlement."

"Agreed."

Erin leaned her head on Nolan's shoulder and closed her eyes. The case against Heather and Stirling had been stressful but clean-cut. Both had been forced to pay a hefty sum in punitive damages. Last she heard, Stirling had been forced to sell his company. She almost felt sorry for him in the end. It was hard to stay angry when she was so happy.

"I'm looking forward to your grand re-opening," Olivia remarked, tossing a bag of balloons at Nolan. "Here, Casanova. Blow these up. You're here to help with party prep, not to distract the head baker."

Nolan made a face and tore into the bag of balloons.

"So, what's the theme for the re-opening?" Olivia asked. "I'm sure Abby would love it if you went with dino-corns but it might not be consistent with your brand."

"You'd be surprised what people are into," Nolan muttered, stretching a balloon vigorously.

"Ok, I'm withdrawing your speaking privileges, little brother. *Erin*, what's the theme of your re-opening?"

Erin looked across at her future husband, a smile slowly spreading across her face.

"I think," she said dreamily. "It can only be—new beginnings."

ABOUT THE AUTHOR

Monica is a writer of romance novels and short stories. After spending almost a decade in the postgraduate study of literature and earning her PhD, she left the world of academia to pursue her dream career as a novelist.

She lives in the heart of the Yorkshire Dales with her long-suffering spouse, their furry menagerie and far too many books.

When not writing, Monica can be found walking her dog, devouring romance novels and getting hopelessly lost down internet rabbit holes.

Printed in Great Britain
by Amazon

11772241R00202